The characters in this book are based on historical persons.

The plot is fiction based on historical facts.

Cover design by Nic Wainwright

Library of Congress Cataloging-in-Publication Data

Harem Twins

Dolores Maria Davis

ISBN 978-0-9976240-0-7

Printed in the United States of America

10 9 8 7 6 5 4 3 2 1

♊

Dedication

Writing about 1400 BC Egypt led me to sources where I gained a great deal of knowledge about this period. I learned much from the <u>Egyptian Exploration Organization</u> and its speakers, such as the renowned Dr. Zahi Hawass, the world's living legend on ancient Egypt; Dr. John Gaudet, author of *Papyrus;* and John M. Adams, author of *The Millionaire and the Mummies.* A woman I have never met, and enjoyed studying immeasurably, is Joann Fletcher, who possesses remarkable knowledge about the specific period I write about. This touches on but a few of the authorities I was able to read about or query. With their contribution of knowledge, my book is far richer in archeological setting and facts.

My family still wonders why I choose this period in history to write about, but indulge me. My son, George, and his family, and my daughters, Diana and Juliet, have listened politely about my scheming plots and unusual characters for years.

To my beta readers, Mimi Swan and Eva McAngus, your time has meant much to me. My weekly writing group and marketing group members have been valuable assets as I have trudged through this journey. And Nic Wainwright, a bright young mind, always avails me with expert computer knowledge. I am grateful.

Special accolades go to Cat Spydell and Paula Reuben, my editors. They follow this ancient time period unwaveringly and keep me on track regarding story. I know I am not an easy writer to edit, as I am often rushing off to write the next chapter thinking somehow it will get away from me. Thank you both.

Author's Note

♊

Pharaoh Amenhotep III (circa 1400 BC) moved Egypt's capitol, Memphis, from the Nile Delta south to Thebes. Colossi statues sixty feet high flanked the Palace entrance. The Fortress of Eternity and surrounding gardens comprised approximately seventy acres and included his Mortuary Temple estimated by archeologists to be seventy football fields in length. Amenhotep III allowed his Queen a personal chef, the first in the known world, and her cartouche imprinted on the building blocks of her apartments. As one archeologist put it, "The man had taste." Pharaoh accepted foreign women into his harem to bolster alliances with past enemies, unusual for Egypt.

Most of the characters in this book lived in and around Pharaoh's Court. I added twins, considered lucky during this time, to fictionalize my story. I hope you find this period as fascinating as I did.

Dolores Maria Davis

Harem Twins

♊

Dolores Maria Davis

Prologue

⚊⚊ (Gemini symbol)

Egypt's sun god Ra was rising in the eastern sky to cast his vibrant rays on the white walls of Pharaoh Amenhotep III's grand new house. A newborn, about to arrive at sunrise in Pharaoh's Harem, would fortel of exceptional heavenly influences.

The mother, Princess Attah of Mitanni, was twelve summers old. Her diminutive frame carried the belly of a hippopotamus. Gaunt and exhausted from slow labor, her birthing was half a moon cycle early, the baby large.

Maja, Attah's only slave, tried to comfort her princess with damp cloths and soothing words as Attah suffered strong and rapid thrusts. Maja overheard two women sitting on their cots watching her princess struggle.

"The foreigner slept with Pharaoh but once, and is bearing his child. Luck is with her. She hasn't even learned to speak in Egyptian yet," one said.

The other pregnant woman said, "I feel sorry for her. No one has brought effigies of Goddess Hathor to bring the sweet north wind, or God Bes to aid her in her childbearing. The tattoo artist is coming in two Ras to

1

paint my breasts with pictures of God Bes so the magic will be with me when I give birth."

Slave Maja was on her knees at Attah's cot asking all the gods she had ever heard of not to let her mistress die in childbirth.

"Don't pray in our Mitanni tongue," Attah said sharply. "If I die, promise me you will always claim this baby Pharaoh's child. Raise my child like an Egyptian with Pharaoh's language and teach him to pray to Egyptian gods." Maja held Attah's hand, replying yes with her large frightened eyes. Attah pulled Maja close and whispered into her ear. "Keep the secret I am about to tell you, forever more, promise?" Maja nodded, her black eyes growing wider as Princess Attah whispered in her ear.

Attah was soon attended by eunuchs who hung wet linen panels surrounding her birthing area to provide coolness and privacy. The women in the harem talked of how Attah labored on in pain and silence. Then a midwife arrived.

Standing tall, the Harem Keeper drew back one of the curtains. "When will this be done?" he asked.

"Very soon," said Maja, looking up with fear as she mopped up the blood that flowed from Attah. "My mistress is opening like a well spring now."

It was an important moment for the keeper when a child was born into Pharaoh's Harem, especially if it was a boy. At last the wailing of a new life resounded. The Mitanni Princess delivered a girl-child. Not a boy,

2

but still an important birth because she had arrived with the rise of the sun god, Ra.

The Keeper smoothed his linen kilt, secured his gold cuffs and adjusted his cropped wig. Leaving his Harem duties to his assistant, he took long, hurried strides to the entrance of the royal audience chamber. A pair of Nubian sentries guarded the entrance. Towering over the Harem Keeper, in his leopard kilt, one guard said, "Halt!"

"A royal child arrived as Ra graced our skies. The omen is great!"

The Royal Guards looked at one another with understanding. "Follow me," said one who promptly escorted the Keeper to Pharaoh's Bedchamber Steward.

Pharaoh's Steward first showed annoyance, then seemed to grasp the importance of such an event. "Wait here," he said with enthusiasm. The Keeper was soon guided through several turns and into Pharaoh's private bedchamber. When he came upon the sight of the Living God's golden bed, he dropped to his knees and performed a great and proper prostration.

"Oh Son of Ra, Great Amenhotep III, Ruler of Thebes, Lord of Truth, King of Upper and Lower Egypt, Strong Bull, He who Establishes Laws and Pacifies the Two Lands, Smiter of the Asiatics: A girl-child has been born this day, at the rise of Ra, and at the New Moon, Year of the Great Harvest."

Strewn with linens and cheetah skins, Pharaoh's gilded lounge was shared by Lady Mui, the royal cat,

3

and two young boys who scurried from his sheets as the clamor of quickening footsteps brought Pharaoh's Vizier and Chancellor. Both were paramount officials of the land and responsible advisors to the King, in charge of Royal storerooms, treasury and more. Lastly, the Court Astrologer strode in.

One by one, other chief advisors to Pharaoh began to appear and praise the young King on his fertile prowess. The Court Astrologer Abu, moved his large frame forward, glared at the Harem Keeper and boomed, "My calculations show two infants born to the Royal House this day."

The Keeper demurred with a deep bow and a submissive voice. "Royal Astrologer, when I left the Harem I saw but one Royal girl child, and no other women are in their final days of birthing."

A commotion came from the bedchamber portal and drew the attention to those gathered. A breathless assistant Harem Keeper came forward. His prostration before the King was inept. He quickly rose and stuttered, "Attah se– se–second child, a boy, Attah– ha– had twins! Princess At. . . tah is dead."

The Astrologer glared at the Harem Keeper.

This news brought Pharaoh to a sitting position. As he rose, he motioned the two Keepers away. He turned his youthful and glistening body that had lived through but fourteen inundations toward his Vizier with a questioning look.

The Vizier stepped forward and said, "My Lord, the

4

minor Princess that has delivered you twins is a woman from your vassal state, Mitanni in Babylon. She came as a war reparation presented to My Lord a season ago by her King."

"Ah, yes of course," replied Pharaoh. He stood and stretched his body that was in transition from a boy to manhood. His Butler moved to his side, offering him an ornate robe heavily embroidered with gold threads.

Then, with rare animation, Pharaoh motioned for his Astrologer. "Abu, my twins have arrived with the rise of Ra and the new moon. Is that not correct?" Not waiting for an answer, he added, "They bear omnipotence from me and regal blood from their Mitanni mother, a Princess in her land. Return to Court in two Ras with the heavenly chart stories of my Royal Twins. Also deliver me a selection of pleasant names to choose from."

Chapter 1

♊

Princess Becataten and Prince Jobutaten walked toward a nearby garden to soak their feet at midday. Both bare-chested. He wore a loincloth and she had removed her shift. Their nanny, an illiterate woman of foreign birth, had given them diminutive names, as she could not manage the long titles that Pharaoh had bestowed them. Prince Jobutaten became Jobu and Princess Becataten became Taten.

"How many steps to the pond is it, Jobu?"

Jobu kicked the sand with his long skinny feet and said, "Maybe thirty or forty steps."

"Do you know that's how wide the stones are that are stacked to make columns," Taten said, in a serious voice.

"No, but you do," scoffed Jobu.

Taten tickled Jobu hard in his ribs then tripped her gangly brother, wrestling him to the ground. They both sat up laughing and spitting sand. Jobu rubbed his scuffed knees, and his left eye wobbled, which happened when he grew excited. "Race you to the pond," Jobu said, as he ran off on his long legs. Taten couldn't catch him.

The twins were sitting at the pool's edge when a garden worker wandered by. "Those are nice rose buds popping out on your chest, little one."

Jobu postured. His lean and boyish body showed anger. "Old man, go away from us or I will call your master on you."

"So you are the big man?"

"The Royal Gardener Sennejem is our good friend, and I will tell him of your words to my sister if you do not leave now!" Jobu said in a voice that cracked, revealing his near manhood.

The worker delivered a lewd grin before walking away.

Becataten looked differently at her brother. "Jobu, you really sounded tough, and look, the man is leaving."

They were silent for a while. "Jobu, I have been wondering. Is that strange royal scribe who comes to see you all the time teaching you his craft?" Taten said.

Jobu offered little enthusiasm. "Not exactly, we're just friends."

"You know you could become a scribe. If you went to Thoth's Royal Scribe School, you could even work in the Palace," Taten said.

Avoiding her question, Jobu kicked his feet in the water. "Let's see who can make the water splash the highest!"

The day passed peacefully as they played with few

words between them until Ra's light grew dim, and they walked home arm in arm to their modest royal apartment situated within the walls of Amenhotep III's grand palatial compound.

Standing with hands on hips, Dwarf Beset greeted Taten and Jobu at the door with her usual cheer. "What have my lovely twins been up to today?" she said in her scratchy voice, looking up at them.

Beset had grown up in Pharaoh's Court and was a gift sent to the Royal Nursery from the King when the children were infants. Dwarf Beset was well educated and greatly revered. Her image was that of the male God Bes but in the female version, he who protected women in childbirth as well as households.

Slave Maja put down a jug of beer she had hauled to the apartment and rushed to Jobu. "You fell and hurt your knees, Jobu? Let me wash and bandage them. And Taten, how am I going to get you clean tonight?" Maja always fussed over the children like a nervous monkey. Dark skinned and bent in posture, she often appeared tired, looking many season beyond her two decades. Maja had accompanied the twin's mother, Princess Attah to Egypt from remote Mitanni. Over the years she had come to be called "Nanny Maja" instead of "Slave".

A few days had passed when Maja decided to make the long walk to the Royal Nursery. She remembered her earlier years there with much happiness, and never forgot the exceptional attention given all the royal children. When she had first arrived, the royal eunuchs that cared for the children disturbed her. But over time, she learned that they were loving caretakers. Maja had made the trek to the nursery to seek out the man who knew much about herbs. She was speaking to him when the Royal Nurse, Heqarneheh, approached.

"Maja, I haven't seen you since you and Dwarf Beset left the nursery with the Prince and Princess."

Maja was careful to bow with reverence to the Royal Nurse, the one in charge of Pharaoh's infants, mothers, teachers, and wet nurses.

"I hardly recognized you, but I knew you by your voice right away," he said.

Maja knew she looked older and emaciated, her posture more bent.

"Maja, you must take more rest and food. You know that twins are considered great gifts of fertility and fortune to the Court, and you will not serve them well unless you stay healthy. Walk with my sister, Lady Norfet, in Pharaoh's garden. In two suns I will tell her to meet with you, and give you one of her famous tonics. I will tell her to expect you."

Maja's eyes widened and she bowed again, thanking him for taking such an interest.

"How old are the young royals now, Maja?"

"The babies, I mean the children, have lived through twelve inundations," Maja said.

"And it seems only a few moons ago that you and Dwarf Beset left to live in your royal apartment. Where are you located within the Palace grounds?"

"We are at the west gate," Maja said.

"Say that again, Maja." The Nurse looked perplexed.

Maja repeated their location. Westerly located apartments were the most distant from Pharaoh's quarters, and where many menial workers were housed.

"Ask Dwarf Beset to come to me when Ra's rays are long, so we may dine. I have things to discuss with her." Turning to the herbalist that Maja had come to see, Nurse Heqarneheh motioned to him. "Give Maja anything she needs." Before he walked away, he shook his head, a mystified expression on his face. Maja was unaware of Nurse Heqarneheh's shock and disbelief of the location and housing of the twins.

Before leaving, Maja passed through the nursery where busy eunuchs were changing linens of the cots and cradles. She missed this place! An abundance of floor pillows supported harem-mothers nursing their offspring. In a smaller area, wet nurses sat and nourished babies born from mothers who failed to live through childbearing. This was where Princess Becataten and Prince Jobutaten had been suckled. Pausing to watch early walkers at play with a basket of kittens, Maja neared the exit, but lingered. Children learning their lessons under the tutelage of able scribes were hard at work. When slaves began rolling in with

10

an elaborate midday meal from the royal kitchen, it was time to leave. Attendants took their food in one quadrant, mothers and children in another. Scribes, along with their students would eat together. Maja knew a long nap would follow. Maja grew sad knowing that she no longer had a place here. When she turned away to make the long walk home with her medicinal herbs, Nurse Heqarneheh called out, "Don't forget to tell Dwarf Beset what I said."

"Beset, Beset! Can Jobu and I go with you to visit the Royal Nursery?" asked Taten.

"I don't want to visit the Royal Nursery," Jobu said. "But I will hail a litter for you Beset, it's a long way."

"Yes it is Jobu, and my short legs could not carry me there." Dwarf Beset looked forward to her meeting with the Royal Nurse, and she suspected he had something of importance to tell her. He was a man who did not chat idly. As Ra's rays grew long in Egypt, it was with anticipation that Beset stepped off her transport carried by two slaves and entered the Royal Nursery.

All the babes were down for the night and a rare quiet filled the nursery. A slave set their table and placed the last meal of the Ra before the nurse and the dwarf.

Staring into the distance, Nurse Heqarneheh took a deep breath. "I have many things to discuss with you, Beset, so please listen carefully. Twelve years ago I

11

settled Maja the slave woman and the twins in the Royal Nursery, making sure their every need was met as soon as they arrived. Their mother had just died in childbirth and was never spoken of again. You remember her, she was that insignificant Mitanni princess."

Beset nodded. "I never knew her, but yes I know of her." Beset tore her flat bread into bite-sized pieces, drawn in by his serious expression.

The nurse continued. "I arranged and supplied the infants with wet nurses; one robust woman and one slender, both with ample breast milk, and the softest linens lined the gilded cradles of the twins. Pharaoh's gifts were received, like you, Dwarf Beset."

Beset set her beer cup down and said, "I remember you doing everything for them and continued to do so." Beset was puzzled. What was he trying to say?

The nurse's hands were folded tight before him. "I personally added to their young bodies Pharaoh's gifts of golden anklets and bracelets that were engraved with their heavenly names. Prince Jobutaten and Princess Becataten suckled into healthy children, each with a separate fan bearer for their cradles. I even saw that the royal kittens from Pharaoh's Lady Mui, another of his gifts, stayed with the children," the Nurse drolled on.

"Yes, we still have Lady Mui's offspring. The original cats have grown quite old," Beset said, to assure the nurse she understood him.

"And I, Nurse Heqarneheh, dictated their progress at every new moon to a scribe. Those scrolls were delivered to Abu, the Royal Astrologer. He was my liaison that would deliver our Lord my reports."

"I believe I remember you telling me that too," Beset assured the nurse.

With steely eyes the Nurse looked both angry and puzzled. "Yet, not long before you and the twins moved to your apartment, Pharaoh informed me that he had heard little of his children. How could Pharaoh not know of the progress of his Royal twins?"

"Indeed, how could Pharaoh not know," said Beset, beginning to understand the mystery.

"That was several innundations ago, Beset, and when you and the children moved to a royal apartment, I thought no more of it."

Beset nodded, urging the Nurse to continue. Nurse Heqarneheh added, "Then, a few Ras ago, Maja told me that you live near the west gate. That is as far from Pharaoh's personal chambers as one can be moved! And it is the least favorable place to live in all of the Palace grounds."

Dwarf Beset had wondered many times why her beloved twins never enjoyed a regal apartment near Pharaoh, and she squinted up at the Nurse, hoping for an answer. "You are right, Nurse and I have found no reason why my twins should live so distant from our Lord."

The Nurse glared at Dwarf Beset. "And are you

13

going to do something about this? It is out of my hands now."

Forced to take in Nurse Heqarneheh's words, Beset rubbed her mouth. "I know a dwarf in Royal Astrologer Abu's household named Dwarf Heby. He is a friend. Sometimes we take beer in one of the gardens after Ra has departed. I will speak with him and learn more about this."

"As well you should, Beset. This treatment of esteemed royal twins cannot be tolerated."

Later Dwarf Beset's litter ride back to their meager apartment filled her with sadness. It was true. Her twins had been left behind to be reared in obscurity, and why? Who was plotting against them to keep them from their true position in the royal Court? Beset's mind turned as she wondered how she could find out.

Chapter 2

Ⅱ

Two evenings had passed when Maja walked with Lady Norfet. She breathed in the exotic perfumes of the area planted adjacent to the nursery. "It is beautiful here and the big pool of lotus flowers smell so, so . . ." Maja still struggled with the Egyptian language, searching for words which never came to her. Her face flushed red.

Lady Norfet took Maja's hand and squeezed it gently. "You have been an attentive nanny to the Royal twins. My brother, Nurse Heqarneheh, has always said so. Your dead mistress would be proud. I can promise you that news of your unfailing care of Pharaoh's twins, is known by many. I hear Pharaoh held Princess Becataten in the nursery once and spoke boastfully of her green eyes. Green as emeralds, he said."

Maja stood as erect as she could and wanted to thank Lady Norfet for the tonic, yet once again her words were inadequate. She wiped tears of happiness from her brown cheeks just as the Royal Gardener passed by on his nightly tour. "Good evening, Royal Gardener," Lady Norfet said. "I would like you to meet

Nanny Maja of Mitanni, in care of Pharaoh's Royal twins." Maja perked at the name nanny, when often she had been referred to as slave. She flushed.

The Royal Gardener appeared a humble man with a slight build, sun-worn skin and rough hands. He met Maja's gaze with eyes as black as olives imported from across the Great Sea. Maja and the Royal Gardener could have been mistaken for brother and sister, as they shared a common birthplace near the great Tigris and Euphrates Rivers.

"It is my great pleasure to meet you, Nanny Maja, and to congratulate you on the care of your wards. I hear many people speak of your loyalty to the children." A man of his rank did not have to bow formally to a nanny, but he did. "My name is Sennejem."

Maja blinked in surprise, bowed deeply and said, "It is kind what you say. I only have poor words in Egyptian."

The leathery skinned gardener smiled. "Is your native land where the two giant rivers cross?"

Maja nodded with widened eyes.

"I can translate for you, Maja. What would you like me to tell Lady Norfet?"

Maja took a deep breath. "Please thank her for giving me her special tonic, and tell her that I will take it every Ra, as she suggests, and thank her brother, Nurse Heqarneheh too," Maja said with much relief.

Sennejem was quiet and soft-spoken, not like some

of the Royal appointees. His dress was impeccable, and his deep sunken eyes bore an extraordinary amount of kohl. He smelled faintly of the castor bean oil that all garden workers wore to protect them against the strong rays of Ra. The Egyptians had learned how to prepare the oil so it was not poisonous. Maja lowered her eyes, as she realized she had been staring at Sennejem.

"Thank you for helping me with my words, Sennejem. After so many years I still need help with the Egyptian language," Maja said.

"It is my honor, Maja." His words made her checks redden as she left the walled garden, parting ways.

Once in her chamber, Maja opened the small jar Lady Norfet gave her. Inside was a dark brown paste. She was to take a spoonful at the rise and set of Ra. It was very sweet and thick. Maja pushed her finger into the mixture and brought it to her lips. Lady Norfet had masked the taste of the healing herbs with dates, raisins, and honey. The aroma was that of the bark of cinnamon, berries from the juniper bush and the herb, sweet flag. There were many more other ingredients, and Maja couldn't detect them all. But she knew how knowledgeable the Egyptians were, and was grateful for something to ease her ills. She thought of Sennejem and Lady Norfet and the help they had given to her and she flushed, remembering Princess Atta and feeling proud that she had done her best to help the Royal twins throughout the years.

Chapter 3

♊

Beset woke early to gather her shawl around her. The thick-walled apartment was chilly, as God Ra had not yet reached them. Their modest dwelling, although within the Palace walls, was a long litter ride from Pharaoh's 'House of Rejoicing.'

Beset had played with Pharaoh when they were children in those Royal chambers, even in the treasury rooms and apartments for concubines. Only Queen Tiy's apartment, Pharaoh's first wife with her venerated staff, was off limits.

As Dwarf Beset busied herself gathering up clay vessels to fill with beer at the local brewery, she mulled over her evening visit with the Royal Nurse. The twins had never seen the areas of the Palace that she knew. She wondered again why they were located in this far corner of the compound. Multiple births were a great omen of prosperity, and twins were always housed near Pharaoh.

Twins Suti and Hor had been educated since birth to be Royal Architects. Royal Architect Suti was even awarded a massive land holding, where he raised celebrated cattle, while his twin, Hor, enjoyed a lavish royal apartment near Pharaoh.

When Beset returned with their drink for the day, the morning sky was still dark, but Taten was sitting up in her cot blinking her eyes while their two old cats slept soundly at Jobu's feet. Their kittens were tumbling on the floor with one another. "Good morning, Beset!" Taten whispered, trying not to wake Jobu, as she rubbed her sleepy face.

"I see you two slept together again. Don't you think you are getting a bit big to sleep in one cot?" Beset asked.

"I know, but Jobu likes to talk at night, you know how he is. He never says much during the day," Taten said.

Beset smiled and nodded. "My precious Taten, Ra has barely shown himself! You may sleep yet," she said placing her small, plump hand on Taten's cheek.

"I can't sleep. I want to visit the architects now!" She pulled her child-like, brown legs from the bed linens and jumped up.

Jobu poked his head out from the covers; his eyes were squinted with sleep.

"Jobu, my brother, you must join me today! I know you would find the work of the Royal Architects exciting."

Jobu grumbled, his thick sidelock covering his face. He turned to face the wall and mumbled, "Beset is correct, Ra has barely shown himself. Go yourself, quietly."

Undeterred, Taten started to dress. "Where are the Architects today, Beset?" Taten asked in an anxious voice.

Beset fussed with her matted braids. "One day soon we will shave your head and find you a wig, as you are nearing womanhood, but all you care about are Architects! I should keep mute and make you wonder about your Architects," she teased.

"Please, Beset!" Taten whined.

"Architects Suti and Hor are setting an obelisk at Karnak Temple, but use care when crossing the Nile, child."

Taten rushed out the door, grabbing a handful of dates on her way. Beset watched her go. Taten wouldn't return until the dark threatened the light. Children were safe to roam and play in most parts of Egypt, although Beset had often expressed concern about how far Taten traveled. Taten often watched the Royal Architects Suti and Hor at work. They could have kept an eye on the roving child, but they were busy and had never been introduced to the young Princess.

Taten's nose took her to the nearest bakery, the one next to a brewery where the yeast from the bread was used to make daily beer. Beer was the preferred drink of Egyptians, as Nile water was not potable. The baker was pulling his first morning batch of aromatic flatbreads from his clay oven with a long pallet. As he stacked the golden rounds, Taten waited eagerly. She grabbed the one on top, shoved a few dates into her mouth, and off she went. Juggling the hot morning delight from one hand to another, she headed to the Nile barge. She knew the short way to the river, but barely made it before the raft launched from the bank with a rocking jolt. As they moved along, the sun's long rays were beginning to turn the water into shimmering silver. This was a peaceful time of day with no wind and no human sounds. Only ripples from the bargeman's pole and early fowls offered quiet sounds, and even the few boats with their single sails moved about mutely. Marching into the inky soil and anchoring their roots into the mud, papyri lined the Nile's banks as far as she could see. She breathed the cool fresh air and felt one with the river.

Holding her flatbread with one hand and shading her brow with the other, she looked for the activity of an obelisk being put in place. Workmen traversing the river with their tools and supplies stood alongside the girl who came early in the morning to watch the work of the Architects. When she stepped off the barge, she ran as fast as her young legs would carry her to the temple.

For the whole day, Taten watched the workers as they moved heavy stones and the architects as they oversaw the projects, always checking calulations on their scrolls and barking orders. She ate no midday

21

meal but filled herself with the views of building projects at Karnak Temple. That evening, when Taten arrived home, she was eager to talk about her day. Excited about what she had seen she could hardly contain herself. "I was out before Ra's rays and by the time I got to the Karnak Temple, Architects Suti and Hor were overseeing the setting of a column, Beset, not an obelisk." She took a deep breath. "You should see how they set the big round stones on top of one another to erect a tall pillar. The pre-cut cyllinders that arrive from the Royal workshops look like huge drums that are carved with the words of Pharaoh and all the other gods. The stone carvers ream holes into some of the drumstones and carve knobs on others, like hyena tits, so they will fit together. Then the workers make ramps of sand so they can roll the drums up, stack one on top of another, then they make the ramps higher, and when they have set all the rounds, they are standing where the ceiling will be placed. After that, painters arrive and the sand is slowly removed, as they paint glyphs on their way down." Out of breath, she said, "And I can read them all. Architect Suti says they will never come down."

Beset's eyes widened, "You met the Architect Suti?"

"No," Taten admitted. "But I could hear all he said,"

Jobu sat in a quiet mood as Taten yammered on.

"That's very fine," Maja scoffed, looking at the disheveled Taten. "But I want to know, how will we ever get your tunic clean?"

After their bath, the children stepped out of a small copper tub of dirty water, and Beset and Maja took turns rubbing them dry with coarse linen. Jobu ran to the large cushion and settled himself, excited to hear the magical story to come.

"What is the story about tonight, Beset?" Jobu asked, as he rocked back and forth on the goose-down pillow.

"Have I told you about the priest who lived many dynasties ago, with powers so great he could turn wax animal figures into real live ones?" Beset asked as she reached for an effigy of a small crocodile.

Jobu's eyes grew wide. "No. No, Beset, you haven't told us that one. Come sit."

Beset plopped next to Jobu. Taten yawned and sat on the other side of Beset.

Beset always began her stories with the phrase, "Many dynasties ago..." And when she finished, she ended with, "The gods let them live a long, happy life."

After the stories, lighted pots of tallow were extinguished, and the children found their way to bed. Snuggling in together, the children spoke in quiet voices.

"You act more like a boy than a girl, sister, always talking about building. You may as well have come with me today to learn the art of fighting other boys."

"Jobu, just because you don't like architecture, and I do, doesn't mean I am acting like a boy. Queen

Nefrititi was very interested in architecture and oversaw all of her own building projects."

"Oh, so now you are a queen."

Taten jumped on him, pinning him to the cot. "I don't have to go with you to watch boys wrestle. I can fight with you anytime."

"Children, children," Beset said, separating them. "You are both in need of sleep."

Later, when they were settled in the same cot, Taten said, "Did you really go and watch boys oppose each other today, Jobu?"

"I went with my scribe friend, and we watched some practice bouts. The best of the wrestlers will perform at Court."

Taten sounded surprised. "Really, are you going to be able to attend?"

"I don't think so, but the preliminary bouts are very interesting."

"Is that scribe with the strange name, Tiurek, the one who took you?"

Jobu nodded.

"Is he a Royal Scribe?"

Jobu nodded again.

"Where does he work?"

"I don't know exactly."

"You must know where he works, Jobu. You're not stupid."

"I think he does special scroll work in the royal apartments."

"Really? Have you been there?"

"No."

"His name isn't Egyptian. Jobu. What is it?"

"How would I know? You want to know a lot, sister."

Taten knew he was keeping something from her. She wanted to ask more. There was something about that scribe that made her feel uneasy.

"But . . ."

"Hush now."

Jobu turned away to sleep on his side. She could hear Beset, who had been quietly listening at their door, turn toward her cubicle for sleep too.

Chapter 4

♊

Beset sat in a garden admiring the blooming iris, taking beer with her friend Dwarf Heby of the Royal Astrologer's house.

The Egyptian Court considered dwarves magical people and had imported them from the land of Punt for several generations. They resided in the households of royal appointees and nobles but were gifted only by Pharaoh.

Beset loudly slurped her beer. "Dwarf Heby, do you remember anything about the connection between the Royal Astrologer and the Royal twins?"

Heby was much larger than Beset, with the torso of an average man, but with short legs. He looked nervous as he sat on the stone bench, swinging his legs back and forth.

"I don't know what you want me to tell you, Beset."

Heby took a long draught of his beer through a drinking reed to avoid the chafe atop the quickly-made brew.

"I'm just curious. I know it was a long time ago, but can you remember what happened the day the twins were born? That would be the day the Royal Astrologer would have been asked to prepare their heavenly charts at Pharaoh's request."

"I do remember that afternoon quite well. The Royal Astrologer Abu pounded his way across the gardens from Pharaoh's chamber. It's about three hundred steps, and he didn't wait for a parasol bearer. He's an impatient man, you know. When he arrived, his body was running with sweat with kohl streaming down his face. Ill-tempered and overheated, he was quick to step out of his kilt, remove his cuffs and toss his wig. Two of us worked with haste to cool him down, using wet linen scented with peppermint oil. Another attendant reapplied fresh kohl to his eyes, and wrapped him with a clean kilt. With little reason he can explode like a wounded lion." After drawing more beer from his reed, Heby looked to be recalling something. "The Astrologer entered his work chamber and snapped at his waiting scribe. I remember him saying, 'This day we will all work until Ra leaves us and returns again to brighten the sky.' When the aged butler saw us hovering and listening at Abu's chamber door, he shooed us away."

Beset sat rapt, caught up in Heby's story. Her mind quickened. "Then what happened?"

"Then Butler Farafar moved a stool to sit on and peer through a gap between the door and the wall and listen alone," Heby continued. "The old butler may tell you something if you ask him, but I doubt it. What I do know is that for many Ras there has been a secret air

27

growing within the Astrologer's household about his interests in the slave trade, as well as a heap of correspondence coming and going between here and Memphis with the Amun Clergy." Heby looked around as if to make sure no one else had heard his confessions.

Beset sat quietly, absorbing his tale. "What does it all mean?" she asked in a quiet voice.

"I don't know exactly," said Heby. "But I do know that overly curious members of the Astrologer's household tend to disappear."

The two spent the rest of the afternoon talking about other things, although Beset's mind kept taking her back to the picture of the Astrologer's unusual behavior after the twins were born. Later, Heby offered Beset his torch to light her path home. As she walked in the dark, she realized how vividly Heby had recalled his facts from many innundations back. Abu's household was a busy one with much scrollwork always being produced. But what was the correspondence with Memphis all about? She thought that Abu mainly handled Pharaoh's personal correspondence and heavenly birth charts. Everyone knew Pharaoh was always distancing himself from the Amun Clergy, in favor of the Aten Clergy here in Thebes, and that was the main reason he moved the capitol away from Memphis. These thoughts consumed her as she found her way back to the apartment.

After a moon cycle of taking Lady Norfet's tonic, Maja moved about with new energy. She felt eager to walk with Sennejem in the Palace gardens now that she seemed young again.

As they strolled after sunset, Sennejem grew serious and said quietly, "Maja, because you are in charge of Royals, I want to warn you about something. Our Living God is a great Pharaoh, but his Court is often a place of intrigue. Try to understand that. Be on guard against those who would use the tactics of a scorpion to sting you, or your charges."

Maja stared at him, hoping he'd explain, but instead Sennejem grew quiet. "What are you saying?" Maja asked.

"I cannot say more, but heed my words," said Sennejem. "Soon you will learn to read and write the Egyptian language. It is not so difficult because the language is one of pictures," he added, changing the subject.

Still stirred from his earlier comment, Maja tried to keep up with Sennejem's faster pace. "I promised myself I would learn with Taten and Jobu when their tutors came but..." her voice trailed off.

"Is that what you call the Prince Jobutaten and Princess Becataten?" Sennejem asked with a laugh.

"Yes, my little names for them." Maja blushed. "I love my twins but I am not sure I love Dwarf Beset. I would prefer to care for them by myself."

Sennejem's face clouded. "Dwarf Beset is linked to

the important male God, Bes. She is one who can be of much help to you."

"I don't need help!" Maja protested.

"It is considered lucky to have a dwarf in the household," Sennejem said.

Maja showed tears of frustration. "I would like to care for my twins alone."

Sennejem continued, "In Egypt, you must learn that it is a great honor to live with a dwarf."

"What will become of me if Beset is so important?" Maja whispered. Once again she was reminded of her roots as a mere slave.

"Do not fear, Maja, you will still be needed. Dwarf Beset will help them in other ways, especially as they grow older. Remember she was raised at Court and can navigate the dark politics of the Royals."

"I suppose. I hope you are right." Maja stood but stumbled; Sennejem reached to steady her and said, "You will appreciate the assistance, Maja. Trust me."

Maja nodded, and she suddenly felt faint. She looked up at Sennejem, and he became a blur before her. Shaking, she felt herself sinking to her knees.

Chapter 5

♊

When Beset returned to the apartment that evening, Maja was being helped onto her cot by Sennejem. Taten was trying to draw her attention, patting her hand and talking to her, while Jobu stood back with a frightened look and watched. Maja's gray color and moist face caused Beset to turn to Sennejem.

Beset's heart raced as she said, "Quickly, Sennejem, find a healer for her. She looks to have fallen seriously ill." Maja appeared to be in much pain, doubling up, and moaning.

The twins were hovering with frightened faces. Beset scurried them to their beds. Once in their cots, Becataten looked into Beset's eyes. "Will Maja die?" she asked, clutching Beset's tunic as she turned to go back to struggling Maja.

"I do not think so, but help me, child, before I return to her side. Did you or Jobu see her eat or drink anything?"

Taten scrunched her face in thought. "There was some pomegranate juice that was delivered by a royal scribe. I think he said it was from Lady Norfet. The scribe said this crop of pomegranates was supposed to be very special and made from fruit that had recently arrived from the finest trees grown in the delta. Maja sipped some from a cup, just before her walk with Sennejem."

Jobu was anxious to add his thoughts. "I remember she said it tasted bitter, told us not to drink it and she set it aside."

Beset left the twins and discovered the cupful of blood red liquid. Sennejem returned, out of breath with a healer from the Royal house that rushed to Maja's side to assist her as she moaned in pain. Beset sniffed the cup's content and called Sennejem over. "Sennejem, smell this and tell me if you think this pomegranate juice is poisoned?" she asked in a quiet voice, so as to not disturb the children in the next room. Sennejem took a long whiff touched the liquid with his finger, and tasted it. He looked up with a serious face, and nodded. Beset gasped. "Inform the healer at once so he knows how to cure her," Beset said, wringing her hands. *And so it begins,* she thought. *Someone must know about my recent inquiries about the twins.*

The next morning, Maja could barely raise herself from her cot, and her health was still in a rapid fall.

The healer explained her vision was blurred and she suffered a knot of pain in her stomach. He said the juice was badly tainted and prescribed an herb mixture

32

that would make her vomit. She did so, but with little relief. "We must wait and see if she survives the poison," he said with a shrug before leaving. It was a miracle that Maja did survive the second long night, though she was fevered and in much distress.

Sennejem arrived the next day with a basket of figs. Maja could hardly speak. His gnarled brow conveyed his alarm. Sennejem took her hand. "I expected you to be better, Maja! There is another healer from the Court, who understands many potions and draws on all the proper chants to bring the healing gods. I will summon him for you."

Lady Norfet also came to see Maja. When she stood next to Sennejem she, too, was in great shock over Maja's failing health. "And after my tonic had revitalized her so. What could be wrong?" she asked.

"Please step outside with me," Sennejem asked. They walked together to a small garden area. "I must speak very plainly to you, Lady Norfet. Nanny Maja has been poisoned."

"Poisoned? Impossible!"

"Yes, being around plants all my life, I know a little about poison. Did you send the pomegranate juice to Maja?" Sennejem asked.

"Yes, I often do when we have a good crop."

"Is there anyone new working in your household, Lady Norfet?" Sennejem felt nervous asking the question.

"Only a scribe I recently hired to help me with

research on herbs. Why, what are you saying?"

"Lady, I am not accusing. Is he still in your employ?"

"No, he just worked for me a few days."

"Have you seen him since?"

"No." Lady Norfet said slowly. "I am embarrassed to say that I do not know his name, but I think someone at the royal library may."

Sennejem added, "I know Royal Astrologer Abu and meet with him from time to time. He uses many scribes, I will speak with him."

Lady Norfet looked concerned. "Please report back to me, Sennejem, and use caution when you speak to others of this matter."

"Yes, let us keep this matter between us, Lady Norfet. So far it is only the healers, myself, and Beset who know what happened."

"Let us keep it that way," Lady Norfet said, taking her leave.

Chapter 6

♊

During Maja's slow recovery, Beset made every effort to make life normal for the children and to distract them from the fact that Maja had nearly died. Since they loved evening story time, she increased her telling until Jobu fell asleep each night. Once his gentle sleeping breath filled the room, Becataten would ask questions of Beset.

"Will you tell me about the time when we lived in the nursery and Pharaoh held me?" Becataten said.

"Of course I will, sweet Taten. You just lay down on your cot."

Taten sank down into the goose down cot and covered herself. Beset began, making great use of her facial expressions and pantomiming with her small hands.

"You twins were living just past your second Nile rising when Pharaoh arrived late one afternoon at the portal of the Royal Nursery." Beset pointed to their door opening. "He chose not to have his visit announced but stood quietly with his retinue behind him. With his arms crossed, he scanned his offspring." With a serious face Beset turned her head about, scouring their

35

environs.

Taten watched with wide eyes as she snuggled in deeper. This story was better than a magical one, for it was true.

"All the infants were being rocked in their cradles to the music of lyres and harps. Their wet nurses had fed them all, and it was time to nap. A few children were at play on the floor with dolls, spinning tops, balls of hide and a basket of fluffy kittens." Beset fluttered her hands above the floor then pointed to one of their kittens, asleep next to Jobu. "In a far corner, a few older children were seated on goose-down cushions listening to their tutors. They were telling stories that were illuminated by colorful wall paintings. Pharaoh surprised Nurse Heqarneheh, and when he saw Pharaoh, the esteemed Royal Nurse prostrated himself before his youthful God. The King surveyed his nursery with a broad smile, and you, Princess Becataten, wiggled out of Maja's arms and waddled over to Pharaoh himself, tripping over his feet when you reached him." Beset squeezed Taten's toes and giggled. "You righted yourself by grabbing at Pharaoh's kilt."

Taten covered her mouth and laughed. Beset continued, "Then Pharaoh barked a laugh and picked you up and you tried to imitate him, which made him laugh harder. Maja held back her smile. Everyone in the nursery gasped. Maja froze, uncertain whether to retrieve you. Jobu hid behind her, sucking his thumb." Beset pretended to put her thumb in her mouth. "Then

36

Pharaoh said as he picked you up, 'Who is this little kitten with green eyes?' Beset pointed to Taten's bright eyes. Nurse Heqarneheh approached Pharaoh and said, 'This is your Princess Becataten, twin to her brother, Prince Jobutaten.'"

Taten was enthralled with Beset's telling of this story, even though she had heard it many times. She drew her knees up to her belly, listened to every word and watched every movement Beset made.

"Pharaoh stood holding you, studying your face. You drooled and fondled the golden pectoral he wore on his chest, and he let you." Beset formed her hands into a circle at her chest. "It was inlayed with a falcon and imbedded with colorful stones. The wings, eyes and talons of the bird were studded with lapis lazuli, carnelian, turquoise and gold. When Pharaoh gently handed you back to the Royal Nurse, he whispered something."

"What did he say, Beset, what did he say?" Taten knew the answer but always wanted to hear it again.

"'Which twin is the most gifted?' asked our Pharaoh, and Nurse Heqarneheh answered. 'The Princess Becataten, my Lord.'"

Taten was falling asleep when she said, "And our Lord really liked me?"

"Yes," whispered Dwarf Beset. "Now sleep, my Princess, for the next Ra is another day." She laid her hand against Taten's forehead as she took her leave, wiping tears from her own cheeks as she padded off to her sleeping cubicle. Once in her own cot, Beset went over in her mind that beautiful day in the Royal Nursery. A large wall garden grew there, with a lotus pool stocked with golden fish. Eunuchs gave exceptional care to all the children. She remembered boys wrestling, playing leapfrog and attacking each other with miniature weapons as monkeys romped alongside them. Smaller children pulled string toys: mechanical wooden cats and crocodiles with moving jaws. A few girls danced about to the music of a flutist, while others jumped rope and ran foot races. A colorful parrot hollered from his cage aloft in a nearby tree. A huge black cat, with an elegant gold collar, amused herself watching the activity from atop a high wall as her tailed switched.

Before falling asleep, Beset savored her fondest memory of that that fine day when she had approached Pharaoh to affirm her pledge to care for and protect the twins as he had instructed her.

Pharaoh had told her that he was confident that she was a fine companion and protector to the twins, as he had been to her when they played together as children.

His conversation with the Royal Nurse suddenly grew more vivid in her mind, and she pledged right then that she would make it her mission to learn why the crown had not acknowledged the twins.

Chapter 7

♊

At the rise of Ra, Beset saw Becataten off to spend the day watching the Royal Architects. While Jobu and Maja were still asleep, she rushed from the apartment and hailed the first litter carried by slaves that came her way. "To the Royal Astrologer's apartment," Beset said as she settled herself in the swaying seat.

Butler Farafar was sweeping the threshold of Abu's large apartment when Beset arrived. Situated on a long colonnade, these Royal residences faced a pond stocked with fish and planted with lotus flowers. This long elegant walkway was where Palace officials lived in large apartments befitting their importance and to accommodate their numerous attendants.

"Greetings, Butler Farafar," said Beset as she slipped off her litter.

"Greetings, Dwarf Beset. What brings you to my household?" asked the butler, as the bearers moved on.

"I have come to ask you a few questions about a time long ago when my wards, the royal twins, were born."

Butler Farafar looked nervously toward Pharaoh's distant receiving chambers. He did not invite Beset into the apartment.

"Yes," he said, speaking rapidly. "I remember well when they arrived. There was much to do about your twins from their birth on. First, their heavenly charts were cast, which took a great deal of time, and the Royal Astrologer is never happy when casting this information." He leaned his worn body against a column and continued to watch for the Royal Astrologer.

"Why do you say he is never happy about creating birth stories?" Beset asked.

Butler Farafar frowned before answering, again scanning the distance between Abu's apartment and Pharaoh's Palace where his master was conducting business.

"For important Royal childbirths, like twins, he uses certain articles he keeps in a small chest. The Royal Astrologer removes these items: a plait of Pharaoh's hair, a nugget of gold, a stone of turquoise and the tooth of a lion. He gathers them in his hand and gently tosses them onto a fabric with gold and silver threads that outline the Zodiac." Farafar used his bony hands to demonstrate. "When my master cast your wards' horoscopes, he gasped after the pieces fell into place on the cloth, then quickly put the items away. He translated the information to his scribes, what seemed to me to be very fast. It sounded false. Then, of course, the scribes transcribed his words on the finest of papyrus, but something strange happened afterwards.

He dismissed all but one of his scribes and told him to cast a second set of charts for the twins."

"You mean a duplicate set?" Dwarf Beset asked.

"No, the way I understood it Scribe Tiurek, his senior and most loyal scribe, was going to cast true charts for your twins. The Astrologer's descriptions of the charts of the twins took much longer the second time. I know that sounds strange, but that's the way I understood him."

"Really, you remember all that, Butler Farafar?" Beset raised an eyebrow and looked at him with a harsh glance, but Farafar nodded resolutely.

"Yes, I do. Scribes are constantly at work in this apartment. I know that of late there has been much reference to these charts in the ongoing correspondence of scrolls sent to Memphis. But I have told you a great deal, probably much more than I should."

"If I could just ask one more thing..." Beset began, but Farafar looked around nervously.

"I must go now, Dwarf Beset. I have no more to say to you on this subject," Farafar whispered, glancing around the sun-soaked garden.

"You have a keen memory, Butler Farafar."

The butler raised his eyebrows, "In this household you will be beaten if you forget something."

"Many thanks to you for your information, Butler Farafar, as you know what a dwarf hears will stay with a dwarf."

The two bowed to one another and Beset left the garden, her mind full of questions that she had no way of answering herself.

The following day, Beset followed the twins out for a walk and noticed Sennejem seated where he was surveying a newly planted garden. He helped Beset as she struggled to climb up onto the stone bench and sit next to him. In silence, they watched the twins swim in a large pond nearby.

Taten swam across the pool underwater and asked Jobu to count and see how long it took. Then she did the same for him. They came up sputtering, laughing in the shimmering gold light of Ra. Taten found a lotus flower floating nearby and held it in her mouth, swimming the distance of the pool once more as Jobu giggled at her antics. Beset noted with fondness how Princess Becataten could make her brother laugh when no one else could.

Beset swung her stubby legs while sitting on the stone bench watching the children play. "The Royal Astrologer was responsible for helping you rise to the position of Royal Gardener, was he not, Sennejem?" Beset finally asked after compiling her thoughts.

"Yes, I believe you could call him my mentor,"

Sennejem replied.

"So you know the Astrologer quite well, do you?"

"I do."

Beset knew the Royal Gardener held a prestigious position, especially given Pharaoh's interest in all growing things. With Abu's high ranking at Court, Sennejem was wellplaced to have him as a mentor. Of course, Sennejem was also of high rank; he knew his job well, was greatly devoted to his work and presented himself as an equal to those in the Court when necessary.

The two sat for some time in silence as the children splashed lazily along the side of the pool, the glimmering water stirred by their presence. Beset's thoughts too stirred; she wondered how to ask him if he knew of the intrigue surrounding the twins' charts, but his close position to Abu caused her to hesitate. She was surprised, then, when he asked her a question first.

"I have been wondering, Dwarf Beset, why would someone want to poison Nanny Maja?" Sennejem asked.

"I don't think it was meant for her," Beset said. "Do you know that I believe that the pomegranate juice was for the twins?" Beset asked in a high-pitched whisper.

Sennejem looked stunned. He shook his head.

Beset added, "It is but speculation. Thanks to the gods that Maja is well now. Sadly she is left with a limp and a fallen eye lid, but the twins would have certainly died if they had taken the drink."

Sennejem watched the twins lying beside the pool, warming in Ra's rays.

"I hope to find the culprit, Sennejem, but I, as a lowly dwarf, am not connected enough to hear the Court gossip about such matters."

Sennejem lowered his head. "It pains me greatly to hear this ill news. I promise I will endeavor to learn who tried to harm the children, too. I know from Lady Norfet that a royal scribe delivered the juice, and I now have decided to ask the Royal Astrologer Abu, who knows many scribes, his opinion as to who this might have been."

Beset's heart soared; this was her opportunity! "Take me with you, Royal Gardener," Beset said. "People are willing to tell me things they may not tell others."

The Royal Gardener said nothing. Beset sighed as they sat in silence.

Beset withheld the conversation from Sennejem that she had with Butler Farafar about the Astrologer. Her long ago declaration to Pharaoh to protect the twins was proving to be tricky and working its way into tangled circumstances. But Dwarf Beset knew, now more than ever, to keep her word, and her secrets.

Later that evening, she sent a message to Dwarf Heby to meet her. Beset asked him to listen to the conversation when Sennejem and Abu dined.

Once back in their apartment Beset called Taten to her side. "Taten, on the next Ra I am going to join you on your trip across the Nile and to the sites where the Royal Architects are working."

Taten was surprised, and pleased. "But it's a very long walk, Beset."

"By the heavens, I am not walking, I am taking a litter and you are welcome to join me, child. And today I want you to wear a shift, not a kilt. Come, I bought one in a merchant's stall the other day."

Taten pulled the linen garment, which was loose fitting, sheer and knee length, over her head and said, "It's scratchy, Beset."

"Yes, that will change when it gets a washing." Beset stepped back to look at Taten. "A shift makes you look like a young girl, not a child, and those braids will have to go soon. But for now, let's get to the bakery."

A quick stop for bread, and they were off to join Ra and the Royal Architects. Taten managed to direct the four bearers to the exact location where much activity was taking place, impressing Beset. As she licked dripping honey from her flatbread, Beset said, "Isn't this just a restoration project, Taten?"

Taten, exhilarated by watching the work, apparently didn't hear Beset. As the litter came to a stop, Beset said, "Have you met either of the Architects, Taten?"

"Oh no. Could you introduce them to me, Beset?"

"I certainly think it's time. All we ever hear from you

45

in the evening is about the glorious work of these Royal Architects."

Taten jumped off the litter and took Beset's hand.

Architect Suti looked up from his renderings as Dwarf Beset climbed over rubble with the child.

"Greetings, Dwarf Beset, what brings you to our site today?"

"Greetings Architects, I thought it was time that you meet your most enthusiastic follower, Princess Becataten."

"Greetings, Princess, I have noticed you, of course. You have always seemed interested in our work, and it is nice to see you are not running naked today."

Becataten's face reddened. Becataten was beginning to show signs of beauty and in her shift looked less like a street child. Hor acknowledged her with a nod and a clearing of this throat.

Suti smiled warmly. "I have seen you watching us build and restore for many Ras now." Taten blushed and stared at the ground.

Beset turned enthusiastically toward Taten. "Becataten, did you know that Suti has a huge Estate and is also famous for his tender beef that he raises on his land?"

Becataten shyly shook her head as Beset continued.

"You know, Royal Architect, Becataten is a fine student. I wonder if you would allow her some of your time, and perhaps even give her a few lessons that she could take home and work on."

"Oh, I think that is quite possible, Dwarf Beset," his eyes wrinkling in bemusement. Taten wiggled her sandals into the sand with joy and squeezed Beset's hand.

Beset asked Suti to step aside with her. "I know this is sudden and may even seem bold, but Princess Becataten and Prince Jobutaten are in need of mentors," Beset whispered to Suti, as his plump body leaned down to listen. "Because the Princess is so enamored with architecture and your work, not to mention that you and Hor are twins, I thought it a beneficial time to get you to meet one another. Should you know of anyone who may want to sponsor them, I would be forever grateful. Thank you, Royal Architect Suti."

Suti stood erect, raised an eyebrow, but said nothing. Beset made her farewells to the architects while Taten stayed to enjoy a wonderful new day where she could now feel free to ask questions, and would be privileged to take home lessons.

On Beset's hot and dusty ride back to their little apartment, she smiled as she thought of her progress that day. She wondered, how could a girl with an interest in architecture use such a talent? Now at least Becataten was able to talk to Royals about what she truly loved. Getting a bright young Princess noticed was possible, but would it all just end in a trip to Pharaoh's bedchamber? There she would be planted with the royal seed, and never be heard from again. Beset's smile faded. Pharaoh's house was replete with highly ranked Princesses. That fate couldn't happen to Taten. On the other hand, if Becataten could get along well enough with Suti, just maybe he could become her mentor. Another playing piece in her game to get the twins recognized by the Court began to form in Beset's mind.

After Beset had gone, Taten followed the Royal Architects like a hyena pup trails its mother. She ran toward them and began her fast-talking inquiries. "Architect Suti, can I help you roll out your papyri for your plans today? When you work in the open Court at Karnak Temple, how many people will be able to come and stand in the Court? Is this the plan that Queen Hatshepsut was working on when she died? Will you use the stone from but one quarry?" Taten had the need to question everything, and Suti appeared tolerant of her inquisitiveness. Unlike his lank twin Hor, who avoided Becataten as though she carried a plague.

When Ra was low in the sky, Suti motioned Taten his way. She came running down a hillside toward him. A frown creased his leathery round face as he placed a hand on her shoulder. "How old are you, Becataten?"

"I have lived through twelve innundations, Royal Architect."

"Do you continue to study your lessons,

Becataten?"

She replied in her fast speech, "When we moved to our royal apartment, no teaching scribe came with us, so I go to the Royal Library to read. But it's a long way from the west gate where we live, and sometimes they won't let me in unless Beset goes with me and has a fit like a cat."

Taten watched as Suti hid his smile. Then he set his pudgy fingers to work at a shaded field table, a broad plank across two drums of stone shaded with a thick linen canopy. He reached for a writing stick and an ink pot to scribe some problems on papyrus, then handed the small scroll to Taten. "Calculate these and bring them to me at the next Ra. You may observe our work until Ra leaves, but stay in the background and no more questions."

Taten did exactly as she was told and kept her distance, sitting on a nearby wall. Hor arrived and began speaking in an animated way to Suti. Taten wished she could hear every word. She was surprised when Suti pointed at her. When she saw Suti and Hor gather their scrolls to leave the site, she vigorously waved goodbye. She turned and skipped back to her apartment hugging the papyrus Suti had prepared for her.

Chapter 8

♊

Sennejem stood at the portal of Abu's large apartment as the great sun was leaving Egypt. A tall door carved of imported cedar marked the entrance. Abu's pet baboon heard him before Sennejem knocked and began to whimper.

It was well known that a few seasons back, Abu claimed the young animal from a date farm where his breed was raised and used as labor. The young beast he chose was castrated and delivered to Abu within a moon cycle. Awaiting the animal was a golden collar tagged with the name, Huni.

Sennejem's mouth watered, knowing that dining with Abu would be a sumptuous experience because the food came from Pharaoh's kitchen. When the door opened, Sennejem handed the butler a basket of ripe figs and said, "These are for Huni." The butler nodded, bowed as deep as his old body allowed, then with a scrawny arm silently offered Sennejem entrance. The cool rooms, like all the Royal apartments, were insulated from the heat of the desert with massively thick walls of whitewashed mud brick.

Before greeting Sennejem, Abu clapped his hands.

That produced four lean attendants, standing at attention. Pulling his rotund frame tall, Abu boomed his food order as the slaves listened.

"Two knuckles of Suti beef, four pigeons, a goose, and a crock of goat cheese with a cone of bread. A pot of olives and bunches of mint, parsley and dill. Bring green onions and radishes too. Choose the ripest melons, and don't forget honey cakes." Abu sat back down but had not yet given the order for his attendants to go.

Sennejem was excited when the words "Suti beef" were called out, knowing the meat was from cattle raised on the huge estate that Pharaoh had gifted his Royal Architect. Richly marbled, it was beef reserved mainly for the Court.

Abu turned to his butler, "We have sma, do we not?" Sma was blended wine of preferred vintages, found only in Pharaoh's cellar. How Abu got sma wine on his table, Sennejem wanted to know, but did not ask. The butler nodded that they did stock Pharaoh's vintage. Abu then motioned for the four young men to retrieve the food order from the royal kitchen, some three hundred steps away. They took off running, empty baskets in hand. Slaves sprinted to Pharaoh's kitchen lest they forget Abu's order, in which case they were beaten. Although all kitchens in Egypt were out doors, none was greater or larger than that of Pharaohs.'

Only then did Abu motion Sennejem to be seated.

"How goes your life, Gardener?"

"It goes well, thank you, Astrologer. It is always a pleasure to dine with you. You can call a menu faster and better than anyone I have ever known. Your food choices are always excellent."

With his large hand, Abu filled his mouth with almonds from a nearby bowl, taking his time to chew them. "You could, too, if you used Pharaoh's kitchen."

"Oh, I could never do that. I have a woman outside my quarters who has a small brazier and I pay her to cook for me from time to time. I fear that I would be taking from Pharaoh's table."

"Don't be stupid, Sennejem, Pharaoh's staff would just cook more food," said Abu.

Butler Farafar struggled with sturdy tables of mahogany that he placed before Abu and Sennejem. He set calcite bowls lined with rose petals for hand washing, pouring water over their hands as they held them above the bowls. Handing each man a square of linen, he placed a jeweled handled knife and a goblet of thinly crafted alabaster on each table, carefully filling them with sma.

Once the meal was served, Abu used his knife deftly on joints of Suti beef, poking large pieces into his mouth with the point of the blade. He tore apart the pigeons with his big hands and chomped them to the bone. He groaned sounds of pleasure like a man who hadn't eaten in days. He ripped the goose apart and ate the flesh off both legs and thighs. Sennejem ate with reserve, but his eyes grew wide as he tasted the beef. When Abu seemed to be slowing down, Sennejem spoke.

"I do not know if you have heard, but a terrible thing happened to Nanny Maja several Ras ago. She is the woman that came from Mitanni a few years ago with a little-known princess who died bearing Pharaoh's twins."

Abu grunted what sounded like a yes. "Of course, I know of the twins. I cast their charts and chose their names at Pharaoh's requests, many inundations ago."

Sennejem nodded and continued, "The nanny was sent pomegranate juice for the children. She tasted it first, as she always does, and grew deathly ill. She nearly died. Later it was found that the juice had been poisoned!"

Abu straightened in his chair and flatly answered, "Really? That is a shock. Who would do such a thing? Are you sure the juice was poisoned?"

"Oh yes. There was no doubt. An herbalist came to examine it. And I even tasted it."

"Who delivered the drink to this nanny?"

"It was a Royal Scribe who had worked briefly for Lady Norfet and who had knowledge of herbs. On occasion this scribe frequented the Royal Library. I was wondering if you may be aware of a Royal Scribe with knowledge of poison."

This time Abu did not look up and said in a low growling tone, "What makes you think I would know of such a scribe?"

"My pardon, Royal Astrologer, I just thought because you know and use so many Royal scribes, you may..."

Abu interrupted, "Do you have any idea how many Royal scribes work within the Palace, Sennejem?"

Sennejem shook his head.

"Of course you don't, Gardener. Your question is that of a fool. If you are so interested in finding such a person, why don't you ask the Overseer of All Works, and not me?"

"I would not trouble the Overseer of All Works, and I am sorry I troubled you. Please forgive me. But may I humbly ask you how many libraries there are in the Palace?"

Abu seemed less annoyed at this question. "You know of the Royal Library? I have a library for my work, and Pharaoh has a personal library on botany." Sarcastically he added. "Perhaps you would like to ask Pharaoh your question."

Sennejem quickly changed the subject, and with continued drinking the subject seemed to diminish Abu's outrage.

The end of the evening came when Abu clapped his hands, signaling his butler to unleash his baboon. This brought his pet running to his side where he sat attentatively. Abu fed the plump figs to the dun-colored beast that danced and begged for each piece of fruit. When Huni had devoured them, Abu stood and turned toward his bedchamber to retire, Huni at his side. Sennejem promptly left.

At the next leave of Ra, Sennejem reported back to Dwarf Beset. He said he had learned nothing from the Royal Astrologer about the scribe in question and had succeeded only in angering Abu with his query. Heby reported to Beset the same story.

Beset said to Sennejem, "Why do you suppose he was angered over such a matter?"

Sennejem shook his head and shrugged.

Chapter 9

♊

Maja's poisoning slowly became a memory, and the little family of four did not mention it further. Taten and Jobu had lived through almost thirteen inundations while Nanny Maja and Beset had lived through twice that many river risings.

"I've packed our midday meal so we can spend time at the river today," Maja said with enthusiasm.

"Do we have to go?" whispered Jobu to Taten.

"Of course we do, Jobu," Taten whispered back.

"But she gets sad when we go to the river and starts talking about our dead mother," Jobu said.

"Our dead mother, as you call her, was Princess Attah of Mitanni in the great empire of Babylon," said Taten indignantly. "Besides, the only other person you want to be with is that scribe that you won't talk to anyone about."

Avoiding Taten, Jobu walked to Maja, and said, "I'll carry the basket of food, Maja."

Maja had regained her health, and loved walking with the children the long distance to the opposite end of the Palace where the Mother Nile flowed. Once on the shore, Maja would repeat the story about their mother,

Princess Attah, who had come from a land where two great rivers crossed one another and where the water raged.

"The Nile is calm today, so we can walk into the mud. It softens the skin on our feet, and we can watch the fishing boats and water birds." Maja would show delight at outings like these, but her memory of Princess Attah would tend to sadden her as she told her tale of a long-dead princess and a land far away.

Beset liked trekking the Palace grounds, but because it took her an entire day get to the Palace apartments on foot, she began using traveling chairs. At the opposite end of the compound, near Pharaoh's chambers, she could move about the halls among the Royals and Nobles. She was forever seeking a way to get the twins recognized by means of a significant liaison who could take them to Court. This meant listening to much gossip and accepting invitations of refreshments and attending small social gatherings. Beset paused in the halls to rest one afternoon when Queen Tiy walked past with her entourage. She saw Beset and stooped low to speak with her. "Are you lost, Dwarf Beset?" the Queen asked.

"Oh, no, queen, I am merely resting my short legs," Beset answered, lowering her eyes in a humble way.

"It is good fortune I have found you, Dwarf Beset," the Queen said. "You must come to my gathering this

57

evening, then you shall stay in my Royal apartments overnight."

Beset agreed and sent word to Maja that she would not return that evening. Maybe the gods would smile upon her today, and she could find a way to discuss the twins, even get them invited to a Royal event.

In the Queen's chambers, candles blazed and scores of floor pillows were strewn about. Gathered nobles and high-ranking guests nibbled on tidbits of exotic nuts, figs, grapes, honey cakes and sipped sma wine. The guests' garments shimmered with golden threads and rich colors as the gossip flowed.

"Now that Queen Tiy's apartment is complete, I'm sure you have all noticed that Pharaoh has let her mark every building brick with her cartouche," said one sparkling guest.

"And Pharaoh allows the Queen her own cook. His name is Chef Bakenamun."

"He cooks well enough, but he is ill tempered," another regal-looking woman whispered.

"Has anyone seen the goods that arrived a few Ras ago from Anatolia?" A woman giggled, covering her mouth as bangles clanged on her wrists, "My friend entertained a captain from one of the ships the other night, and he brought her woven fabrics and jewelry like we have never seen in Egypt."

A eunuch added, "I have heard it said that if a captain can forge the Great Sea with exceptional goods from the Mycenaean Empire and trade his shipments here in Egypt for gold, he can retire for life."

"Don't forget the exotic cargo that arrives from caravans overland from our eastern shores like Punt," said the eunuch's companion, holding hands with his male friend.

Beset almost interrupted to say *she* was one of those exotic items that had arrived from Punt many years ago, but instead decided to listen. She learned Pharaoh had scores of vassal states beyond the Great Sea, divided into three administrative areas. These were called the eastern countries, with Egyptian overseerers who were responsible for regular tribute. These vassal states returned to Egypt all manner of goods, livestock and slaves.

Beset lazed sleepily on a huge pillow as more eunuchs entertained everyone with stories of Pharaoh.

"My Lady, you know that Pharaoh's butler bathes and dresses our Lord but is never allowed to touch his skin?" said an elderly man. The Queen nodded her head knowingly.

Someone blurted, "Everyone in Egypt has piss a pot, but Pharaoh has a bathing room with a drainage trough that takes away the Royal waste."

"That will be enough chatter," said the Queen.

"But may I say one last thing, My Lady," offered a young girl. "I think it was a lovely gesture that Pharaoh announced his marriage to you, Queen Tiy, by sending inscribed scarabs throughout his lands."

Beset soon found the stories of the rich and noble

redundant and tiresome. Where was the intrigue? She smiled at everyone, yawned and slipped away quietly. She tightened her small fists as an attendant directed her toward her assigned cot in the Queen's suites.

Yet as she pondered all she had just heard and seen, she wondered: Why were her sweet twins never to know this life of leisure? Why had they forever been ignored? And why had the gods not allowed them to be introduced not once at Court? She set her jaw and decided that it was her duty to correct these injustices as she crawled into the lavish cot appointed to her.

Beset awoke the following Ra to the view of many bodies of soundly sleeping guests. Some were in cubicles on cots, others in larger beds. Most had fallen asleep in their jewels and fine clothing with too much sma in their bellies. She quickly dressed and took a last look about at the beautiful items that adorned the Queen's apartment. The sumptuous rugs from eastern provences covered the floors, hanging silks from caravan traders danced in the morning breeze, and massive art objects of carved stone from exotic locales stood against the walls. Attendants had begun to arrive with trays of grapes, watermelon, pomegranates, and plums. Others brought pots of tamarind and hibiscus teas with baskets of freshly baked lotus-flower bread.

Beset heaved a great sigh as she headed outdoors.

Not wanting to stand in the halls for a litter outside the queen's apartment, Beset slipped into a small garden and climbed onto a bench. She knew a litter would soon come along, and the planted area seemed such a refreshing place after her night with the noble and royal.

Four runners, manning a wicker chair, soon approached. She hailed them with a wave of her short arms. "Bearers, do you know the way to the royal kitchen?" Beset called.

The lead man bowed deeply and said, "I do, Dwarf Beset, and it would be an honor to take you there."

"Thank you," Beset said as she seated herself in the chair, adjusting the animal hide pillows for comfort. She hadn't slept well, and her body was sore and tired.

"You have not been to the royal kitchen before?" the bearer asked.

"No, I have not. But last night I learned how large it is and that Pharaoh has allowed Queen Tiy her own private chef."

"Yes, that is true, and if you don't mind my saying so, Chef is a tyrant."

Beset laughed and said she had heard that last night, too. The bearer went on, "Pharaoh's chef works at one end of the Royal Kitchen and is of a good nature. Chef Bakenamun cooks for the Queen, at the other end. May I suggest that I deliver you to the—"

Beset interrupted him. "You may indeed deliver me to Pharaoh's chef."

Her conveyance moved down the shady side of the Queen's apartment where the great Ra had not yet arrived. Here there was a long view of the Mother Nile on her right. Living at the opposite end of Pharaoh's Palace compound, Beset rarely saw the river. She felt a sense of reverence when she viewed the Great Mother and spoke a quiet prayer to her.

Then, into view came an open roof of at least two hundred steps long. The sounds of utensils, chopping, and pounding grew louder as they neared. When Beset stepped off her litter and inhaled, her mouth watered and she licked her lips and entered. Scores of workers were cutting vegetables, boning fish, and bisecting the carcasses of cows, pigs, sheep and wild game. The calling of orders was deafening. She stood watching, her mouth agape. Once the Royal Chef saw Beset he took long, swift steps to greet her. Smiling broadly, he revealed several missing teeth.

He was a tall man with a low-hung belly. His unique and colorful head covering identified him as Royal Chef. To add to his importance, he also wore a gold medallion dangling from a chain around his neck that designated him 'Cook Supreme'.

"Greetings, Dwarf Beset. What brings you to the Royal Kitchen? Do you have a special order for me?" He said, in a low deep voice.

Beset was nervous and her voice shrieked higher

than usual. "No, Royal Chef, I am on tour and..."

He boomed, "Well, then, let me give you a proper tour. I do not have many visitors, and it will be a pleasure to show you my kitchen."

Beset relaxed. This was not Queen Tiy's chef. "Oh, that would please me very much, Royal Chef."

Above the long roof were working fans, manned by slaves who pumped them rigorously. These giants wafted the air about, and spanned the length of the long roof, but still the flies came. "Your kitchen is so big, Royal Chef."

"I imagine it must seem even bigger to a small person such as yourself, Beset." Chef laughed as he led the way. He snapped his fingers at a lanky Nubian, ordering him to carry Beset on his shoulder so she could have a proper view of his domain. The Nubian lifted Beset like a feather and adjusted her short legs around his neck. Looking down she viewed the long tables beneath the lengthy linen covering that afforded the workers shade. Chef patted her back, smiled and pointed to the areas where his vast staff cleaned and prepared vegetables, broke down animal carcasses, and butchered poultry. On the ground were baskets of fruits and clay tubs of water to soak off black soil from root vegetables. At one table, a baboon carefully removed dates from a sack then stacked them on plates. Beset noticed that he intermittently popped a ripe one into his mouth. Rows of donkeys stood outside the covered area and were being off-loaded of their

63

precious fuel: wood and dung to feed the large cooking braziers. Squawking ducks and geese were hanging upside down, awaiting the knife. In the distance she could see a small herd of cows being milked. Goats were tethered nearby for their milk. Butter was churned, and cheese was housed in a shed near them. Different varieties of flour were being ground next to breadmakers who created many forms of dough and flatbreads, readying them for clay kilns. Runners stood patiently as food orders were being prepared for their noble masters.

"You have everything here, Royal Chef, but how do you cook for so many?"

He stood tall and said, "I cook first for Pharaoh and his guests. For example, last night Viceroy Merymose from Kush was with our King, and I served them a sumptuous dinner. I cook next for Pharaoh's Court. Everyone else waits. But if one day you, Dwarf Beset, want an order you will not wait." He snapped his fingers again and Beset was gently lowered to the ground. "Now come and sit with me for a midday meal. Fresh baby eels have arrived. I will treat you to my favorite delicacy since you have graced my kitchen with your presence."

Pleased, Beset nodded and allowed herself to be catered to as she enjoyed the rich and delicious fare. Being in the presence of Pharaoh's Chef made her more determined than ever to bring the twins to their proper station. They had never tasted a fine meal nor seen

64

exotic foods. They had no knowledge beyond the education they had received in the Royal Nursery. No runners ever graced their apartment, no servants brought them prepared delicacies. *Yes,* thought Beset as she feasted on the tasty eel dish in front of her. *The twins will have all this, and more.*

Chapter 10

♊

Beset soon left her conveyance to walk off the heavy midday meal the Royal Chef had prepared for her. Along the way, the sumptuous tastes remained with her, and she felt a bit guilty at consuming such a lavish meal.

It was quiet as she strolled. Most Palace occupants were napping this time of day. Stopping to rest, she leaned into a column, and discovered on the other side a group of young scribes seated on stone benches, having a hushed conversation. They had not seen her approach. She heard a voice whisper, "I know of a minor harem Prince named Jobutaten that I can bring to our next evening at the great pond. He is a young and tender thing, and we can induct him into our way of life."

Beset recognized the voice as the scribe whom Jobutaten had befriended.

Another voice asked, "Is he interested in boys?"

Beset held her breath through a short silence, and then the older voice spoke again. "Trust me, I will bring this princeling to our gathering and bet you a gold debon he becomes one of us. We'd best get back to our duties."

Beset covered her mouth with her hand and clutched the column for support, her knees buckling as the scribes stood to leave. From their words she gleaned the older scribes were trying to make Jobu their sexual pet. She stood still as a stone. When the young scribes left, she huffed her way toward home with renewed energy.

After a sleepless night of worry about the scribes and the twins' place in the Palace, Beset rose and trod to the nearest baker, who fired up his oven well before the light of day. There she found bread, cheese, plenty of honey and butter. In a nearby garden, she used a tree stump as a table and settled herself on the ground to take an early breakfast with a cup of beer. While cursing aloud over the young boy's words of yesterday, she heard someone ask, "Is that you, Beset?"

With a mouthful she mumbled, "Yes."

"Are you alone, or am I disturbing you?" asked Sennejem.

"I am alone. I am angry and I have a serious problem with no answer in sight. And when a dwarf cannot see a solution, it is a very bad day."

"Can I help?"

"I'm not sure, Sennejem, but you may be able to answer a few questions for me." Beset related the conversation she had overheard involving Jobutaten. "Do you know if the scribes in Abu's house are mostly interested in boys, not girls?"

Sennejem looked flustered. "I... I really couldn't say, Beset," he stammered.

"Yes, you can, Sennejem. It is a simple question," she said.

"Well, yes, I guess you could say that the older of the scribes probably prefers his own gender. Why do you want to know?" Sennejem asked.

"I want to know because I think that older scribe is interested in Jobu for that reason alone, and I don't believe Jobu knows that is why the scribe associates with him."

"It is not uncommon for boys to experiment in their early years with their friends, Beset," Sennejem said.

"Yes, I know that. I am not judging the scribe, but I feel Jobu is about to be used, and for another reason."

"Are you sure Jobu's not just wanting to become a scribe and is associating with the boy for that reason?" Sennejem asked.

She shook her head and rubbed her nose. "I do not know what is happening yet. I need more facts," Beset said, firmly.

"I agree," said Sennejem. "But I am not the one with the knowledge you seek."

As she and Sennejem made more small talk over their meal, Beset's mind began to wander as to whom she might speak with next.

Beset sat waiting in their favorite garden for Dwarf Heby.

"I hope you haven't been here long, Beset," Heby said, as he stepped off a litter with a basket.

"No, no, I was just enjoying the shade. Ra is strong today."

Heby reached into the carrier which held a pitcher of beer, a cone of bread, pickles, and a round of fresh goat cheese.

"Mmmm, this smells like good cheese, Heby." Beset inhaled deeply.

"It's the finest from Pharaoh's kitchen, and that's what the Royal Astrologer demands." Heby said.

They settled on benches to drink beer and munch on the bread and cheese.

A friendship had developed between them, and when they met, it was in this secluded garden. Heby found it more difficult to be away from his duties than Beset. But when they got together it was midway between Abu's grand dwelling and the humble apartment at the back end of the Palace grounds where Beset lived.

"What is it like living on that long colonnade among those elite Royal residences?" Beset asked.

Heby took a deep breath. "Busy."

"Doesn't Architect Hor live on that beautiful arcade too?"

69

"Yes, he lives at the other end. His twin, Suti spends many nights there as it takes half a Ra to drive his chariot home to his Estate. It's a huge land holding that Pharaoh awarded him where vast amounts of food are grown, and many animals are herded. It is said that Architect Suti has a wife who is an able overseer, but a difficult woman," Heby said, taking a big bite of cheese.

"Yes, I have heard that, too," Beset agreed, nibbling the end of a sour pickle. A warm breeze reached her face. "Is Hor involved in the Estate?" Dwarf Beset asked, trying to gather as much information as she could, especially about the twin architects.

"No. I worked in Architect Hor's household for a brief time, and I heard him say to his twin, 'There is no farmer in me, Brother.' His apartment is very elegant, and he enjoys entertaining. He has a lot of male friends."

"Speaking of male friends does the scribe called Tiurek have many?" Beset asked.

Heby scratched at his nose and cleared his throat. "He's Abu's favorite scribe and very smart, but he can also be very mean. Why do you ask?"

"Tiurek has been spending time with Jobutaten, and I think he wants to control, even dominate, him."

"If Tiurek spends time with someone, that is what he wants to do, you are correct."

"Why does Abu keep him, if he is so mean, Heby?"

"I think he finds him loyal, and he keeps the Astrologer's secrets. They are somewhat alike."

"What kind of secrets?" Beset asked in a quiet voice. She tried to stay still to hide her impatience as Heby readjusted himself on the bench. Finally he spoke in lower tones. "The Royal Astrologer recently ordered a large raft to be built by his Nubian slaves. He has had a long-standing business in the slave trade, and, I think a clandestine one."

"Why do you suppose he keeps such an operation secret?" Beset asked.

"My guess is that Abu is about to move his human cargo to Memphis. He could barter the Nubians for higher prices there. He bought them in Kush, for but a few trade goods, and without Pharaoh's knowledge."

"You would think that he would not go behind Pharaoh to do this." Beset said.

"Greed is a common trait among the rich, Beset, you know that."

Another soft breeze passed over them, and they sat quietly for a time before Beset said, "If you ever hear any talk about my twins in your household, I would greatly appreciate knowing about it."

Heby nodded, patting Beset's hand. "I know. I will tell you."

Heby was outside getting a breath of fresh air one warm evening, inhaling the aroma from a nearby rose garden. He watched the lotus blossoms slowly close

71

with the falling darkness. It had been a long hard day of work, and the heat had been strong. He heard short swift steps on the arcade that stopped at Abu's apartment. It was architect Suti who looked to be in deep thought.

Suti knocked on Abu's door. The aged Butler Farafar welcomed him into the stark receiving chamber, announced him then disappeared.

Heby entered the apartment through the servant's entrance, and watched through a crack in a warped door as Suti entered.

Abu looked up from a papyrus. Heby watched as Suti reacted to the pungent animal smell in the apartment, then peered around and looked surprised to see a sleeping baboon in the corner. With a pitcher of wine and a fine goblet before him, Abu sat at his bench. The only light in his chamber came from a few saucers of tallow with burning wicks. There were few adornments within, no statues of gods, not even a wall painting. An ample library chamber lay beyond, crowded with rolled papyri. But, glistening high on a shelf, was a collection of jewel-handled daggers.

Receiving Suti with surprise, Abu rose to tower over him. "You have a heavenly chart you require of me, Royal Architect?"

As Suti stepped forward, he straightened his posture. "No, no, but you do know the heavenly chart of the child I wish to speak to you about. It is the Princess Becataten, born in the harem of a Mitanni

Princess."

Heby's interest grew, and he listened to what he knew he would pass on to Dwarf Beset.

Abu stood more erect, and his left eye twitched. Then he spoke without animation. "The charts of Royal children are privy only to Pharaoh," Abu said with authority.

"I understand, Royal Astrologer, and I do not come to infringe on that privacy. I come to discuss the child because she is one who learns quickly and shows much promise. I knew you would understand this from casting her birth record. I thought that perhaps, since you and I were playmates as children, I might ask a favor of you."

"A favor? What kind of favor?" Abu asked with suspicion in his voice.

"I thought that you and I might mentor the young Princess Becataten."

With a sour expression, Abu sat, and did not offer Suti a chair.

"But I know how very busy you are with the demands of the Court. One can just look around and see the vast number of scrolls you and your scribes are working on," Suti gestured.

Remaining on his bench, Abu said, "I will think about this, and we will talk again, but now I am occupied."

Suti reacted to his dismissal with a polite bow and

left the apartment. Heby watched the Architect pause to listen to Abu call a food order to the butler, "A plate of pickled meats, a stack of bread and two jugs of beer."

Heby then observed Suti standing outside with a pensive expression, staring into the distance.

Later that evening, Beset and Heby drank beer late into the evening under a pomegranate tree in their midway garden meeting place.

Heby explained how he overheard Suti's request, and Abu's aloof response toward the idea of mentoring Princess Becataten.

"That is a disturbing conversation that the Astrologer and the Architect had, don't you think, Heby?"

Dwarf Heby set his cup of beer down on their bench. "Beset, you may be expecting too much of architect Suti, and the astrologer as well, to be mentors to the Princess. Even though Suti has no children, he is a very busy royal and knows he can't support your Princess alone. Mentoring is very rare, Beset."

Beset was quiet for a long while. "It's not just getting Becataten and Jobutaten mentored. There more to it than that, Heby. It's getting them recognized by the Court."

74

"You do live humbly and distant from of all the Royals," Heby said. "I believe you told me that they have never been received at Court. Why do you think that is, Beset?"

Beset, her voice shrill, said, "That's what I am trying to find out!" Her beer sloshed as she grabbed the bench with her free hand so she wouldn't fall off.

Chapter 11

♊

Suti spent the night in his brother's apartment. When he awoke, he was a man in low spirits. A large cup of cool beer, warm bread and ripe figs were left at his bedside table by Hor's butler. As Suti sat up in bed, he absently took his breakfast, drank a little brew and nibbled at the fruit. After he bathed and dressed, a resource came to him. Out the door he went with a piece of flatbread, his short-stepped pace quickening as he ate and walked. The journey to the gardens next to Pharaoh's audience chamber was invigorating, coupled with a warm Nile breeze that carried the scent of narcissus mixed with castor bean oil. The army of Pharaoh's gardeners all lathered their backs with the oil to stave off the Egyptian sun. Strutting peacocks screeching to their peahens brought a smile to Suti, as did an abundance of fish jumping in a nearby pond.

His mood changed from dark to light.

When Suti peeked into Pharaoh's audience chamber, luck was with him as he caught the eye of Vizier Huy, the man he wanted to see. Vizier busied himself with scribes but turned to Suti with an expression that said he would get away sometime soon.

A nearby stone bench at the far end of the chamber seemed an inauspicious place to wait. Suti found himself staring at the ornate stone floor he and Hor had designed for the audience chamber. He and his twin had chosen the finest artisans to paint their renderings. The floor depicted a colorful Mother Nile with her verdant banks, teeming fish, water fowl and flourishing papyrus plants.

After finishing his business, the Vizier took quick steps toward Suti. As he approached him, he was both walking and reading a scroll. Rushing to step into his cadence, Suti said, "Vizier, I have a request for you to make on my behalf to Pharaoh."

The Vizier didn't look up, but grunted.

With a direct approach and speaking quickly, Suti began, "Lady Nagara and I would like to request that we mentor Princess Becataten for a few inundations while she lives on my estate. I need not tell you that Lady Nagara is a talented woman of nobility, and could be instrumental to the Princess during her transition to womanhood. As you know, we are without children."

The Vizier stopped and looked up from his scroll to scrutinize Suti's face. "Why do you think Pharaoh would want this, Royal Architect?"

The Vizier always wanted to present a good case when asking a request from Pharaoh. Suti stood as tall as his short frame allowed. "I would hope mentoring the Princess would give Lady Nagara and me the opportunity to serve our Living God in yet another way

77

for the kindnesses and gifts that he has bestowed on us."

Satisfied, the Vizier returned to the audience chamber to present Suti's request that very morning. Suti took the bench to wait for his bid to be heard.

In the gleaming hall, the Vizier gave his list of warrants and information to The Living God. Abu and others stood near as the King sat upon his golden throne, looking somewhat bored as the list went on. Nearby many slaves tended to any possible need he may have had and his glance went occasionally to a much-painted harem girl across the room that seemed to be flirting with him. The Vizier ended his business with Pharaoh with Suti's proposal. "Lastly, My Lord, I have a request for mentoring a little known Princess by Royal Architect Suti and Lady Nagara."

Abu's frame grew rigid. He drew close to Pharaoh's ear and whispered at length to him.

The Vizier's eyes were cold, and he carried a sour look, unaccustomed to being interceded by anyone. Abu delivered what clearly was a rebuttal as the Vizier tightly rolled a scroll he held behind him.

Pharaoh looked off into the distance with a pensive air after listening to the royal astrologer, and finally said, "I grant Architect Suti his request."

Abu's face showed defeat. He stepped back from Pharaoh, his left eye twitching.

At first light, Suti rushed home to his vast landholding bequeathed to him by Pharaoh for his lifetime. The land was south of Thebes on the Nile. To arrive there, traveling by chair, it took a full day, and runners had to be replaced several times during the journey. The crowded Mother Nile sometimes offered a comfortable craft, but not always. Suti chose a two-horse chariot that was always available, and the ride took but half the time.

Although he and Hor were in the middle of an important restoration project at the Karnak temple, he left for his property, driving his horses hard. It was important to explain to Lady Nagara personally that she was to be responsible for mentoring a royal child. Pharaoh had decreed it, and it would likely involve two inundations. That sort of commitment meant sitting with Lady Nagara to explain why he made this request. Suti had reasoned that because they had been childless, mentoring Princess Becataten could have rewarding benefits for them both.

At midday, near the end of his drive, Suti's land came into view. Here hundreds of workers watched over the cattle that grazed his fields. The site was majestic, manned with slaves and able attendants who cared for Suti's smaller animal herds and growing fields as well as his grand residence. His land was important as it produced famous beef, and he was proud the Court had titled it, 'Suti Beef.' At a small knoll, Suti always stopped to view his farm workers toiling to produce barley, flax, vegetables, fruits, and flowers for the glory of Egypt. He did not linger long to observe their efforts on this day, however, but instead rushed to meet with his Lady, his competent overseer in his absence.

News of his arrival always preceded him, and when he drove his chariot to the steps of his grand house, Lady Nagara waited at the entrance.

Her face was fully painted, her eyes outlined heavily with kohl; cobalt blue colored her eyelids, and her checks were flush with a dusting of ocher, the color of apricots. Not wearing a wig in the extreme heat of this land, south of the Thebian Palace, she stood like an Egyptian goddess in her kilt and silver sandals. Nearly thirty innundations in age, she still dressed bare-breasted and turned many a man's head. From her ears dangled lapis and carnelian earrings. Cuffs of solid gold studded her wrists. A necklace of turquoise collared her neck and the top of her breasts.

As Suti climbed the stairs to greet her, with her usual coolness, she turned a cheek for him to kiss.

"Greetings, Honey Cakes, I arrive with special news."

"I am sure you do. You were not scheduled to arrive for many moons."

Suti stood half a head shorter than she, marveling

80

at her beauty. "Come," he said placing his chubby arm around her waist, "Someone, find me my scribe and a cool goblet of wine."

Once settled in their formal chamber, Suti began to ramble about what he was working on at the Karnak Temple, and explained that he and Hor were not arguing as much as they used to, that new projects were coming faster than they could keep up with when Lady Nagara interrupted him.

"Suti, tell me what you have come all this way to say."

"Well, my Honey Cakes." Suti wiped his head with a damp linen cloth a slave offered. "Pharaoh has granted a request of mine - actually I had the Vizier present the request, as ours, to Pharaoh."

"Go on, Suti," Lady Nagara said, her eyes narrowing as she sat a bit taller on the edge of her seat.

Suti rushed his words. "It seems that there is a little-known harem princess named Becataten. She is a very bright young girl about to come into her womanhood. She has never been properly recognized by the Court and is a bit of a waif. Like me, she is a twin. Their mother died in childbirth. For many moons, she has been interested in our work at the Karnak Temple and..." Suti used the cloth again on his face and head.

"Suti, are you saying she is to live here?"

"Exactly, my darling, we are to mentor her."

"We?" Lady Nagara said.

"Yes, my Honey Cakes, she would reside here and you would be largely responsible for her upbringing and education."

Lady Nagara sat back on her lounge, but said nothing, and Suti rose to busy himself with his scribe, wanting to get away from her kohl black narrowed eyes.

Becataten arrived in the beginning light at the Karnak Temple where Hor worked on a restoration project. She approached him slowly but he chose to ignore her. "Greetings, Architect Hor," Becataten said politely. "Will Architect Suti be joining you this Ra?"

"Suti is at his Estate," grumbled Hor.

Becataten hesitated, not liking to talk too much to the ever-annoyed Hor. "When will he return, Architect Hor?" she quickly asked.

Hor's glare took Becataten aback. "Many pardons, I do not wish to be interruptive; I just have my completed lesson to give to him." She held out her scroll.

"You will have much time for scrolls." Hor said with a mocking smile.

"I do not understand, Architect."

Hor spoke loudly. "Suti is at his Estate explaining *you* to Lady Nagara."

"Who is Lady Nagara? Does this mean I have done something wrong?"

Hor grew irritated. "Lady Nagara is an intelligent and noble woman."

"But who is she?" Becataten felt hot tears in her eyes.

Shaking his head, Hor huffed. "You *are* an ignorant one, aren't you? She is Suti's wife."

Becataten wiped tears from her checks with the back of her hand while she crumpled her lesson-scroll in the other. She stood there mute, not knowing what to say.

Adjusting his stance and pretending to work at his drafting table, he responded, "Stop sniveling, the Gods have smiled upon you. You are to be mentored by Suti and Lady Nagara, but I know not why."

Taten covered her mouth with her hands, then stood straight and said, "Thank you, thank you very much for telling me, Architect Hor." She turned and ran as fast as she could to share her good fortune with her little family, her tears drying quickly in the hot sun of Ra.

Full of her breathtaking news, Taten raced to the river raft and jumped aboard. Crossing to the other side of the Nile, she thought she had never seen it move more slowly. Leaping off well before the barge touched the shore, she ran home so fast she lost a sandal along the way and hopped across the hard hot sand. Arriving at her apartment, she leaned into her doorway breathing like a spent jackal and clutched at a biting pain in her side, her foot burning.

"Maja! Jobu! Beset!" called Taten breathlessly. "I'm going to live with Royal Architect Suti and Lady Nagara on their Estate!" Becataten rambled. Her brother and Tiurek were on the floor playing a game of senet, and were momentarily distracted. The room fell silent.

"What do you go on about?" Maja finally asked.

"I'm going to live on a grand state, Architect Suti's Estate, Maja."

"Who told you that?" asked Maja.

"Architect Hor, Suti's twin. Isn't it wonderful?"

"Why you going there?" asked Maja.

"They are going to mentor me," Becataten said with elation.

"What is mentor?" Maja asked.

Still out of breath, Becataten said, "It means I get to study more, learn more and I will be taught how to be a lady who can one day be received at Court."

Beset screeched as she hobbled in from her sleeping alcove. "That is wonderful, Taten! You will learn much, and I have heard Suti's Estate is beautiful with a huge villa. Lady Nagara even grows special flowers for Pharaoh. I have also heard they raise cattle and many exotic animals for Pharaoh's zoo."

84

Jobu eyes began to water and his scribe friend patted his hand. "When will you leave?" Jobu asked, quietly.

"Soon, but I am not sure exactly what Ra."

The boy playing with Jobu stood then left, nodding as he exited. Beset squealed with delight, but Jobu looked crushed. Taten went to him and placed her hand on his shoulder.

Of late, Jobu's new friend had appeared at their apartment often, taking Jobu away to games and sometimes keeping him out late at night. Taten believed Jobu seemed joyless around this scribe, but he seemed to have a relationship of sorts with him. She argued with Jobu many times, trying to convince him not to associate with the scribe. But Jobu, who was never adamant about anything, continued to visit with this youth.

Jobu's head lowered as he fiddled with the sticks of the board game.

Beset said, "Jobu, you can visit Taten at the Estate. Would you like that?" But Jobu didn't answer.

Beset turned to Taten, looking at her as if she were for the last time. "What I have worked for is about to happen! You are to be become educated, a lady," said Beset in a whisper.

Maja fell silent and quietly retired to her small bedchamber. Beset, holding back tears, hugged Taten. Beset pulled Jobu next to her, his waist at her shoulder. Tearfully she shooed the twins to their chamber for their evening bath. Taten realized that this was one of the last times the little family would be together, and she fought the lump in her throat as she and Jobu went toward their rooms.

As Beset wrung out linen clothes from a water pot for the twins to wash themselves, Becataten tried to get Jobu to talk to her.

"Aren't you happy for me, Jobu? Please speak to me." She turned to Beset, who shook her head then held a finger before her lips, asking Becataten not to query Jobu further.

The three ate dinner in silence. Then Beset promised her usual, a bedtime story. Taten and Jobu enjoyed the larger bedchamber with two down-filled cots, a chest each, a chair and some shelves. Jobu's toys filled a small basket, but the shelves were crowded with Taten's scrolls, her brushes and inkpots that she used to keep notes and drawings about the architects' progress on the Karnak temple.

Beset's story began as she sat on a big cushion below their cots. "A beautiful young princess went to a huge estate to grow into a grand lady. Her brother, who was a handsome prince, came to visit her..." she began. Taten knew that Beset told these stories mainly for Jobu because it was his happy time.

After storytelling, Beset told Taten how wonderful her mentoring would be and how happy she was for her. She kissed Taten on the forehead before heading for her own bedchamber.

"Goodnight, Beset," Taten said, her throat tight again at the thought that her days here with Jobu, Beset and Maja were few.

"Goodnight, sweet Princess," Beset whispered as she left the room.

Taten crept onto Jobu's cot, hauling one of the old cats. Jobu turned away, sniveling.

"Jobu, don't cry. I love you and as Beset said, you can come and visit. I know you can. Architect Suti is a kind man. And it will only be for a few Nile risings. Then I will return, and you and I will live together forever." He still had his back to her and wouldn't turn around. She moved closer and hugged him in her protective way, her hand on his scrawny dark shoulder. "Jobu, that older scribe Tiurek who always comes to visit you seems strange. Do you like him?"

Jobu was silent for a time and then said in a choked voice, "Don't go, Taten."

"Jobu, it will just be for a little while, just until I get my moon visits, and when I return our lives will be as they have always been."

He drew away from her and remained silent.

She tried to think of something else to say, but began to imagine the new life she was about to enter when sleep arrived.

Chapter 12

♊

The day had arrived for Taten to leave for Suti's estate. She called anxiously to her family from the apartment doorway. "I promised Suti that I would be at his litter before Ra shows himself. Please, hurry everyone."

Earlier, Becataten had packed her possessions in a small bundle that included two linen shifts, a comb, one pair of papyrus sandals and her nursery gifts of gold bracelets from Pharaoh.

Jobu staggered from his bedchamber, rubbing sleep from his eyes. Maja dragged herself to the door with Taten's small bag of belongings. Beset, while smoothing her shift, hurried toward their exit. The cats cried and weaved between Becataten's legs, their tails held high.

"Let's go. If we go now I think we will have time to stop at the bakers." They walked to the end of their apartment complex and stopped at the nearby bakery where an assistant was pulling flatbread from a round clay oven with his long wooden pallet. Maja and Jobu each grabbed a piece. Beset took two, lathering them with butter, grunting with sounds of delight as she ate. Taten was ahead of them, bread in one hand, a fig in the other.

They walked in a line as commoners did, a disheveled bunch, as they moved toward the west. They edged around some new plantings where desert sand had been laced with black soil from the Nile, and the smell of clean rich earth filled the air. Becataten thought it must be a large herb garden, because the aroma of rosemary and peppermint was strong. She watched the Royal Gardener Sennejem directing a crew, and when he saw them, he swiftly headed their way. When he caught up to the small group, he placed a gentle hand on Maja's shoulder.

"Is Becataten going somewhere, Maja?" inquired Sennejem softly.

"Yes, Taten goes away to the big Estate, a whole Ra away. She will not come back until she is a woman."

"What large Estate, Maja?

"Architect Suti's, who she now loves more than she loves us," Maja said, weeping.

Sennejem drew in a heavy breath, which he covered with a cough. "Of course, I remember now. He's the one mentoring her," said Sennejem.

"Yes. That is what Taten calls it. What is mentoring, Sennejem?"

"It is when someone helps another to rise in education and status."

Maja asked, "Do you know if Architect Suti and his Lady are loving people?"

"They are very rich and well-placed people who can

help the princess in many ways."

"But are they loving people, Sennejem?"

Softly he replied, "No, Maja. I hear Lady Nagara is quite firm in her ways."

Maja wept again.

At the west gate were two sleeping guards that Sennejem awakened. The embarrassed sentries quickly stood, bowed to the Royal Gardener, and opened both doors wide. This was a little used access as it faced the desert, not the Mother Nile.

Once outside the walls, Taten scanned the area for Suti. She didn't have to look far. There he sat in a two-chair, canopied litter. Eight glistening Nubians stood at attention; two at each corner of the conveyance. Their black skins shone purple as the early light began to put down long rays across the desert.

When Suti noticed Taten and her family in the early light, he smiled and rolled his round body off the parked litter. "You are here with Ra, as I requested Princess, and that is good. We must get an early start. We will arrive at my Estate just as Ra departs."

Becataten walked toward Suti with a brave smile, but with less confidence than she had felt earlier. She wanted to hug Suti, but decided that might be undignified, and she knew that would hurt Maja's feelings. Not having chewed her bread well, she had the hiccups and her stomach jumped like a frog. She turned, realizing she must say goodbye to her family, and be away from them for two inundations. Maja stood bent and gloomy with Sennejem a few steps behind her. Beset smiled through tears of joy. Jobu stood stoically. Taten was now ashamed to have earlier shown such enthusiasm to leave. Realizing what a small but loving family she had, she rushed to them, arms stretched.

Maja shook with silent sobs as they embraced. When Becataten bent to squeeze Beset, the dwarf whispered, "I'll miss you so. We must keep in touch with scrolls. The estate is always running correspondence back and forth so use their envoys." Taten promised in a choked voice.

She turned and walked to Jobu, who was staring at the ground.

"You won't forget me, will you Jobu?" He flung his arms around her, squeezing her tight. By the gods, she thought, Jobu was the hardest to leave behind. "Oh Jobu, you must come to visit me. Please promise me you will come. You and I cannot be apart for two innundations."

Why did she suddenly feel something was very wrong with Jobu? She knew he didn't want her to go. She was sad to leave him, too. There had been a vagueness about him lately that she had never known before. When they lay in bed the other night, she wished she could have prodded him to speak about why he didn't want her to go to Suti's estate. It wasn't like Jobu not speak of his feelings to her, especially late at night when they shared talk. But as she released him from her embrace, she knew there would be no answers. It was time to go.

Suti settled himself into their litter chairs. One of the Nubian runners bowed deeply before Taten, taking her bundle and helping her to step onto the conveyance. He lowered his head again before her when placing her parcel at her feet. No one had ever shown her this respect before. Was this the way a princess was treated? Would people at Suti's Estate behave this way too?

In unison, Suti's eight Nubians lifted their litter poles, which were carved with the heads of long-billed geese. Taten and Suti were tussled toward one another, holding on to the arms of their chairs. The runners took up a silent cadence, pounding their large feet into sand as they moved into a smooth jog. They headed down the side of the Palace walls and followed the Mother Nile south. The calm river, with a silvery surface, rippled and glistened by the light of the emerging rays of Ra. Taten looked up at the canopy overhead as the fringe danced. Looking to her side, she could see Nubians' backs dripping with sweat.

Catching herself in a daydream, she turned to look back and see the portrait of her small family against the Palace wall, now diminished by one, and she was struck with a hurt deep inside her chest. The only family she'd known stood huddled in the barren sand at the back end of the west gate. She waved vigorously then turned away. But Becataten had to look back one last time to keep the picture of their memory as bright rays washed over them. They stood bent, looking forlorn.

There would be no more talks with Beset who could always answer any of her questions. She would miss the love that Maja poured over her, and she saw that Maja was already lost without her. And Jobu, her beloved twin, the other half of her, whom she had loved and counted on since they were toddling about the Royal Nursery together...her heart seized as she knew she and Jobu had unfinished business. What was he involved in? What was so secret, he couldn't even tell her? The thought of Jobu's recent distant manner returned to disturb her greatly.

Becataten looked back once more and her chest tightened. The scribe, whom Beset did not like, appeared and stood with his arm around Jobu. Older and taller than Jobu, he almost showed possession over her twin. She mistrusted him and regretted that she hadn't asked Beset more about this scribe, as the Palace walls enveloped her family from view.

Refocusing her attention on the swaying litter, Becataten turned to Suti between hiccups and asked, "The Nubian bearer was very polite to me. Are they as kind to everyone?"

"These Nubians are my slaves and have been informed that you are a royal princess." Suti turned to look directly at her. "Princess Becataten, let me begin your education here and now."

Becataten found it hard to look directly into Suti's eyes. She shifted uncomfortably in her seat.

"Because you have been blessed with Pharaoh's blood you will always be respected more than most people, at Court or elsewhere. You have lived too long with but two low women; Dwarf Beset, a mere gift from Pharaoh, and Maja, who is called your nanny. We both know she is but a slave who accompanied your mother to Egypt."

It was hard to hear her small family described so harshly and with no sentiment. She looked out at the passing desert and tried to find something to focus on other than Suti's blunt words.

"When your Mother died bearing you and your twin, Maja simply inherited your care. Death is a hard thing for the people who are left behind. But it is common that mothers die when giving birth to twins. Hor and I were orphaned at birth for the same reason. Because you and your brother suffered the same fate, I believe you have been much insulated and coddled by these two women. It is time that you grow into a Royal Princess with proper attendants and a larger view of Egypt."

The sun now illuminated everything. Small houses came into view, but try as she might, Becataten could not concentrate on them or anything else except what Suti was saying.

"Henceforth you will never be referred to again as Taten, as that is a name you will leave behind. You will

94

be referred to as Princess Becataten. Lady Nagara will instruct you in royal etiquette, how to dress and speak, play instruments and dance, not to mention the continuation of academic schooling. When you return to Court you will return a lady, knowledgeable about many subjects with proper deportment, fine wigs, the wardrobe of a lady and attractive facial accents. Now observe your surroundings on our journey to my Estate. This is the first time you have been further than the Karnak Temple, is that not correct?"

Becataten nodded. She had never heard Suti speak so firmly to her. It was clear much was to be expected of her from this day forward. She promised herself she would do everything she was told, and prove that royal blood indeed flowed through her. Raising her head a bit higher, she began to take in the desert, the Mother Nile, its people and smells. She had much to think about, and she knew change was coming, and coming fast.

Becataten's thoughts about her new life were soon diverted by an Egypt she had never before imagined. Fleeting by were things she had only read about. The Egyptian houses were small square dwellings, sometimes two stories, made of mud brick but not whitewashed, and not of thick walls like the Palace buildings. There were many false starts, leaving abandoned buildings. Room additions to existing homes looked shabby. As they passed small villages, Becataten saw entire families, from small children to

95

aged grandparents, all working Pharaoh's fields. Men and donkeys carried items many times their size. She saw an occasional cow being milked by small children. But goats were everywhere. With just a stick, the youth herded them along with sheep and pigs. Animal pens on some of the plots confined geese and ducks. Egyptians loved all animals and penned many. She remembered reading in the royal library that it was not possible to raise the hyena, however, as they would not procreate in captivity, but almost every other kind of animal was being kept by the commoners here.

Fishermen dotted the Nile in small boats where fish and fowl abounded. A small market would come into view from time to time where barter was taking place for produce and game. The smells of the verdant riverbanks, of freshly dug canals and the warm desert air gave her the feeling of tranquility and a quiet strength.

Egypt was in her blood, and now it was speaking to her.

Watching these scenes of Egyptian life, Becataten sat back in her chair and the lull of her transport soon put her into a pleasant sleep. It was quite warm and growing more so when she was awakened by a gentle nudge from Suti. Midday was long past. Curiously, she found people running alongside her to keep up with their conveyance.

Straightening in her chair she turned to Suti. "May I ask who are these people that follow us?" she quietly asked.

"They are workers from my Estate who have come to meet us and are interested in seeing the Princess that I am mentoring. They are paying homage to you, and are curious about you."

Becataten watched as they stopped their fieldwork and ran alongside her transport to stare and smile at her. As they drifted back to work, others would pick up the pace, and so it went on the last leg of the journey to the villa.

Becataten politely nodded to the people with as much reserve as she could muster, and decided to ask no more questions in front of them, lest she appear ignorant. As their chair pulled toward Suti's grand home, Becataten took in the wide, tall steps of the villa in the distance. They passed gardens, a fishery, an aviary, many trees, and the air was heavy with the scent of flowers. The grounds were expansive, and without walls like she was used to seeing at the Palace. Channeled waterways from the Mother Nile extended as far as she could see. Cattle grazed in the distance. Pointing off into the horizon, she called excitedly, "Suti, what is that huge animal with the long, long neck?" She forgot her oath to ask no more questions.

"Those are giraffes. We are gathering animals for Pharaoh from the lands to the south so he may have a zoo."

"What is a zoo?"

"No more questions now, we are nearly at your new

home."

Standing at the top of the stone steps was a slim woman dressed elegantly in a crisply pleated, white shift, wearing a gold collar. Her painted face showed the work of a fine makeup artist. She wore no wig. She waved with reserve as footmen rushed down the steps toward the litter.

Becataten stepped off the conveyance and reached for her bundle, but a house slave quickly retrieved it. Embarrassed, she pulled her hand away. She had never known such attention, and it made her feel uncomfortable.

She mounted the stairs with Suti, and when they reached the woman at the top, Becataten realized how stunning she was.

"Lady Nagara, I deliver you Princess Becataten," Suti said as he kissed his wife's cheek.

Becataten was not prepared for what came next. Lady Nagara did not speak but scrutinized her. Becataten's face burned. She had never been looked at like that before, and didn't know if she should bow, or when to look away. Self-consciously she touched her frizzy braids. She felt sure about only one thing, at the moment, and that was not to reach out for Lady Nagara.

Suti broke the silence. "I will leave you ladies to become acquainted. I have plans to review and reports to write. Where is my scribe?" At Suti's words, a male attendant went running into the house in search of his assistant. Lady Nagara lightly clapped her hands and a girl, younger than Becataten, appeared, awaiting instructions. With little expression, and not taking her eyes off Becataten, Lady Nagara said, "A bath, shave her head, oil her body, especially her feet, tend to her nails and dress her in fine linen. No facial paint or jewelry." Then Lady Nagara turned and walked inside, leaving Becataten alone with the slave.

Chapter 13

Ⅱ

Becataten soon found herself in a large stone tub with three attendants; one working on her hands and feet, another shaving her head with a copper razor. The scrape of the copper blade on her scalp made a rasping sound and Becataten shivered. Then a softer shave followed with another cutting tool that was not as harsh. Becataten saw that it was a piece of obsidian, shiny and black. She had read about this stone. It had been spit from a fiery mountain and had come out like glass. Special stonecutters chipped it, and it was the preferred implement of surgeons. How difficult it was not asking questions, but she decided she wanted to see and hold the black blade. "May I see the obsidian?" Becataten said pointing to the object. Her attendants didn't know what she was referring to. With wide eyes, one of them handed it to her. Becataten felt its hardness and saw how brightly it glistened.

Once out of the tub, the two slaves rubbed her dry then lathered an aromatic unguence on her body. Another woman dressed her in a long white, transparent shift with deep pleats. Looking at the dirty bath water with two floating braids, Becataten felt embarrassed to see how soiled and shoddy she must have appeared when she arrived. What must she have looked like standing before Lady Nagara?

After Taten and Suti's chair disappeared on the horizon, Beset looked toward Jobu and called, "Jobu, come, let's walk and talk!" He shook his head and turned away, walking off with his older scribe friend. Beset shook her head and tightened her lips. She marched away with no destination in mind, walking off her frustration with Jobu.

Dwarf Beset knew the challenge that lay ahead. She must find a place in the Palace for Jobu, just as she had found a place for Taten. To Dwarf Beset, that meant she would begin by learning more about his new companion. It plagued her that this young man seemed to have been one of the scribes she overheard in the halls of the Palace whispering with one another about making Jobu their pet. But she wasn't quite sure, and didn't know what to do about it.

Soon she needed to sit, and found herself in the same garden where she and Heby often met. Settling under a morenga tree at the edge of a pool, she sighed and sank her feet into the water as she rubbed her sore legs.

"Beset, there you are. I sent a runner with a

message that I would be free this Ra, but I was told you were not at home," said Dwarf Heby as he approached, sweating with effort in the hot sun. "How lucky that I found you here."

"Yes, we were busy seeing Taten off to the Suti Estate."

"You are looking quite gloomy, if you don't mind my saying so, Beset." Heby hauled himself up onto the bench beside to her.

"I am, but my gloom is mixed with joy. Today Princess Becataten left for a better life."

"Let me guess. Now it is the boy twin you are worried about," said Heby.

With a wan smile, Beset nodded. "It is not that I am worried, it is that I find I am dealing with a mystery."

"Then you are in your element. Ever since I have known you, Beset, you have savored a puzzle."

"Have I really?"

"Yes, Beset, really. So what is it this time?"

Beset was quiet for a time. When she spoke it was with a faraway look. "I took a chair the other Ra to a quay where royal cargo is unloaded from distant lands. As an infant, I was delivered there from the land of Punt. That was twenty-five innundations ago. I was told a huge amount of gold debon was paid to my parents for the privilege of owning me. My parents reluctantly released me so I could grow up in the renowned Court Egypt – so I was told. I was educated among Royals and often played with Pharaoh,

102

as we are the same age. When he was crowned at twelve, he gave me as a gift to the twins, along with two of Lady Mui's kittens. I was considered clever, intelligent even intrepid, by Pharaoh, and I have always tried to live up to Pharaoh's standard. I felt lucky to escape being taught the craft of jewelry making or keepers of household pets, and instead be gifted to the royal twins."

"That's a lot of words," Heby said, as he swung his legs. "But they are melancholy words, Beset."

"Yes, I suspect that I am melancholy this Ra, Heby."

"I had hoped to break bread with you but was unable to find you, and now I see that you are in no mood for company. I am going to leave you to your thoughts. I am only guessing, but I think you need time alone."

Heby climbed down off the bench and wandered back to the Palace corridor. After Heby left, Beset looked into the pool at her image and prayed, "Sweet Isis, you gave me the twins along with a conundrum didn't you? Is it because you know I can solve it?" Tears welled as she thought of her beloved Taten, gone, and Jobu, so distant.

A craftsman delivering goods passed by and waved from a distance. "Beset, I have your cane ready, but it is at my workshop. I just need you to come and lean on it and tell me if it feels like it is the right height," he called.

Beset waved back and said, "Come, and sit."

The small brown man with large hands walked spryly to the pond. He set his bundle of goods; cooking bowls, small elaborate boxes filled with combs and carved hair ornaments on the ground. He sat next to her, plunging his feet into the pool, without removing his sandals.

"Thank you for recognizing I needed a cane, Royal Craftsman. My spine is not as straight as yours, and I know my walk has become crooked." Beset said.

"The cane will help," he said, "I have made many canes and they always help."

"Just walking short distances lately causes my back and hips to ache. I hope you are right."

"It is a privilege to make a cane for you, Dwarf Beset. If you ever need a woodcarving, just ask me. I carve many things: inlayed cosmetic boxes for the Court ladies, chests for noble households, tools for the royal kitchen, and cylinders for the scribe's papyri and..."

Beset interrupted him. "What scribes do you carve for, Craftsman?"

"I carve containers for all the royal scribes in the Palace."

"I can see by your work that you are a good carver. I think you must have a long list of clients."

"Oh yes, Dwarf Beset, I do. When you come to pick up your cane, I will show you all my clients. I have listed them on a long papyrus that hangs in my stall."

"I will indeed come and see you very soon. My guess

is that your names all have a title as well as who they work for."

The woodworker so enjoyed soaking his feet, he failed to answer, but Beset knew the answer. Her spirits lifted. Perhaps Isis was guiding her to the help she needed after all.

Chapter 14

♊

After Becataten's bath and grooming, it was already late evening. She was shown her ample sleeping chamber on the second floor of the Suti residence, where her cot and a chest stood. Paintings on the walls showed the Goddess Hathor, the Mother of love, fertility, sexuality, music and dance. Becataten stared at the images and wondered, was her new life to engage in these things, with no more scholarly learning? *Is that what I am to become, a woman of beauty?* She felt saddened by this thought when the butler arrived with her dinner.

"I have brought you your dinner, Princess Becataten," the lean, dark servant said as he bowed. He had an important bearing, and arrived with two assistants. One held trays of food, while the second carried her dining table and bench. They proceeded to set her a lavish meal of far more food than she could consume. Her tabletop was crowded, with a basket of warm flat bread, thin slices of skewered beef, freshly cut herbs, cultured milk, and a chickpea sauce. A pomegranate had been seeded for her and sparkled like gems in a small calcite bowl. Other unrecognizable fruits filled a tray. She sat alone, chewing pieces of beef as tender as she had ever eaten. As good as the food was, she sat wondering where Suti was, and why she must eat by herself. After her dinner table was cleared away, other servants attended her and helped to change her into nightclothes before she lay on her cot of goose down with the finest linen bedding. Left in the dark, she watched the stars appear through her high clerestory window. The stars reminded her of Beset's magical story-telling time, Maja's hugs, and cuddling with Jobu. She buried her head into her pillow as the tears came. She sobbed until she heard a knock at her door.

"Hello, Princess," said a cheerful Suti, as he entered and sat on the edge of her cot. Attendants bustled in behind him, lighting the oil lamps until the room was brightly lit.

"No tears now," Suti said, holding rolled up scrolls under his arm. "You are to live a life of luxury, Becataten, and I assure you this new life will be one that you will soon enjoy. I have brought you scrolls with maps of the estate and the surrounding grounds. I thought you would enjoy them, and they would help you to orient yourself."

Becataten wiped her tears and reached for the scrolls, fingering the fine papyrus. Suti took her hand. "I know Lady Nagara can be strict at times, but she has your best interest at heart, so give her time to warm to you. You both are bright women with similar talents,

107

you know."

Becataten couldn't think of anything she had in common with Lady Nagara.

Suti leaned toward her and kissed her on the forehead. "Sleep well, Princess." Then he stood and spoke softly to the waiting butler before leaving.

After viewing most of the scrolls with Suti, her mind still crowed with the events of the day leaving her unable to sleep. Becataten tossed in her cot when she heard another knock at her door.

"Yes," she said, wondering whom this could be. The butler stepped into her chamber. "Princess, Master Suti has instructed me to give you a potion for sleep, and a slave girl to stay with you as you rest. She will lie on the floor at the end of your bed should you need anything in the night." Princess Becataten reached for the terra cotta cup he extended. "What is the potion made from, Butler?"

"It is made from the poppy seed, and I have brewed it myself."

Becataten had heard about the flower and how it could have powerful effects. "Should I drink it all?"

"Yes, Princess, drink all of it. You will sleep well and feel refreshed in the morning, as it is my talent to brew the potion properly."

Becataten finished the brew and settled back into her cot. Her new slave lay on the floor as instructed, but did not sleep as she awaited her mistress' slumber. A strange yet comfortable fog filled Becataten's mind until she knew no more.

The next morning, Becataten was asked to follow an attendant to Lady Nagara's sitting chamber where she was told to wait. The room was huge and contained the longest shelf Becataten had ever seen. It was lined with scores of Lady Nagara's elegant wigs. Several chests sat against the walls. A standing copper mirror stood in a corner next to a lounge chair covered with silk pillows of bright colors. Becataten wanted to touch the cushions, but she had been asked to sit on a bench next to a large wooden container. A homely attendant sat opposite her and when she saw Becataten enter, the woman rose to bow. Her long face bore no facial paint. Her thin lips showed a smile. Becataten nodded to her, but was trying hard not to become friendly with the household attendants because she felt Lady Nagara would not approve. She tried to sit still but since the shaving of her scalp she couldn't resist scratching at her head. Looking about she found lavishly painted Egyptian gods on the walls and tall braziers that smoldered incense, giving off exotic scents.

The plain woman wore a shortcropped wig, and between them sat an inlaid cosmetic chest. Once the chest was open, intoxicating fragrances filled the air. Becataten couldn't resist saying, "It smells so good."

She looked down to stare into the large box at the many containers.

"Are you the facial painter?" Becataten asked.

The woman nodded.

"What is kept in the blown glass containers?"

"Kohl, to paint the eye like the one Pharaoh is now wearing," the painter said in her deep voice.

"And what's in the alabaster pots?"

"Sticky paint, to line your eye lids."

Becataten pointed, and said, "Those are clods of ochre in the baskets, are they not?"

"Yes, and gold dust in the little boxes."

"Gold dust," Becataten said with reverence.

The painter pulled out a drawer that held a cache of copper tweezers, razors and hair pins, all polished bright orange. She drew open another that held combs and cosmetic brushes. Applicators delicately fashioned of bird bone, reeds and shell were kept in a basket with a long tangle-comb of ivory that had a carved bird on top. Large pinfeathers from a bird were used to stir and mix colors.

"May I touch the box?"

"Of course, you are a princess."

Becataten ran a finger along the chest's fine grain. "I think this is wood from the precious mahogany tree, from Beset's land in Punt."

"Who is, Beset?" asked the painter.

"Beset is my loving dwarf. I miss her so. She would love to see this."

110

The painter held up colored, blown glass bottles and said, "These contain floral essences of the lotus, the desert lily, and even oil of the rose. Smell them." Becataten took a small dark blue perfume bottle in her hand.

"It is the color of the sky just before Ra joins us," she said. Becataten held it up, admiring the way the light sparkled through it. Tears filled her eyes. "It is all quite beautiful."

With an affectionate smile, the painter watched Becataten.

They heard the soft slap of Lady Nagara's silver sandals in the outside hall. She entered, followed by her butler, who promptly placed an inlaid chair before her. Lady Nagara, beautiful in her blue gown, sat and said, "This Ra, you appear far more civilized, Princess Becataten. Now we will see what you look like with facial paint. You will not wear a painted face every Ra, but you will when you leave the Estate or when you receive someone. Is that understood?"

Becataten nodded.

"Here, we do not nod, we speak,"

Becataten quickly replied, "Yes, Lady Nagara, I understand."

"Painter, let us begin."

Princess Becataten was slowly and artfully made anew. The silvery paste, mixed with kohl was made from ground galena, and carefully applied with the small bone of a bird's leg. The painter, with her small finger, deftly rubbed ground malachite mixed with almond oil to the lids of Becataten's eyes, that gave her a dreamy, exotic look to her almond shaped eyes. A glistening red paste of ochre was rubbed on her lips with an applicator from the stub of a goose quill. The painter reached for a round of linen that was tied with a string and held ochre-dust, the color of apricots, and gently powdered her face. With a smaller ball of red ochre mixed with a modicum of gold dust, she powdered her cheekbones until just the right amount escaped the linen to give her face a light glow.

The artist stepped back to look at her work and said, "Finished." She held a large copper mirror before Becataten, who stared in disbelief at her new glamorous image. "You made me look like a different person, a woman of beauty, Painter. Thank you for this gift."

Lady Nagara scrutinized Becataten's face, adjusted herself in her chair and revealed a quick crooked smile. She stood, turnd away and took a few steps toward her walled patio.

"Lady Nagara, I could finish her face with more gold dust, if you like," the painter said,

"Leave us, Painter." Lady Nagara said. The painter left, and Becataten felt like she now deserved to be in the company of the beautiful but distant Lady Nagara.

Chapter 15

♊

Beset wasted no time in taking a litter to the Craftsman's Village to pick up her leaning stick from the woodcarver. She was looking for the long list on papyrus the craftsman had boasted held the names of his clients. There was a jangle of noise coming from the village stalls of the working artisans when Beset stepped off her conveyance. Faced with a warren of endless booths, several people stepped back to allow her passage. But it was crowded and hot, and she wrinkled her brow, wondering how she would find the lone craftsman who carved her cane. She had no idea the collection of artist's stations, all in the middle of the Palace grounds, were so numerous. The square held scores of coppersmiths who pounded out large cauldrons, while others created weapons, kitchen implements, even small tools such as razors. Wood carvers were chopping at blocks to create effigies of all sizes, and delicate musical instruments. Jewelry makers were inlaying gems into gold and silver. Beset stopped briefly to observe ivory workers polishing legs for stools, from antlers and horns.

She pushed on, but the day grew hotter and her

path grew narrower until she found herself among foreign artisans with whom she couldn't communicate. Hot and exhausted, Beset plopped herself on a bale of flax. She was at a weaver's stall, and the stern woman glared at her, obviously having no proper reverence for a dwarf. A small boy with a finger in his mouth stood at his mother's side, also staring. Feeling uncomfortable, Beset slowly raised herself to leave, unsure where to turn next. She walked a short distance and felt someone at her side. It was the small boy from the last stall. He smiled at her and managed to speak a few Egyptian words.

"I am seeking a woodworker who made me a cane," said Beset, pantomiming as she spoke. Though he probably only recognized a few of her words, the boy took her hand he led her to the woodworkers.

"Thank the gods for children," Beset whispered, as she reached into her pouch and placed a good-sized piece of copper debon in his hand.

Beset stood before the woodworking shop and slowly scanned the area as the woodworkers looked up, acknowledged Beset. Seeing that she was not a paying customer, however, they quickly returned to their labors. Then she saw it on the inside of the stall wall; a long, well-worn papyrus painted with many names. Finally she had arrived at the right spot! She wove her way to the stand and stood staring at the long list.

The humble carver she had met before spied her. "Welcome, Dwarf Beset!" he said as he bowed before

114

her. "I am happy to receive you. Let me get you your staff." He stepped behind a hanging goat hide at the rear of his stall. Quick to return, he proudly presented her with a far more handsome walking aid than she had imagined.

"This is more than a cane, it is an elegant staff," she said, smiling at him, "Thank you, Craftsman, for this aid. I know it will help me when I walk."

"I carved a place, here, where you can easily clutch the staff. Try walking with it. I want to be sure it is the proper height for you, Dwarf Beset."

Beset strutted about with the stick and said, "This seems just right, Craftsman. I can see you have taken much time making me this fine walking stick. And what is that bit of carving I see at the top?"

The craftsman grinned with a toothless smile. "It is your sacred name, Goddess Beset."

Beset rubbed her stubby fingers over the letters of her name. "May I pay you for this fine piece of craftsmanship?"

"No, but you may leave me with a blessing for my wife, who is about to have our fifth child."

Beset reached up and touched his shoulder. "I bless you, and your pregnant wife."

He bowed and thanked her.

Beset moved to the hanging papyrus, and leaned against a table in his stall to admire it. "My, you have many clients written on this long papyrus."

"Yes, Dwarf Beset, I work for many scribes, and

115

they all keep records for Pharaoh's royal house. They are in constant need of scroll holders, some elegant, some plain."

"Really," Beset said. "And who gives you the most work?"

"That would be hard to say, but the Vizier, the Royal Astrologer, and the Director of Public Works keep me very busy."

Beset perked, "How many assistants does the Royal Astrologer employ?"

"Not too many, but he works them hard."

"Where are they listed?"

The carver pointed to a title and said, "Scribe Tiurek, the head scribe of the Royal Astrologer's house, is the only one who is allowed to assign work to me."

Beset said, "Isn't his name also a place in Babylon?"

"Yes. It is said that the Royal Astrologer bought him in a slave market when he was a small boy, imported from the land of Tiurek, and named him after the city. The young man once told me that it is where two great rivers flow, in the small province of Mitanni, I think."

Beset nodded then purposefully leaned on her staff and said, "I cannot thank you enough for carving me this valuable leaning-stick."

The carver bowed to her again and said, "I consider it an honor."

Beset walked away with her new staff feeling a bit grander. She ambled to a nearby bench, on the outskirts of the craftsman's village. It was good to escape the noise and closeness. A vendor passed offering pomegranate juice. She pressed a piece of debon into his hand, and sat enjoying her refreshment and rest.

Beset closed her eyes to think: The small country of Mitanni in Babylon was a place that linked several people. Princess Attah, the twin's mother, and Maja, along with Sennejem were all born there. Scribe Tiurek, Abu's favored scribe, bore the name of a city in the land of Mitanni. When Sennejem dined with the Royal Astrologer, they spoke in a common tongue from that land. Why so many connections to this place? She remembered that Abu and Pharaoh were half-brothers, with the same father, but with different mothers. Maybe Abu's mother had been a princess from Mitanni. She needed to know more about this land, and much more about Abu, the Royal Astrologer.

Early the next day, Beset walked through the garden, her short legs growing weary with each step, although her walking stick kept her from faltering. She found a secluded bench to rest on, hidden in a stand of palms. She was taking in the warm rays of Ra when she heard voices. She jumped down from her bench and crouched, spying through waxy fronds. Sennejem and Maja settled on a nearby bench. Beset strained to hear their conversation.

117

"Don't cry, Maja," soothed Sennejem. "Taten will be back before you know it, and she will return a refined and royal princess. It is a talent only the rich can teach."

Tearful, Maja said, "I miss Taten so much. Now just Jobu is here, and how will he become a grand prince? He has no, what you call mentor? They took Taten from me because I didn't learn picture writing like I should have, Sennejem, and because I don't understand all the gods of Egypt, and because I don't like Dwarf Beset enough."

"Now, Maja, that's not true." Sennejem said.

Maja shook her head. "I know Beset was a special gift from Pharaoh for the twins when we lived in the nursery, but we were happy without her."

"Maja, dwarves are a good omen, and a god in the family of Egyptian gods."

Maja looked doubtful and hung her head. "I know it, but now we only have one twin," she said. Sennejem and Maja lapsed into their native tongue and Beset moved away so she would not encounter them. She walked slowly back to the apartment leaning on her staff with each step. Her mind filled with the conversation she just heard.

Beset already knew Maja didn't care for her, and she realized she would like to change that because their lives were to be forever intertwined. It was also time to ask Maja some questions about Babylon. A plan was beginning to unfold that the dwarf knew

118

would include a generous amount of wine.

When Beset arrived home, she was pleased to see that an envoy from the Suti Estate had delivered a scroll from Becataten. She quickly read it:

Dear Maja and Beset,

I miss you both so much. No one here at the Estate is anything like you two, and yet I have to say much care is taken with me. Scholars teach me, attendants dress me in the finest clothing, and a makeup artist has painted my face many times. I am learning to become a refined Lady. I am taught how to play musical instruments and to dance. Here, one is served delicious foods and items I have never before known.

Please tell Jobu to write me.

I love you both and I think of you always, especially before I go to sleep.

May the gods keep you,
Taten

Beset put the scroll down and called for a slave. She ordered him to bring a sumptuous selection of foods to their apartment, along with three pitchers of sma, all from Pharaoh's kitchen. The slave's mouth dropped open as she ordered. "And tell Pharaoh's chef that the order is for Dwarf Beset," she said, handing him lage woven baskets. She gave the slave a few pieces of copper debon so he could hire a litter. She led him outside and hailed the nearest one. Never having been on a conveyance before his face widened into a huge grin as he climbed aboard and was carried off.

When the food arrived, Maja's eyes bulged. "Who is this for, Beset?" Maja asked. Beset layed out roasted birds, flowers stuffed with seasoned grain and fried eels. Maja sat eagerly at her bench, reached for a bird leg, and began chewing it with delight. "Mmmm, tastes good, Beset. This food is better than any before. What kitchen?"

Proudly, Beset said in her high pitch, "This food comes from Pharaoh's kitchen."

Maja dropped the leg. "No! We cannot eat the God's food. Can we?"

With confidence Beset said, "Of course we can. I have arranged it so. Enjoy yourself and try some of Pharaoh's wine."

With eagerness Maja watched as Beset poured her cup full. "This is called sma, Maja, and is a blend using many grapes." She paused, and patted Maja's hand. "It is the custom in Egypt to drink the first cup without stopping," Beset fibbed, with a sly grin.

"That is hard to do," said Maja.

"Just try," Beset encouraged.

Maja did, smiled broadly, and ate more. She seemed fascinated by the skin on the small game and at first stared to pull it off but after tasting it, she devoured it, making happy eating sounds. Licking the fat from her fingers, she said, "Any more of Pharaoh's drink in the jar, Beset?"

Beset smiled as she filled Maja's cup, knowing there were two more jars at her feet. Half of Maja's face showed enjoyment, the other side still dropped from the past poisoning. All Maja had ever drunk was the common barley beer of the workers that was made quickly with little time to ferment. Soon she was a different person, speaking amiably to Beset, smiling and laughing.

Beset read Becataten's scroll to Maja, and they both lamented how much they missed her. Beset poured more wine for Maja, avoiding drinking too much herself, and decided it was time to ask her some questions.

"Maja, you know that you have never told me about the time you entered Egypt from your country of Mitanni."

Maja stopped smiling, drained her cup then sighed as she stared across the room. She spoke in a monotone, as though she was under the spell of a sorcerer, and Beset needed to ask no more.

"We rode in a big veiled cage pulled by oxen, and it was so hot. We held each other and cried for days. The drivers of the caravan felt sorry for us because the trip was so long and we had never been anywhere, but they wouldn't take us back to Mitanni. In two moons we ran out of water, our chest of clothes all lost. We were filthy when we arrived, and Princess Attah's lips were cracked and bleeding.

"My beautiful Princess Attah and I arrived looking

for the Palace harem, but it was only half built and couldn't keep all of Pharaoh's women yet. Outside, a big tent was set to take the women who were not so important. Attah was not special; she was but a war-reparation from our Mitanni King, so we lived in this outdoor place for two moon cycles. Scribes from the Court came to count women and their slaves. The man in charge was the one who fell in love with my Attah. They became secret lovers, and he visited her many times. He was a strict man but tender when near my Attah. Mitanni was the birthplace of this man's mother so he spoke in our tongue. Attah told me that he asked the great Pharaoh if he could take my Princess for his wife, but Pharaoh refused him. This man of the Court was very angry because Pharaoh was still a boy, not yet able to couple with his women. When we moved into the finished harem, my Princess was one of the first that Pharaoh took to his bed. Attah told me that Pharaoh thought he had made love to her, but she shook her head. On Attah's dying cot, she told me her lover was the father of her unborn, but I must treat her child as Pharaoh's offspring. She never said her lover's name. He was a big man for an Egyptian, and he wore fancy kilts; someone very important, I think"

Maja stood looking exhausted and said, "I go to my cot now."

Beset reached across the table for Maja's hand. "Maja, you never told me all of this. You have had to carry this for a long time."

Maja stared into space.

Beset asked softly. "Maja, have you seen this man since you have lived in Egypt?"

Maja shook her head.

Beset continued, "And you are sure that this man's mother was from Mitanni?"

Maja nodded. She stood and swayed. Beset moved to her side to assist her to her sleeping chamber.

Alone at the table, Beset poured herself a full cup of sma and sighed.

So it was Abu, she was sure, who fathered the twins. Did he know they were his children? Abu was appointed intermediary between Nurse Heqarneheh and Pharaoh, yet he passed on no information about them. Why did he secrete the children's progress? Withholding that information led them to live a life of mediocrity. Did he carry a vehement grudge against Pharaoh because he had been refused a request to marry Princess Attah? Could he be so vengeful that he was punishing his own offspring? And how could he do this after having cast their heavenly charts, which must have been impressive. Beset was stymied.

Chapter 16

♊

Becataten saw little of Lady Nagara, for at least two moon cycles, and only when she came to observe the progress of her lessons. Her teachers gave her high marks and explained that her only weakness lay in knowing foreign tongues. But they added, because her memorization was great, she was gaining on her language abilities. And having mastered reading, writing and her number skills some time ago, she often finished her lesson early. With this free time, Becataten delighted in touring the grounds of the Suti Estate.

Becataten had pored over the scrolls Suti had left her that mapped the Estate, and walked with confidence in her new surroundings. Lady Nagara insisted that she wore a painted face and a fresh linen shift when she left to tour the grounds. She preferred not to be encumbered by a wig but wore long earrings.

Leaving the grand house one afternoon after her lessons, she hesitated at the top of the steps, deciding which way to walk. The butler came up behind her clearing his throat.

"Hello, Butler, how are you today?" Becataten said. "I should enjoy going out today."

The butler nodded politely. "Would you like me to secure a chair for you?"

"Yes, that would be wonderful. Is it best to use a chair, to travel the grounds, Butler? I don't mind walking."

"Yes, I believe a chair is best, Princess."

An elaborate litter arrived, rigged with a parasol, carried by four Nubian bearers. She grinned as the bearers lifted the poles of her conveyance on their shoulders. One bearer asked where she wanted to go. Becataten had them take her to the end of one of the many of the canals. Here the Nile water and rich, black soil produced a riot of colorful flowers and vegetables that grew in abundance.

With her leather sandals in hand, she stepped off her litter and approached a worker. "What are the names of the tall purple flowers," she asked the laborer, "and what are you planting there?" But unlike Sennejem, they didn't know, and they seemed uncomfortable speaking with a princess. Gathering up her shift she bent down to smell the fragrance of a row of the plant she now recognized as iris. Hearing a clattering noise, she looked up to see a chariot.

"Greetings, chariot driver," she said, as he drew his vehicle to a halt and bowed. "May I ride with you for a time?"

"Of course, you are Princess Becataten, are you not?" he said. Becataten nodded as she climbed aboard the ornately crafted vehicle. With these words of exchange, the litter bearers stared at one another, uncertain what to do with their lost charge.

Becataten grinned as they took off at a trot toward the cattle yards where the chariot driver told her scribes were recording each steer, cow, and calf.

"I must deliver these extra scrolls to the counting platform, Princess. Do you want to ride that distance with me?"

"I do. Please, drive on."

From her view Becataten could see the activities of the hundreds of people it took to manage the Estate: the massive barley fields, cattle herds, the fisheries, the paddocks and stables; the enclosures for ducks and geese, the yards and coops for chickens, even a house for the butchering of game, along with cheese-making areas. And in the far distance, once again she could see those exotic animals that were penned for Pharaoh's zoo.

When the driver stopped, Becataten stepped off the chariot and walked to the activity where Suti's herds were being recorded. "Greetings to you all," she said, smiling.

As the scribes and workmen stared at Becataten, work stopped. "Please don't let me disturb you, I am just here to observe." Becataten said. Slowly their work commenced, but the workers showed

126

discomfort with a Royal so close. Becataten strolled and watched the men expertly count the cattle and record their findings, but she felt like an outsider in the hot dry lands and as if she were intruding somehow with her mere presence. Usually she was an ignored child, a foundling; today she made grown men uncomfortable. It was disconcerting, and soon she felt the need to leave the area. She motioned for the chariot driver who spoke with a foreman nearby, and he escorted her back to the carriage.

On the ride home Becataten watched the driver's hands for some time then asked, "Do you think I could take the reins for a little while?" With a worried look, the driver drew his horse to a slow trot and cautiously handed Becataten the reins. She was easy on the horse's bit, and drove well until they arrived at the stairs of the Estate. The Butler stood in a stiff posture, waiting at the bottom of the stairs for her return. He stepped quickly toward the chariot as she pulled up.

Once the chariot driver dropped her off, the Butler held Becataten by the arm. "Lady Nagara is quite angry with you," he said in a low voice as he led her up the stairs. "Go directly to your chamber." His face held a scornful glare for the chariot driver who was leaving the estate in the distance.

When Becataten entered the chamber, she could smell a burning rope before she saw it. Her heart quickened; what was going to happen to her? An

127

attendant, one she had never seen before, sternly motioned her to kneel on small, sharp rocks that had been laid on the hard floor. The pain was instant, and she longed to stand, but the servant handed her two heavy rocks, one to hold in each hand. Crying out in more pain, Becataten's heart raced. She winced, again and again in the kneeling position she was forced to take. Holding the cumbersome stones, her knees dug further into the sharp stones. Her eyes widened as the servant reached for the burning rope; what further torture could she endure? Flinching, Becataten let out a breath of relief to discover the burning rope was to time her punishment. The smoldering cord was marked with an orange ochre line, several feet from where it was burning. It was clear she was to be punished until the braided fibers burned to that spot. Everyone left the room except for her personal slave, who bit her lip and wept for her mistress. Tears soon trailed Becataten's checks too, not just from the excruciating pain, but as she realized how far she had drifted from the role of a lady today. She had humiliated herself by wondering too far and engaging with the outdoor staff. *What have I done, and how can I apologize for this? I have become undignified to all, even to the butler.* Lady Nagara had said she must carry herself above all workers and slaves, never speaking as an equal to them. Becataten had found that very difficult and now was paying the price.

Into the dark, her punishment continued. When it finally ended, she stood with the help of her slave, who picked the small stones from her bleeding knees. Silently she shook with sobs while she was bathed and dressed. Afraid to speak to her own servant now, she whispered, "If I am sent home, I will be a disgrace. Oh, what have I done? I must learn to live here in a proper way. Please, oh please, Goddess Isis, allow me to stay here, and do not let Lady Nagara send me away." The tending slave's lips pursed tight. Becataten allowed herself to be restored, except for the ugly cuts and gashes on her knees, an example of her punishment for all to see.

Soon the painter entered her chamber to restore her facial paint. The painter worked in dull silence. After she finished, a beautiful new wig was perfectly secured on Becataten's head. Standing tall, Becataten was led silently down the hallway by her slave to see the formidable Lady Nagara.

Just outside Lady Nagara's sitting chamber Becataten garnered all the strength she had so as to not appear weak, or to cry and spoil her freshly painted face. The sour faced butler stood at the doorway, and escorted Becataten inside Lady Nagara's chamber. Becataten bowed to the tall stern figure before her. She sat with considerable pain on the floor before Lady Nagara on pillows made from the hide of the hunted zebra. Lady Nagara sat looking like a statue. With her stern expression and no wig, she looked intimidating. In a freshly pleated, linen shift and perfect facial colors, her gold collar and cuffs shining brightly, Becataten could feel her blackened eyes glaring down on her.

After a deep breath, Lady Nagara set her jaw. "For every conversation you have with a worker on my Estate, you will be punished accordingly. Do you understand this?"

Oh, thank the Gods, maybe she is not going to send me home.

"Yes, Lady Nagara."

"Why do you question the workers, and sometimes even the slaves? I am told you were in the fields and even on the cattle platform where the herdsmen drive the animals to tally them. You were handling the palette of the counting scribe and discussing his work. That, to me, is shocking, and in no means keeping with the standards of a lady."

"Lady Nagara, I mean not to offend you, I am just interested in what they do."

"It is not your place to be interested in what estate workers do. You do not yet understand why you are here, Becataten. Nor do you comprehend that you are being groomed for the Royal Court? It is not even clear to you that you are a princess. You are here to learn how to conduct yourself at an audience with your Pharaoh, and to receive his royal commands. Engaging with people beneath your station has no place in your learning. You are to adorn Pharaoh's Court, to please him. You are to refine yourself, your beauty and your feminine talents."

Becataten kept her head bowed and could smell Lady Nagara's exotic perfume. The scent reminded her of her early days in the nursery with the harem mothers all around her. Would her mother be this age if she were alive? Would she be this strict? Her memory was jarred by Lady Nagara's quiet but stern voice.

"Today we start on a new regime. Before Ra greets us, you will awake, bathe, dress and complete your music and dance lessons, then practice proper walking and speaking skills. You will take a mid-day meal, and rest, after which you will dress again, wear proper facial colors and tour parts of the Estate, in a *chair* that you will not *leave*. You will give no special instructions to your attendants. Upon your return, you will bathe and dress again. We will dine and be entertained by musicians and dancers. And you will learn to perform for Pharaoh privately. Your performance for our Living God will be far more genteel, however, than those who dance before us."

Becataten stared, trying to take in all that Lady Nagara said.

"Lady Nagara, may I ask you a question?"

With reluctance, Lady Nagara nodded.

131

"Is it not proper for me to know the business of running an Estate in case I may be given that position one day?"

Lady Nagara shook her head, "Again, Becataten, you do not understand your position. You are Pharaoh's possession, and the chances of the Living God bestowing an estate upon you are as unlikely as one who tries plucking a tail feather from a running ostrich."

Becataten hadn't heard that expression before and tried to put it together with what Lady Nagara was saying. "Your duty is to become an asset at Court, where there is much competition."

Will I go into Pharaoh's Court with other women, and will he make choices of which woman he wants? A shiver of fear ran through her.

Lady Nagara rose and stared out the window into the darkness of night. "As you were born a harem Princess, without the blood of an Egyptian mother, it is the talent that I instill in you that will bring you to Pharaoh's eyes. And that, my ignorant one, is not the running of an Estate."

Becataten adjusted herself on her cushion, careful not to touch her throbbing knees, not knowing what to say, or if she should speak at all.

Lady Nagara continued, "Because my husband finds you quick to learn, and likely because you are a twin, he has decided we mentor you. Think of your poor brother, your twin. Nobody is mentoring him,

132

so he will never be a significant member of the Court, but just a common harem prince, one of many. Do you think you will rise in importance above the hundreds of harem women unless you absorb what I teach you? Suti tells me you are bright, yet that talent alone will not get you to Court, unless you combine my skills and the wisdom I shall pass on to you. Now, are you bright enough to have grasped what I have said?"

Becataten swallowed, caught off guard at being addressed directly. "Yes, Lady Nagara." Her voice was raspy and Becataten struggled to hold in her tears. Hit hard by the mention of Jobu, she was reminded how many moon cycles she had been away and had received no word from him. Beset had responded to her scrolls, always including sentiments from him, but it was not the same as receiving his written words. She thought of broaching the subject with Lady Nagara, asking if he could visit her, but decided this was not the time.

Becataten sighed and said, "Lady Nagara, you are so beautiful and know so much about the Royal way of life, and I know you have so much to teach me. May I ask how you came by all this knowledge?"

With suspicion, Lady Nagara narrowed her eyes and scrutinized Becataten's face. Hoping not to appear divisive, Becataten strained to hold a neutral gaze while their eyes met. Finally, Lady Nagara answered.

133

"I was a Lady in service to Queen Tiy when Pharaoh married her, the same age you are now; twelve inundations. We were all that age. She was from the bureaucratic classes, but wealthy. I was from nobility, and not as wealthy."

Becataten's thoughts wandered to a conversation she had with Beset before leaving for the Estate, and how Beset explained what patience and study it would take to learn how to become a proper princess. She was beginning to understand.

Lady Nagara fingered her cuffs, and her face went dark. "The Court was shaken and greatly surprised when Pharaoh chose Lady Tiy to be his first queen, as she was not of the Noble class." After adjusting the pillows in her chair, Lady Nagara's stare into the distance was long before she added, "He chose her just as he came to kingship. He adores her and his in-laws, who he has placed in high status." With an expression of distaste, she said, "A few seasons after the marriage, Queen Tiy released me from her Court. It happened when Pharaoh had begun to view me with some favor. When that occurred, Pharaoh deemed I should marry Royal Architect Suti, and manage this vast estate in his absence." She heaved a sigh. "Pharaoh used to send me flowers. Now I grow flowers and send them to him." Having drifted into melancholia, she made an abrupt return to curtness. "So, you see, I have spent time in the Royal Court, a place where you will soon find yourself."

Becataten's chest tightened when she saw the hurt look in Lady Nagara's eyes. With her great lands, a Royal Architect for a husband, her beauty largely intact and her lavish surroundings, Lady Nagara bore no happiness. Extravagant clothing from many foreign ports filled her chests. Suti would return to the Estate with newly wrought adornments from the finest craftsman in the artisan village. To Becataten, Lady Nagara had everything, yet sadness filled her. She had missed becoming queen of Egypt, or even second wife.

Timidly, Becataten continued, "Why do you think Pharaoh chose you for this life, Lady Nagara?"

Narrowing her eyes a little less, Lady Nagara said, "I had scribes who taught me and were amazed at the progress I made with calculations, reading, and memorization. I believe that Pharaoh knew I could run this Estate without a man, and certainly that is what I do. Architect Suti, as you must have noticed, is away much of the time."

"Did you love Architect Suti when you were given to him?"

With rigid posture Lady Nagara responded, "You have become impertinent today, Becataten, and have stepped beyond your station inquiring about personal details." With new hardness she said, "However, I will say that if you are fortunate enough to become a favorite of Our Living God, he will eventually choose a husband for you, and you will accept that husband and you will respect him and try to love him."

Becataten didn't dare ask another question. She asked permission to leave, bowed and exited Lady Nagara's sitting chamber with a sense of relief. She felt herself shaking as she returned to her room, her servant holding her up like a living crutch as her legs felt weak beneath her. She was tucked into her bed but awakened after a brief nap. Sadness clutched her heart and a pang to be outdoors. She sat up and her servant, who had been dozing on the floor beside her, jumped to the ready.

"Ask Butler to find me someone to accompany me to the river. I wish to see the Mother Nile. My heart greatly desires it."

"But you will be in trouble, will you not?" asked the soft-spoken slave girl.

"I do not think so, if I ask first."

An appropriate guardian was set to accompany her to the Mother Nile. She stumbled across soft dunes, her heart full of anticipation to see something comforting that she loved. The butler had chosen a senior eunuch. Becataten needed to be near the river and feel its constancy. Together, she and an old eunuch walked in silence, he ahead of her with a firm grip on a high-held torch.

Standing on a hillock viewing the Nile, Becataten watched the soft current. The water gently flowed

136

from origins where the mighty cataracts stood in the land of Kush. The ripples stretched from shore to shore, glistening in the half-moon light, softly moving the river toward the delta where she spilled into the Great Sea.

Looking across the water, Becataten took a deep breath and sang softly into the warm still air. The night was quiet with only an occasional screech from an egret. Her song was the ancient Hymn of the Nile. It took as long to sing as it took for the rope to burn during her punishment, earlier in the day.

The eunuch who accompanied Becataten listened, mouth agape. The next day everyone could hear the old man extoling Princess Becataten's ability to sing the entire anthem to the ancient river, Mother Nile.

Chapter 17

♊

Becataten's studies grew more rigorous. Her music teacher had her pluck the lyre on a daily basis until the effort drew blood from her fingertips. Her legs ached at night from the rigors of her dance instructor, and many pots had fallen from her head to crash on the floor before her walk was proper and her posture erect. Her speech instruction was repetitious because she was told her tongue had grown harsh and crude, never having used the King's vernacular. She was also expected to dress and bathe and dine with Lady Nagara, in the fashion of a lady. Exhausted most evenings, an unexpected surprise occurred one day, so she rallied enough energy one night to compose a scroll. In her candle-lit chamber, she wrote:

Dearest Beset,

I have no word from Jobu – thank the gods I can write you. I have been forced to keep my council because Lady Nagara is not a woman I can share my thoughts. But this Ra something good came from something bad and created my first real audience with her since my arrival, and now I am learning daily how to be a lady. I learned much about her and why she is both sad and sometimes angry. But the best news is the Estate just received an invitation from Pharaoh's Court for she and I to visit the Palace, and I will see you all soon. I am so happy. I can hardly wait. Tell Jobu to go nowhere. I want to see him. But also tell him I love him, as I do you and Maja.

Taten

The day arrived when the invitation to the Palace was a reality. Servants at the Estate had spent the days before readying the most impressive gowns, the best and freshest of make-ups, herbs, perfumes, and oils. Wigs were replaced and tried on, and finally, after the grueling day's travel, they arrived at the Palace where they were offered their own suite. Taten wished to see her family desperately but was watched closely and bathed and pampered up until the moment where she was brought forth, a sparkling being in the finest of garments with the most elaborate face painting and wig, to Pharaoh's hall.

Becataten stepped into Pharaoh's grand hall and found the gathering overwhelming. The air was

139

close, dry and oppressive but Princess Becataten stood perfectly still in the audience hall with Lady Nagara and the Royal Architects Suti and Hor. The huge chamber permeated with smells from foreign dignitaries. Oils of morenga, almond, mint, cardamom and cinnamon, swirled in the air. They were mixed with flower perfumes of jasmine, sweet flag, and lotus. The combinations made her a bit dizzy. She thought men must not have the nose of a woman. They chose the strongest scents.

Becataten stared up at the high ceiling. It was as tall as a palm tree. Up the walls were scenes of papyrus groves and wild flying geese. Just below the ceiling were horizontal rows of painted rosettes. Fine and unusual weavings, fringed with vivid colors, covered the rear wall. They looked foreign and she guessed they were gifts from Pharaoh's vassal states.

Lady Nagara nudged Becataten. "You're staring like a child does at honey cakes," she whispered.

"May I ask if the flowers in the alabaster vases, near the thrones of Pharaoh and Queen Tiy, are from the Estate?"

"Yes, now quiet, and no more staring." Lady Nagara said harshly.

It was Pharaoh's edict that the chamber be filled with his elite group of Egyptian nobles and high-ranking bureaucrats, plucked from his Thebian populous of three million. The crowded hall teamed

140

with five hundred people. Even the most powerful magistrate was in attendance: Viceroy Merymose, who had traveled two Ras from Kush. He had arrived with his son, who was to be educated in Thebes, as was customary among the nobles and rich classes. Pharaoh's Vizier stepped forward, delivering in a strong voice the story of the plentiful bounty of the recent harvest, explaining that the Great Lord would be dispensing some of that largess today.

Suti stood near as Viceroy Merymose was studying Becataten. She could feel the hot gaze of the Viceroy upon her, and struggled to avert her eyes. She knew he was greatly distinguished with the coveted title of King's Son, ranking him paramount among all of Pharaoh's officials. In her studies, she had learned that during the fifth year of Pharaoh's reign, he and the Viceroy had put down an uprising in Kush. They had returned victorious with seventy thousand Nubian slaves. It was said that Pharaoh wore a depiction of that enemy incised on the bottom of his gold sandals.

Her thoughts were diverted when she saw the men from the east that grew black beards that flowed in wavy patterns down their chests. These men dressed in heavy woven robes, and were potentates from Pharaoh's vassal states in the northeast, where his governors expedited regular tribute.

She had to hold back a smile at the strutting merchants, in unusual garb that had sailed the Great Sea to be here on this day. Some wore pounded breast- plates. Others brandished silk robes and vests woven from seashells.

She saw Hor bend down to Suti's ear. "You know those traders have ships moored at the Delta that are crammed with exotic cargo and well-guarded by our militia."

Suti nodded.

Hor continued. "It is known that if a captain from Mycenaean can cross the Great Sea and barter his goods for Egyptian gold, he would never have to trade again."

This was all so fascinating for Becataten to hear, it made it difficult not to stare. It was one thing to read scrolls about all of these people, but to see them close was captivating.

"Who have traveled the farthest to be here?" she whispered in Lady Nagara's ear.

Lady Nagara looked pensive for a moment. "Probably those over there," she said as she nodded toward a group of mahogany-colored traders with wrapped headdresses. "They sail here from a sub-continent to the east where there is also a great river. Once they embark on Egyptian soil, they caravan their goods to the Nile then sail to Thebes. They bring us the weightless silks, lavishly embroidered fabrics and alien hides."

"That would be the Indus River," Becataten said, remembering her geography lessons.

Lady Nagara nodded. "They arrive with strange women who wear gems between their eyes," she whispered with distaste.

Becataten thought these women were alluring with their large black eyes and sensuous mouths. They wore intricate designs painted on their hands and the bottoms of their feet with the paste from the flowering henna plant. More intricate than the Egyptians' tatoos, she thought. Adorned in glittering clothing, they were littered about in cages by their maritime owners.

Still whispering, Lady Nagara covered her lips. "See those men? They are from the northeast where two great rivers cross. They bring their women like dogs on chains, with jewelry pierced to all parts of their body. Look how unclean the men appear with unshaven hair on their heads and body."

This display of women brought Becataten's mother to mind, as she too had been a foreign tribute from the Tigris and Euphrates river valley. Her mother, Princess Attah, had arrived with Maja twelve or more inundations past. Did she resemble these women in some way? Clearly, Lady Nagara has dismissed that possibility.

Then a parade appeared of tall black women, who walked behind their even taller men from Kush. Standing proud and bare-breasted, they wore a

143

hairstyle studded with intricate pieces of carved ivory and brightly colored feathers. Lady Nagara seemed to hold no distain for this group.

Becataten began to carry herself with more esteem as she stood among this amalgam of beauty. A little taller than the average Egyptian with fuller lips and her rare, almond-shaped green eyes, Becataten knew she was impeccably dressed. Lady Nagara had chosen a long shift of translucent linen. Her breasts were visible through the transparent fabric, but not exposed and flaunted like Court women. Minimal gold jewelry, inlaid with lapis lazuli, adorned her neck, and gold bracelets cuffed her wrists. She reached to finger the plaits on her obsidian-colored wig that were interwoven with gold and turquoise beads. The artful headpiece framed her full checks and dreamy gaze with elegance. She could feel Lady Nagara scrutinize her from time to time, but she felt like a Royal and kept her head high.

The Vizier's robust voice drifted into the columned hall delivering from his scroll the designated names of those who were to enjoy gifts from the Living God. Queen Tiy sat like a statue of granite. Pharaoh, posed on his large throne, was far more vibrant as he casually scanned his audience. His favorite feline, old Lady Mui, sat on his lap, adorned for the event wearing her golden earrings and collar. It reminded Becataten of the kittens she

144

and Jobu had been given from one of Lady Mui's litters. She sighed, thinking, *that was a long time ago.* Then she thought she saw Pharaoh pause to view her, but when she turned to look at Lady Nagara, she found her smiling back at Pharaoh. Becataten recalled the history Lady Nagara, Queen Tiy and Pharaoh shared, and how they once played like brothers and sisters. She watched Lady Nagara take in Queen Tiy. Becataten did the same and found the queen less youthful looking than Pharaoh. The beauty she had left was laden with heavy jewelry, an elaborate feathered dress and a huge wig. Pharaoh appeared as a robust figure, muscular, bronze-colored from his regular hunting, charioting and archery prowess. Just the smile lines of his eyes betrayed his age. Sitting on his throne with the strength and self-esteem of all the gods, he was the virile image of a king. His subjects were all told that no man in the Egyptian army could pierce a copper shield from the distance that Pharaoh could. His body glistened from the anointments of perfumed oils and the time he spent in Ra's rays. Long ago Lady Nagara had told Becataten to wear no essence, should she be invited to his bedchamber. Pharaoh always wanted his perfumes to dominate.

It looked as though Lady Nagara was daydreaming. She seemed to return to the present when Architects Suti and Hor were bestowed with funerary gifts; a fine papyrus roll of the *Book of the Dead*, assuring their transition into paradise. The scrolls were hefty with myriad illuminations, executed by Astrologer Abu's able scribes.

Becataten watched as Lady Nagara was offered glistening shaqyu; earrings of gold, turquoise, carnelian and colored glass, fashioned into blossoms, symbolizing her regular gifts of flowers to the Court. They were presented to her on a pillow by a Court attendant, followed by a chest of frankincense, carved of lapis lazuli.

As the event concluded and the crowds began to disperse, Becataten respectfully asked Lady Nagara if she could visit her family before returning to the Estate. Lady Nagara deemed she could, but that she must return before the next rise of Ra. An early start meant the first half of the return trip would not be so hot. "Thank you, Lady Nagara," Becataten replied with a proper bow. Her heart raced. *I can't wait to see Jobu.*

The Viceroy strode toward Becataten. Lady Nagara moved her into the crowd, away from his approach. Shifting her direction, she bumped into a Babylonian potentate, who turned on her with annoyance. Putting a hard hold on her wrist, he spoke harshly to her in his foreign tongue. Then drawing her close to his smelly bearded face, and with a wicked grin, he mauled her breasts. Becataten's face flushed with shock as she tried to

146

free herself.

The Viceroy was quick to reach her, his dagger out of its sheath, and followed by personal Nubian guards, armed with spears. When the foreigner was descended upon, he barked a crude laugh. Then arrogantly he started to speak, but was silenced as the Viceroy held a dagger to the potentate's throat. Nubian guards held spears at his belly.

The Viceroy called for Egyptian sentries. That sparked a commotion in the crowd that the Viceroy quelled with commanding words. "Remove the Babylonian."

The Viceroy turned to her. "Have you in any way been harmed, My Lady?"

Becataten shook her head, stunned.

Lady Nagara said, "We are thankful for your intervention, Viceroy. Now we must go."

Lady Nagara whisked Becataten off to a nearby hall, and required a royal guard to escort them to a nearby vacant apartment used for guests.

Once inside, Lady Nagara said, "You still look well enough. How do you feel?"

Becataten shook her head. "I am still shocked, but that is all. Why did he do that?"

"He was a foreign swine, and we shall speak of him no more. Now use the chamber pot if you must, then we will return to our suites."

Becataten shuddered. "What do you think will happen to him?"

147

Wearing a nondescript expression, Lady Nagara answered. "Considering that you are a Royal Princess, I suspect he shall be castrated and sent home."

Becataten's face reddened as she felt the beginnings of being a Royal.

Chapter 18

♊

Becataten's heart pounded as she rushed to her old apartment in the Palace complex where she grew up. She tried to pass through the throng but after just a few steps she was stuck, standing still. A major ruler was passing through with a large entourage. She overheard a man address Viceroy Merymose. They were having a conversation about the various foreign women who were in the hall that were gifts to Pharaoh. "We have a slave trader who collects the finest women from Kush every season and supplies them to..." They moved on, and she missed the rest of the conversation. Then she heard Hor's voice. "What a transformation Lady Nagara has made of Becataten. She has become quiet, reserved, even appearing regal."

Becataten glanced at Hor as he was appraising her.

"Oh yes," replied Suti, "Lady Nagara could make honey cakes of mud. Look what she has done with me!"

Lanky Hor teased in his deep voice, "She could have made you taller."

Becataten smiled at the banter between the twins. Seeing them together made her even more anxious to see Jobu.

Suti continued, "Becataten was a beauty in the rough, and it is true my Lady has taken that beauty and enhanced it greatly, but I am sure you remember how quickly she learns. She is like a fine sword with both sides now finely hewn." Suti paused a moment, then said, "Hor, how far is your apartment from the boy-twin, Prince Jobutaten?"

The noisy crowd was on the move, people were pushing their way toward litters and chair bearers to transport them to their homes outside the Palace, while those with royal apartments walked toward the coolness of their environs. In the heat, a few women were removing their wigs and handing them off to attendants, and as Lady Nagara watched, she scowled in distaste. Becataten straightened up, and stood absorbing the wealthy mass of humanity that surrounded her. She eavesdropped on the nearby twins, as Suti's mention of Jobu had jolted her. She had never heard him speak of him.

Hor bent to Suti's ear and spoke in a voice she could barely hear. "The boy-twin lives some distance from me, but I see him from time to time. It is hard to believe that he and Princess Becataten are the same age; even related. He runs with some scribes that in my view are too old for him. Like me, he seems to prefer men to women, but I do not approve of his crowd."

Becataten was shocked to hear this claim of Jobu preferring men to women. They must be wrong. Amid the clamor, she edged closer to them, trying not to appear to be eavesdropping.

"What makes you say that, Hor?" Suti asked.

Hor worked his mouth before answering. "My instincts tell me that the boy-twin is being sexually used by these older scribes, and they are reckless types."

With concern, Suti spoke with sensitivity. "Hor, can you look into that matter and let me know more about the boy's day-to-day living habits? As twins, we should foster whatever talents these children may have."

They stepped to an alcove away from the crowd. Becataten slid over and stood outside the recess, unnoticed by Lady Nagara, so she could hear more, but Lady Nagara glanced over and motioned her back by her side. Becataten hesitated before complying and caught a final snippet of the conversation.

Hor sighed and said, "Don't ask me to do your work, Suti. I am not suited to the paternal role."

Becataten could no longer hear them as she returned to Lady Nagara's care. She stared into the distance over the throng of people. *What had happened to Jobu, and was he being used? Why wasn't she told of this?*

151

Lady Nagara noticed the brothers and walked over to them, interrupting them, "What are you brothers conquering?" Becataten followed, seeing her opportunity to learn more.

"Hor was just telling me that he was going to look into how Prince Jobutaten is living his life."

"Hmm! I wouldn't bother," said Lady Nagara. "He has already grown too old to model into anything valuable. It took me two inundations to bring out the best in Princess Becataten."

With a sour look, Hor replied, "I agree with you, Lady Nagara."

Suti stood with a pensive stare, while his brother led his wife away by the arm. Hor's head bent to hers, as they began chatting away. They enjoyed gossiping about all things related to the Court and were catching up. Becataten could tell.

Becataten set her jaw, and pushed past the end of the entourage that passed before her. She was shocked to see a young boy, about Jobu's age, beautifully dressed and cared for, yet not even a prince. With fierce determination, she ran outside, pushing through the masses of people so she could find a litter to carry her away, back to her real home.

When Becataten entered the small apartment she was struck by the familiar smells and the humbleness of the dwelling. She found only Beset asleep. Time was running fast and half the day gone. Becataten's eyes were wild as she searched for her brother. *Where was Jobu?*

"Beset," gently called Becataten to awaken her from her typical midday nap.

Drowsy and not recognizing Becataten, Beset sat up and said, "Yes, my lady, can I help you?"

"Beset, it's me, Taten."

Beset jumped up and screeched, "By the Gods it *is* you, by the Gods you look so, so grown up, so beautiful, Taten. Oh I can't call you that anymore, you really look like a royal princess, Taten, I mean, Princess Becataten."

With tears spilling down her cheeks, Becataten put her arms out and bent down to Beset's stubby frame. "Beset, give me a big hug and call me whatever you want, I have missed you so much! Where is everybody?"

Beset's high-pitched voice was out of control. "Maja went for a walk with Sennejem. Jobu is rarely around anymore. I'm not sure where he ever is."

Becataten wrung her hands. "I want to see Jobu so much, I missed him terribly, and it's so important that we talk. He sent me not one scroll to the Estate. And thank you, Beset for your words.

They meant so much to me."

Beset finished blowing her nose and wiping her eyes. "Becataten, can you stay a few Ras with us? I need to talk to you about Jobu, and his new friends. I think his life may have taken a bad turn, and of course we want to hear all about your life at the Estate," Beset said as she began weeping again.

Becataten wiped her tears carefully so as to not smudge her makeup and walked to the bedchamber that she and Jobu had shared. She touched the edges of the scrolls that had meant so much to her as a child. They were unfurled and dusty.

"Oh, please do tell me about Jobu, I just heard some disturbing news about him. I am due back at a waiting chair to return with Lady Nagara before Ra rises, so we just have the dark time together, Beset."

Beset made an effort to collect her emotions. "Let's go to the garden, at least I think I know where Maja is, and we can talk about Jobu along the way," Beset said. She smoothed her wrinkled shift and wobbled toward the portal, when in walked Jobu. He was holding hands with an older boy. He stared at Becataten, at first not recognizing her, then a rare smile crossed his lips and they fell into each other's arms. His friend touched Jobu with fondness, then turned and left.

Beset stood, wiping more tears from her craggy checks as her beloved twins embraced. "You two talk while I go and get us some beer and find Maja."

154

Jobu had grown taller than Becataten during the two innundations they had been apart. A black fuzz, grew above his upper lip and below his eyes there were dark markings of half-moons, not made by kohl. *He is so thin,* Becataten thought. The royal plait that dangled over his ear was disheveled. His kilt was not fresh.

"Jobu, are you ill?"

He shook his head and spoke in a deeper and new voice. "You look beautiful, Taten, and you smell good, too."

"Jobu, this place is wearing on you. Let me ask Suti if you can come and live with us for the next season. The Estate air would do you good and we could be together. I could show you so many new things and..."

He put a finger to her lips and said. "I am fine where I am, it is you who belongs there. Look what it has done for you! You have become a fine princess. I do not care to become a fine prince, even if I could."

Becataten grew angry. "Jobu, I have heard about your new friends, and I don't like them. It sounds as though they are using you." She stared into his eyes and he looked away.

Jobu took a step back from her, frowned and said, "Where did you hear that?"

"You hear everything at Court. Are these so-called friends using you, Jobu? And who was that boy that just left you were holding hands with?"

Jobu looked uncomfortable studying her and turned away again to reach for a pitcher of beer. She thought she saw fear in him, and knew he was weighing his words. She waited.

"You have returned a different person, Taten. And to answer your question, Royal Scribe Tiurek, who just left, and several others who work for the Royal Astrologer are my friends."

"Jobu, Jobu, I love you and I missed you so much! I don't want to argue, but you didn't send me one scroll, and I worried so about you. Please come back to Suti's Estate with me. You don't look well."

Jobu looked awkward and alarmed at her demand. "That's not possible," he said.

"Why? These friends can't mean more than I do, can they?"

"Of course not, it is just that I cannot leave the Palace now. I am beginning to learn something about us that has been kept secret since our birth and ..."

"What do you mean? You sound mysterious, Jobu."

Beset returned out of breath with fresh barley beer and Maja. They all wept and hugged. Then, sitting on coarse linen floor cushions, they chatted about Becataten's beauty and grace. Maja ran her hands over Becataten's clothing and jewelry. "Can I try on your golden cuffs, Taten?"

156

Becataten took them off and handed them to Maja. She removed her wig and set it on a floor pillow.

"The hair is so fine and the golden beads in the braids are so shiny," said Maja. Becataten watched as they all stroked her wig.

"How calm and regal you have become, Taten," said Beset.

Maja nodded as her eyes shown with tears.

Taten turned to Jobu, wanting to talk privately with him but realizing there was no polite way to leave Maja and Beset. "Jobu, what have you been doing with your life since I have been away?"

"Oh, I spend time with Sennejem, helping with his garden tasks."

Becataten looked briefly at Maja, and saw her say "no" with her eyes.

"And you spoke briefly about new friends, Jobu."

"I told you, I have a few friends who are scribes in the Palace."

She could feel a mounting resistance in her twin. She tried to veer the conversation to his situation of possibly being used by his new friends and of the secret he knew, but Jobu was cautious and his answers were elusive.

The time they had together seemed to fly. Now it was near sunrise, and she knew she must leave. She was so happy to visit with Beset and Maja. Yet she had gotten no information from Jobu about his friends or what was so secret about his life.

Tearfully she made hurried goodbyes. Reaching out to hug Maja and Beset, she whispered in Beset's ear, "I need to get Jobu alone."

"Jobu, walk Becataten to the gate, Maja and I will come with her wig." Beset said.

As the twins walked, Becataten said, "Jobu, you have been vague about your friends and unclear about this secret you started to talk about."

He ignored her comment and stared at the ground.

"Say something, Jobu?"

He looked away from her as they walked.

Becataten decided to try and reach him with another topic as she held his hand. "So Maja still spends time with Sennejem, do you think they are lovers?"

Jobu shrugged his shoulders and said, "I don't think so. He is a nice man but as you know their stations in life are very different. I think it is their common dialect that attracts them most." Jobu slipped and weakly struggled to regain his footing.

"Jobu, stop right here! I will not take another step until you tell me what is wrong!"

"Come on Taten. They will be angry with you if you do not meet them at the gate."

"Angry!" replied Becataten, "If you only knew. I have been castigated in ways you have never been. Lady Nagara makes a Princess not with milk and honey but with harsh punishments I will never forget."

"I am sorry to hear that, Taten." Jobu looked down and shook sand from his sandals. "I have missed you too, but while you were gone..." he paused.

"What? Say it." Becataten urged.

"I think I am close to learning something about our birth records that has been kept from Pharaoh, and maybe about a Court plot too."

Becataten stopped walking, turned to Jobu and said, "Learned what!"

"There is an older scribe that told me that we have two sets of Heavenly Charts, both different."

"Are you sure of this? Who is this person?"

Jobu nodded. "He belongs to Abu, the Court Astrologer and remembers when our birth stories were cast."

"Why would the Court Astrologer keep two sets, and both different?"

"That is what I am about to learn."

"Do you think our scrolls are unfavorable?"

"That's what I am trying to find out."

"And you said that there is something else too. What did you mean?"

"Oh it's nothing, really."

"Jobu!"

He looked down again, and said, "I have heard talk that Memphis priests plot to remove Pharaoh, and that's all I know. I swear by the Gods."

"But how did you find out about the plot, too? Oh, Jobu, I worry so about you. It sounds like you have made friends with a den of scheming people."

In the distance Becataten saw the bearers waiting at attention and Lady Nagara sitting stiff in the large conveyance.

"Don't worry," Jobu said as he squeezed her hand. "I will learn all about this, but do not expect a scroll from me. We must keep this a secret about our Heavenly Charts."

She held his hand to her chest. "I promise, Jobu. Twin of my heart, please be careful. You know how Beset always says the Court can be a treacherous place, and so does Lady Nagara."

He held her hand longer as she stepped onto the chair next to Lady Nagara. Both twins' eyes filled with tears.

After the runners took up their jog, Jobutaten ran alongside Becataten's litter. With fixed glazes they stared at one another. Tears splashed down Becataten's cheek, but she remained stoic in front of Lady Nagara.

Jobu fell back, and as he grew smaller in the distance between them, Becataten recalled a scroll Beset had sent referring to the scribes Jobu called his friends. Beset said they were too old and a manipulative lot. Lady Nagara and Beset were right; the Court was a dangerous place. Becataten's face held a small frown, and on the ride back to the Estate, she was both somber and silent.

Chapter 19

♊

Sennejem arrived to accompany Maja for an evening walk. Occasionally Beset would follow in silence. She knew how much Maja enjoyed these outings, and it was an easy way for Beset to learn of a few Court rumors, especially as Sennejem spoke more and more in Egyptian to Maja.

The Royal Gardener and the nanny were an unlikely pair, yet Beset saw that they had things in common. Maja was inept socially. Sennejem had difficulty looking people in the eye and seemed to hold no one close. Their most common bond seemed to be the Mitanni culture.

"Good evening, Maja," said Sennejem as he handed her a freshly cut iris.

Maja smiled with pleasure. "Thank you, Sennejem," she said in a voice that she reserved for him.

"I have a litter waiting to take us to a place in the Palace garden you have never seen, Maja."

Beset's attention was piqued. "Would you mind if I came along this fine evening. It is so warm in the apartment tonight."

162

Maja looked perturbed, but nodded.

They traveled along quietly. "You like the calm and peace here like I do, don't you, Maja?" Sennejem said.

Maja nodded, "Yes, it is restful here. You are lucky you have this place, Sennejem."

"Yes, and it is an honor to plant the exotic plants that Pharaoh likes. You know he is very knowledgeable about all growing things. I put in the ground exactly what the Crown wants. This moon we received Morenga trees imported from the tropical south. I am told Pharaoh keeps scrolls on its many uses."

"Would you like to see my latest planting of one of the trees, Maja?"

Beset had little interest in plants, and she knew Maja felt the same, but both women agreed.

After a long ride, Sennejem asked the bearers to set the conveyance down, and walked to a recently planted tree. "See this leaf? It can be eaten like a vegetable, and hold the pod; that is where the oil is found. It is used for perfume making and even the chefs like to cook with it. Pharaoh will receive the first crop. I am told he believes it keeps him young by applying the lubricant to his skin."

Beset sighed and stepped off the litter, bored and doubting she would find out anything of intrigue from this pair. She looked around; they were far from the bustle of the Palace. She searched in vain for a second litter to return home on when Maja asked, "Sennejem, can you tell me again about Suti?"

With curiosity, Beset listened as she pretended to show sudden interest in Sennejem's tree.

"Of course," Sennejem said, as he walked over to a garden seat nearby and sat with Maja. "But as you know I have not been the Royal Gardener long. Everyone knows the Royal Architects Suti and Hor are from the Noble class. Hor lives in a large apartment here in the Palace compound."

Beset sneaked behind them and quietly hid well behind foliage to listen.

"How is Noble class different from Royal class, Sennejem?" Maja asked, a dreamy quality to her voice. Beset could tell Maja cared much for the Royal Gardener.

"When you are a Royal, you are blessed with the blood of the Living God, like Jobu and Taten. But when you are Noble in class, you are rich and serve the Royal class."

"So, you, Sennejem, are what?"

"I am only part Royal, as my mother was a harem princess from Mitanni, like Princess Attah was to the twins. I think I am still considered of the Noble class."

"So Taten and Jobu are just part Royal?" Maja asked. Beset could tell she was trying to find out something specific and held her breath.

"Well, yes that is true. To be a full Royal, your mother must be an Egyptian."

"So you work for Pharaoh, and you are part Royal?"

Beset was stunned by Maja's easy manner with Sennejem, and talkativeness.

"I work for Pharaoh because the Royal Astrologer recommended me highly. He is a man who has the ear of Our King, so when it came time to appoint a new gardener, he learned of me and I was chosen," Sennejem answered, shifting uncomfortably. He stood, as if the conversation were too much for him. Maja remained seated.

"I do not understand." Maja shook her head. Beset wondered if Maja really didn't understand or was trying to get more information.

Sennejem took her hand and said, "After the Royal Gardener before me died, the Astrologer interviewed me. He read my heavenly chart and said I could perform the job well. I also think he liked speaking in our native tongue. Most of the slaves who work for me are from the lands of Babylon, and I can speak their languages. But you wanted to know about Suti, didn't you?"

"Yes! What I wish to know...Is this Royal Architect, who took Taten, a good man?"

"Oh yes, I think he must be, Maja. Pharaoh covets multiple births and holds them in high regard. That is why he has made them Royal

Architects."

"Why does Pharaoh not covet Taten and Jobu? We never hear from Pharaoh - not since thirteen inundations ago when he sent birth-gifts to the Royal Nursery."

Beset thought that Maja had made a good point and secretly cheered her on.

"I cannot speak to that, Maja."

Maja stood up. "Maybe everything will change in Taten's life, and I will never see her again."

"Now, now, Maja, don't worry so."

Sennejem was distracted when he noticed Abu crossing the garden in the distance. "Look over there, Maja," he said, pointing into the fading sun light in the distance. "Across the garden, do you see him? The Royal Astrologer, Abu, walks from Pharaoh's Court to his royal apartment. See the torch-bearer running to keep up with his long steps."

Beset peeked behind the dark foliage and watched as Maja strained to see Abu in the twilight. "Yes, I see him, he looks... he looks like someone I saw when Princess Attah and I first came to Egypt. He wears a fancy kilt like that man..." Her hands covered her mouth, she grew silent then faint.

"What is it, Maja?"

"Nothing." Maja swooned a bit but caught herself. "Sennejem, I am sorry. But can we go back to the apartment? I don't feel well."

166

Beset stepped forward, stumbling through the undergrowth. Maja had almost told the secret! "I'll see her home, Sennejem. I think she is becoming ill." Sennejem could not cover his surprise at Beset's sudden appearance.

"No, I will see you both home," he said with concern.

"If you think that is best," said Beset. Sennejem stared at Beset with suspicion, but Beset assisted Maja and helped her onto the litter.

After a bumpy ride that seemed to take forever, Beset rushed Maja into to her bedchamber.

"Maja are you feeling sick? I could bring you back an herbal brew?"

"No, leave me," Maja muttered.

"Sennejem waits outside to see if you need further assistance. I will tell him to leave." Rushing out the door, Beset hurried to find Sennejem sitting on the grounded litter.

"Can we walk?" Beset asked. Sennejem nodded grimly and stepped out of the litter. They walked to a small grove of newly planted palms where a bench stood.

"What is it, Beset? Is Maja ill?"

"I don't think so, but she is upset," Beset said as she struggled to climb onto the bench that was surrounded by overgrown mint.

As he helped her, Sennejem said, "I was pointing out the Royal Astrologer when she said she felt weak and wanted to go home."

"Has she ever met him?"

"No, no. I was just telling her how he helped me to become Royal Gardener, when I saw him in the distance. She said she thought he looked familiar from a long time ago. I didn't understand; something about his fancy kilt."

"You visit with the Royal Astrologer often, don't you, Sennejem?" Beset said as she picked a piece of mint to smell its aroma.

"Not often, but sometimes. You could call him my mentor."

"I'd like to hear your story about him."

Beset wanted to know what kind of a man Abu was and what kind of help he had given Sennejem.

Sennejem settled himself, and began. "We both came from Mitanni mothers and shared the language. I started managing work crews in the gardens and was able to rise quickly in station of Royal Gardener, due to the help of the Astrologer."

Beset listened to Sennejem as she stared at a distant row of olive trees.

"I don't feel I know the Royal Astrologer, Sennejem, but it sounds like he has been good to you."

"Yes, he has, but I don't think he is a very happy man."

"What do you mean?" Beset asked.

"An old scribe once told me that in the early

days of the Palace he experienced a sad event and it changed him, and not for the better." Then he interrupted himself as if realizing the risk of his words and said, "I cannot linger longer Beset, I must be going, I have an early day of work."

"You go, Sennejem, I will sit awhile in this lovely place."

He bid her farewell. Beset remained on the bench in the evening sky, swinging her legs and muttering to herself, "Maja says Princess Attah's lover was Abu, and the twin's father. Butler Farafar says Abu created two sets of heavenly charts for the twins. These charts are supposed to read differently. Sennejem says his mentor is Abu. Scribe Tiurek, who has pushed his way into Jobu's life, is Abu's senior scribe." She counted off the connections on her fingers as she figured it out.

Abu's name comes up far too often, she realized. It sounded as though he was trying to control the destinies of my twins. Why? Beset wondered as she pondered the question far into the night.

Chapter 20

♊

As the morning sky grew brighter, an Egyptian envoy was dispatched to deliver a canister containing Pharaoh's personal seal. His orders were to carry it to the Suti Estate, and to the care of Lady Nagara.

He ran swiftly and tirelessly through the sun's rise and nearly into a faint, with few stops for rest along the way. When he arrived, a watchman at the walled garden of the residence allowed him entrance, where he passed a tree-lined pool full of fish, paddling ducks and lotus flowers, then up the many steps to the walled villa entrance, where he stopped to take many deep breaths. Granted admission by the butler, the runner followed him through a reception area across a glazed tile floor. The household secretary was summoned while he waited. In the grand hall, cool breezes entered the high clerestory window openings and drifted through the villa's rooms that were built of thick mud brick, painted white much like the Palace. It helped to keep the grand house cool. Paintings of plant and animal life adorned the walls, interspersed with depictions of Pharaoh's cartouche, to bring good fortune. A young female servant arrived with a cup of well water for the lean, dark man who waited patiently. She smiled, and he stuttered, "How - many - rooms?" Grinning, she whispered, "Twenty." He rolled his eyes and made a deep clucking sound with his tongue.

Lady Nagara's assistant entered and said she was designated to receive the correspondence and that he could take some refreshments on the roof. The man bowed then unleashed the gem-inlayed metal cylinder from around his neck. He uncapped it and withdrew the papyrus roll, handing it over, bowing again.

Lady Nagara entered and saw the Palace runner. "What brings you from Pharaoh's Palace?" She asked, noting the Royal emblem on the scroll canister.

She reached out for the scroll from her assistant and read it quickly. Lady Nagara heaved a sigh as she rolled the papyrus document tight. Holding the missive close, she turned on her heels and headed toward her quarters.

As she walked she called for her butler, and when he arrived she barked orders: "Tell Chef a celebration is nearing. I want the Stable Master ready with powerful steeds for a drive to the Palace, soon. Have the laundryman and hairdresser attend my wardrobes and those of Princess Becataten, our

171

wigs, too." Lady Nagara stared across the vast room, a thrill running through her as she began preparations in her mind. In countenance, however, she was, as usual, steely and cool.

"You look lovely, Becataten," Suti said, as she joined him on the canopied rooftop at sunset. A low table, set with brightly colored, goose down cushions awaited the diners. With the little movement of air, the candle flames stood bright and still. Becataten wore a fine linen shift that was interwoven with gold threads and cinched tight with a brightly woven red belt. Her face was painted with care - cheeks the color of pomegranate blossoms and lips the shade of the hibiscus flower. She chose lotus oil for her perfume. Delicate, long golden earrings nearly reached her shoulders, and she wore no wig.

"You truly look beautiful on this momentous occasion, Princess."

"Thank you Architect Suti," she said then turned to say good evening to Lady Nagara and Hor, who were seated nearby.

After they were all settled, Suti said, "Tonight is a celebration in your honor, Princess Becataten. Lady Nagara has planned it, and I have chosen the wine and instructed chef to serve us a surprise for dinner."

Becataten was speechless, for in all of her time with Suti and Lady Nagara, she had never been honored before. Lady Nagara spoke. "You recall the envoy from the Palace that came with a scroll for me a few Ras ago?"

Becataten nodded.

"It is an elaborate invitation for you to visit the Palace for an extended stay, and specifically for you to spend time with Pharaoh. He suggests you join him on a hunting trip for lions, riding at his side in the royal chariot. He speaks of a river cruise on the royal barge. He also mentions touring his favorite monuments, acknowledging your interest in architecture." The scroll lay at her side.

Suti interrupted with raised eyebrows "You can thank me for the tour of Pharaoh's latest building sites, Princess," he said, chuckling.

Lady Nagara sat across the candlelit table from Becataten, continuing in her dignified manner. "And of course, this includes visits to Pharaoh's bed chamber. How many, will depend upon you. We have little time to work on preparing for all of these events. You must spend some time in a chariot." She stiffened and continued, "Although I recall you have done that. You'll have no trouble viewing Pharaoh's building projects as you are conversant in architecture, thanks to Suti, and I am sure you must have sailed in a boat before. But, regarding the bedchamber, you must have schooling. I will instruct you."

Suti added, "This is a great privilege, Princess. The women of the harem are just rotated in to Pharaoh's bedchamber. You have a grand invitation by the God himself and an invitation to travel with him as a companion."

"May I see the scroll?" Becataten asked, finding her voice. Her head was swimming with the news. She felt she needed to see it to fully understand it.

Lady Nagara slowly pushed it toward her, narrowing her eyes. By Lady Nagara's expression, Becataten could imagine her thoughts, *if only our lives were reversed.*

The welcomed, sweet north wind began to flutter across the roof, setting the lit candles dancing. Becataten unrolled the thick papyrus roll. With care and reverence she smoothed it out on the table toward Hor, who held it open for her. She fingered Pharaoh's royal seal and noted with interest the entire text.

Lady Nagara grew quiet as she watched Becataten pore over the scroll, noting the attention she paid the hieroglyphs colored in red that specified the most important content.

"How much of that can you read?" Lady Nagara asked.

Not bothering to look up, Becataten said, "All of it, My Lady."

Lady Nagara pointed to a red line of the

hieroglyphs and said, "What does this say?"

"This talks about the royal barge and how we will sail to the land of Kush and..."

Lady Nagara interrupted her and said, "That will be enough."

Suti smiled at his wife. "Remember, I told you she was a talented one."

Lady Nagara responded by clapping her hands for the chef, who arrived with a loaf of bread baked from stone-ground emmer wheat molded in the image of Becataten. This was the custom in Egypt when honoring a guest, and sure confirmation that the evening was an auspicious one. The wine was served in calcite goblets, a light palm wine for Lady Nagara and Becataten, a blended red sma from Pharaoh's cellar for Suti and Hor.

Suti raised his glass and said, "Wine is for offerings, wine is for taxes, wine is for happy returns and merry-making, but tonight it is for my two ladies for a job well done. Now let us dine."

Suti nodded to the harpist who commenced playing and singing a festive hymn to the *Goddess Maat, She Who Keeps Order, Truth And Justice* in the world of Egypt. To the waiting cook, Suti indicated, that dinner begin.

From the roof, orders were signaled to the outdoor kitchen below to begin food service. Trays of cucumbers, chickpeas, lettuces, herbs, olives and a variety of breads were brought upstairs to the rooftop dining table. Roast duck, grilled fish and boiled eggs were served next, then skewers of Suti's tender roasted beef. But a prize was saved for last. Two slaves placed a cedar board in the center of the table that held a roasted, unborn gazelle composed on flowers. Suti picked up a flower and held it above his twin's head in a playful way.

For the first time Becataten watched stoic Hor smile, and joke with his twin. It brought Jobu to her mind, and how complete the evening would be if only Jobu were here, too. She choked back the thought as a portion of gazelle was placed before her.

Everyone ate and drank to their fullest. As the feast wound down, baskets of watermelon, dates, figs, grapes and pomegranates continued to emerge from the kitchen but at a slower pace, due to much wine drinking. The north breeze gained some and gave a light ripple to the colorful canopy above. This merriment was something Becataten had not seen at the Estate, and she sat back in a comfortable haze taking it all in.

Even Lady Nagara became more animated. She and Hor had the same sardonic sense of humor and, as was their custom, the two chatted about Court gossip most of the evening. Hor said, "Did I tell you that Queen Tiy has become aware of this scroll and wants a visit from Becataten when she arrives at the Palace?"

With the look of a sated feline, Lady Nagara said, "Does she? Well, I think we shall avoid that sticky place." Hor agreed, and together they chuckled. Suti had enjoyed much wine and was talking to a household cat sitting on his lap. Becataten had never heard him use this manner of speech before. She giggled, feeling the effects of the wine.

He slurred, "Wouldn't you like to be in Pharaoh's bedchamber with the Princess? You could have a tumble with Lady Mui while Pharaoh and the Princess share the royal bed." His belly bobbed as he chuckled.

The service of honey cakes signaled the end of the meal and the guests, somewhat unsteadily, retreated from the rooftop down a narrow circular stair to their sleeping chambers. Becataten realized she, too, was unsteady from the wine. Hor offered her help to her chamber. He bowed, ever so slightly at her door, and in his deep voice said, "Congratulations, Princess, you have become an elegant lady, befitting your class." Becataten was surprised by his compliment. But a stranger event followed when Lady Nagara approached her and gave her a strong hug and kiss, followed by, "Now, go straight to bed, Becataten."

Once in her cot, Becataten stared at the rendering of the Goddess Hathor, painted on her bedchamber wall. Maybe the Goddess of love, fertility and sexuality would help her to entertain

Pharaoh. She tried to see herself in Pharaoh's bed chamber and envision what it would be like to couple with the lord of the land. But most of all she wanted to know more about coupling. It seemed that everybody around her was excited, even proud that she was about to be intimate with Pharaoh. She had seen cattle and baboons join together and scores of other animals, but it didn't seem very pleasing. Sometimes it even appeared brutal. She had heard mating cats at night, and that sounded horrible. It was clear that Lady Nagara and everyone else thought it was an enticing thing to do. But exactly what to do was an unknown. If only there was a scroll she could read to learn more! What if she failed to please Pharaoh?

She could hear her slave at the bottom of her bed snoring. Becataten got up, used the chamber pot then fetched a cool glass of well water. She wavered as she walked back to her bed.

Becataten knew everyone expected so much from her performance. How had her mother, Princess Attah, pleased Pharaoh? Becataten had never heard anybody speak of her mother, the Mitanni Princess, sent to Pharaoh's harem by her Mitanni King. Did he have any memory of their time together? Not even Maja spoke of that time. She must ask Maja more about her mother. Everyone knew that Pharaoh wanted more sons. He only had two Royal ones. Would she be the one to deliver him another?

Maybe he wanted her in his bedchamber because he thought she could bring him twins. All of Egypt knew the Living Lord coveted multiple births. And worst of all, what if she didn't please him. What would become of her then? Spinning thoughts and too much wine kept sleep away. She got out of bed again, this time to speak to the The Mother of Love who could surely help her to please Pharaoh. Maybe she could even help her deliver him a son. Becataten knelt and appealed to the Goddess.

"Oh great Goddess Hathor, my time with Lady Nagara and my tutors has come to an end with my invitaton from Pharaoh. I think they believe they have tamed the wild child in me, and they probably have. But to be honest Goddess Hathor, I did it much by myself because of the time I spent alone living here. My only time with the family was tonight when I got to read the scroll from Pharaoh. He has beckoned me, and I thank you for that. Now I ask you for help in pleasing Pharaoh by knowing how to properly couple with him. You, Mother of Love, please help Our Great Lord to lust after me." Becataten stared at the painting, which seemed to blink and smile in the wavering light of a tiny oil candle. But no answers came to her. Feeling frightened by the task ahead of her, Becataten returned to the warmth of her covers and looked at Goddess Hathor as she drifted off into an uneasy sleep.

Princess Becataten awoke screaming, shattering the stillness of the night. Lady Nagara rushed to her bedchamber passing sleepy, bowing Estate attendants and the butler, all who had come running from their bed stalls to be of service. The chamber slave who slept at the foot of Becataten's bed tried to console her but could not.

Becataten was sitting up, sobbing and in a dream-terror-state with the fear of all the gods in her eyes. Lady Nagara sat on her bed and shook her firmly with no effect. Then she slapped her hard across the face, bringing Becataten into the present.

Her screams had created a household commotion. The herd of working baboons screeched to one another in the distance. The giant sight hounds in the stables barked their alarm. The parrot on the roof repeated his shrill squawk.

Lady Nagara spoke, "What were you dreaming about, Becataten? You are safe, and all is well."

Through her sobs, Becataten tried to answer, "A young boy lays dying."

"Were you dreaming about your twin, Jobu?"

"No, the boy sleeps in the Royal chamber."

"Jobutaten lives in the Royal apartment you lived in together. Are you sure it isn't Jobutaten?"

"Yes, I know it is not Jobu, this is a very young boy, near death."

180

"You mean one of Pharaoh's sons?"

"Yes, the first-born, the one with an Egyptian mother."

"What else did you see in your dream?"

"There were two snakes."

Lady Nagara took in a guarded breath and sat erect. "What kind of snakes?"

"They were crossed like this." Becataten crossed her arms in the form of an X.

Onlooking attendants grew wide-eyed and mumbled to one another about magic.

Lady Nagara reached for a column to lean on with an expression of concern. She dismissed her staff but not her butler.

Still very frightened, Princess Becataten looked at Lady Nagara with clarity and said, "It was God Heka who came to me, was it not?"

"Go back to sleep, all will be well. You just had too much wine. We will talk when Ra returns." Lady Nagara turned to her butler, looking intense, and whispered, "Brew a drink from the poppy for the Princess. I also want our healer here to deliver one of his protective spells." The butler bowed, turned and left.

The chamber slave returned and settled on the floor near Becataten's bed, but not before she set a pot of frankincense to smolder throughout the night to protect them from evil.

181

Lady Nagara returned to her bed and slipped between her fine linen sheets. Suti said, "Too much wine for the Princess tonight?"

"I don't think it is that simple. Either Becataten has been reading too many scrolls in the library about the God Heka, or she has had a portentous dream. When you leave with Ra for Thebes I want you to return - by the same chair – with the old Heka Priest, the one you grew up with who is a practitioner of the divine knowledge of magic. Do not fail me, Suti, this may be a serious problem, and I want it solved by this priest. I think we can trust him. And does he not have skills in astrology as well?"

Suti yawned and nodded.

"Tell him to say nothing about why he is coming but that he has been invited as an old friend for a social visit. Bribe him if you have to, but I want him here as swiftly as the Gods will permit. Suti, do you hear me?"

"Yes, my Honey Cake," Suti muttered before rolling over to return to his interrupted sleep.

Lady Nagara lay awake as Suti's snoring filled their bedchamber, and she stared at her ceiling.

The ankhs painted there were symbolic of life, yet Lady Nagara had not brought a life to their marriage. She prayed little for a child, often remarking that she did not look forward to childbirth. But tonight she quietly crept out of her bed and knelt before the chamber's altar of Goddess Hathor, and whispered: "Am I barren, and is Becataten to be my only child?"

She clapped her hands. That promptly brought an attendant. "Light my frankincense." And soon a smoldering copper brazier in the corner of her bedchamber wafted the smoke of the protective resin. Lady Nagara drew in the scent, waiting for sleep as she adjusted her ivory headrest.

Chapter 21

♊

Using his young scribe's shoulder to lean on, the elderly Heka Priest limped into Lady Nagara's receiving chamber on the following day. "Thank you for your invitation to stay at the grand Suti Estate, Lady Nagara, I look forward to my time here." He bowed graciously as Lady Nagara took in the old priest's demeanor with a critical eye. He was shaped much like Suti, short and squat but with ruddy skin and penetrating eyes, the color of fine tourmaline gems. His hair was spiky and white. He didn't keep a clean-shaven head, as was the custom among priests.

"You were right to call for me, Lady Nagara. Suti has given me some facts. This sounds like a telling-dream that the Princess had. I think I am going to find these twins interesting, not only because the girl has second-sight but I already feel the boy is involved in something that is going to be informative, if not dangerous. Now, if you will allow me and my scribe some time alone in your library, I need to cast the heavenly charts of the Prince and Princess."

Lady Nagara stood erect, glared at the Priest, adjusted her wrist cuffs and snapped, "How long will that take?"

"Give me until Ra leaves us, and I will have something for you, possibly at the late meal. I look forward to some of the famous Suti beef. It's been a long time." He held her gaze for a while as if reading her face. He wanted the day alone, and he wanted a hearty dinner.

As if understanding his intent, Lady Nagara broke her stare. "Very well," Lady Nagara agreed. She clapped and had the priest attended to, as she paced nervously most of the day, awaiting his results.

The priest arrived for the evening meal with his scribe who sat next to him on the floor. Dinner was served in a small private chamber where the floor was festooned with estate flowers and tall candles. Lady Nagara and the Priest sat on a bench, each with a table set before them. The tall, wax tapers illuminated wall paintings depicting a verdant garden planted with pomegranate trees and date-laden palms. When skewers of beef were placed before the Heka Priest, he rubbed his hands together and salivated. Lady Nagara sat silent with a stern expression, waiting for him to present the story of the dream interpretation, and hopefully the

185

heavenly chart stories of the twins.

"Where is the Princess, Lady Nagara?"

"I didn't feel she needed to be here."

"Oh, but she must. I will not dine without her."

Lady Nagara tightened her lips and sat rigid. He held her gaze again. She complied, as he had information she wanted. A clap of her hands and a toss of her head set her beaded wig clicking. A slave boy appeared. "Summon Princess Becataten," Lady Nagara said. Becataten soon arrived as an attendant placed a bench and table at her disposal. Becataten bowed before the Priest before she sat. Lady Nagara made quick introductions and motioned for the meal to commence. They sat in a triangle, facing one another.

The women watched the Priest consume his meal with vigor. His eating sounds filled the silence. "Delicious meat, delicious," claimed the Priest as he reached for his third skewer, dripping with a chickpea sauce.

Becataten smiled and with politeness said, "Suti enjoys this beef almost as much as you do, Heka Priest."

"My dear Princess and Lady Nagara thank you for allowing an old man the last love of his life, eating." He wiped his chin with a linen cloth. "Now, I will continue to eat a little slower and talk to you both about this event as well as other things I have learned."

Lady Nagara turned to him, expelled a breath and dropped the quail leg she was nibbling on to listen.

The Priest sat forward on his bench, dipped his fingers in a water bowl with floating rose petals and dried his hands. In deep thought, he rubbed his hairy head. "Princess, you had a very telling dream last night that said two things. You have been given the gift of second sight, and you have been chosen, I believe, to deliver information to Pharaoh."

Lady Nagara recoiled and pushed her food dish away, expressing her distaste for the conversation.

The Priest continued. "You told me that you have had this vision before when sleeping, but that last night was the first time the Goddess Heka came to you. Is that correct?

Becataten bit her lower lip. "Yes, Priest."

The Priest nodded his head several times. "Last night the Goddess Heka made your nightmare frightening so as to compel you to listen to her. Pharaoh needs to be told of the imminent seriousness of his son's condition. This means we must proceed with caution and wisdom. But before we can make plans to inform Pharaoh, I want to interpret your birth charts, for they give more information than your dream."

Becataten's eyes were wide, and Lady Nagara leaned toward the Priest.

"The charts for you, as twins, are complex and

tell much. Your lives revolve around Pharaoh. Because you were the first born, Princess, you are affected the most with the strongest connection to Our Lord. Both of your scrolls show two fathers, and I am not sure yet what that means. But something that concerns me more is that your births are auspicious, and that means they must have been know to Pharaoh. If they were, your place in his life would be most prominent. Your heavenly stories reveal an interaction with Pharaoh that supports him, even protects him from danger. You both have strong spirits." He looked into Becataten's eyes and softly said, "Your *Ka* is especially potent, Princess, and virtuous. I understand from Lady Nagara that for the first time in your young life, you will be presented to Our Lord." He continued to rub his head and said in a softer voice, "It appears that Prince Jobutaten is now in the way of much harm."

Becataten braced herself and nodded, unable to hide the fear in her eyes, remembering what Jobu had said about their records and that there may be two sets, one true and one false. She had made him the promise to discuss this with no one. She fidgeted on her stool and was nearing tears.

Lady Nagara said, "I order you to speak your thoughts, Becataten." She looked at the two meek and quiet kitchen attendants who stood in the corner. "Leave us," she barked. The pair silently left the room at a quick pace.

188

The Heka Priest reached across to Becataten with an open hand, and said, "I am your friend. Now speak, Princess. "It will be better for you and your twin if you do as Lady Nagara asks."

Becataten was filled with turmoil and lost all the composure Lady Nagara had instilled in her. Speaking rapidly, she began. "Jobu says the Royal Astrologer's scribes are friends of his. They told him two heavenly charts each exist for us, and he thinks Pharaoh has only seen one." Her cheeks were hot and smeared with kohl from the tears she could no longer hold back.

"That is a shocking betrayal, if it is true," said Lady Nagara.

The Priest held his hand toward Lady Nagara to silence her and turned to Becataten. "Did he know what charts were produced for Pharaoh?"

Becataten shook her head slowly.

"I can tell you that Abu, the Royal Astrologer, did not reveal to Pharaoh the auspicious stories that I cast this day."

Becataten sat on the edge of her stool and bit her lip. "Priest, I don't understand what is true and what is not."

Lady Nagara said, "Be still, Becataten." She placed both hands on the table before her, looked into the Priest's eyes and said, "Are you saying that an undistinguished set of birth charts was put before Pharaoh, and that their true, and exceptional stories have been hidden from our all-powerful God?"

"I am," nodded the Priest.

"So, Abu the Royal Astrologer, is a cunning jackal, but why?" asked Lady Nagara

The Priest rubbed his jaw and nodded. "Yes, why? And why would he want to deceive Pharaoh? That is what we must learn."

"Priest, I have considerable station within the Royal house. I will have a private audience with Vizier Huy to advise Pharaoh of this deceit. Our Living God is a fair ruler, a King who reveres honesty and loyalty. If he believes Abu has lied to him, he will act swiftly," Lady Nagara said.

"I am sure that is true, Lady Nagara, but our first priority is Prince Jobutaten. He appears to be in imminent danger. I would suggest that you bring him to the Estate on your fastest conveyance. We can discuss your influence with the King only after the young Prince arrives. I hope he can avail me with information that will tell us who produced a second set of heavenly charts, and why they tell a false and undistinguished story. And to further discuss this dream of yours, Princess, you say that the child you saw that lay dying is from an Egyptian mother and wears a sidelock."

"Are you sure we must wait for the Prince, Priest?" interrupted Lady Nagara.

The Priest held her gaze again. She stared back

190

briefly then clapped her hands. She called for the butler to order the Stable Master Senzar to ready his fastest chariot, to dispatch it to the Palace, and return with the Prince Jobutaten no matter what the circumstances. Becataten's heart leapt with hope that her beloved brother would soon be joining her. Tears, this time of gratitude, spilled down her cheeks. She wiped them away.

Lady Nagara turned to the Priest. "My interest is in the Princess, who has been with me through two inundations. I have spent time training her for her visit Pharaoh's royal house. And you tell us she would have been there all along, were it not for Abu? Let's deal with him next."

Becataten nodded, in wonder that her life, so far from the main corridors of the Palace, had all been because of one man's actions. What did Abu have against her and Jobu?

"Your dream describes the royal Prince, the one in succession to Pharaoh himself. Do you have any other feelings about this vision?"

Becataten thought a moment. "I don't think he is dying naturally," she said.

Lady Nagara's eyes narrowed as she listened.

"What do you mean by that, Princess?" asked the Priest.

"You asked if I had a feeling, and that is it." Becataten fidgeted with her linen napkin, and added, "I don't know if this means anything, but

191

Jobu said that there is a rumor that the Memphis clergy is plotting against the crown."

The Priest and Lady Nagara stared at one another. The Priest took a large gulp of his wine and wiped his mouth while staring at Becataten, his eyes wide.

The Stable Master that had been summoned to the Palace of the Dazzling Aten was returning to the Suti Estate with Prince Jobutaten. Jobu's friend, the royal scribe Tiurek, insisted he accompany Jobu, and stood in the chariot next to him. The sky, now darkening from a growing sand storm, made it difficult for stable master Senzar to drive his chariot. With but one hand holding the reins, he wrapped his head and much of his face in a white cloth. Grit was obscuring his view and biting at his skin. Looking over his shoulder at the black, encroaching tempest, he turned and whipped at his horse to gain enough speed to outrun the menacing onslaught. Wind raged as eddies drove sand against walls and plants. The farms that crowded along the mother river were no longer visible. Dark gusts billowed so close they obscured Senzar's view of his horse. With powerful arms, the charioteer from Pharaoh's last military campaign somehow kept his stallion going. It was no easy task, as the frightened animal danced more than he galloped.

It was Prince Jobutaten's first ride in a chariot and his hands held hard to the rails. His fright was pervasive as the blowing sand obscured the view. Jobu's face was full of dread. Tiurek wore a hard look as he gripped the rocking chariot with one hand, the other hovering over a jewel-encrusted dagger he wore in a sheath at his waist.

With an abrupt thud, a wheel hit a large rock, and the stallion reared, causing the vehicle to turn onto its side. A chilling cry came from the horse. As Senzar jumped from the conveyance, it rolled over. When he reached the animal, he used all his effort to down the horse by pulling his bridle to the ground. He looked around for his passengers as he crawled atop the beast, but saw no one through the haze of sand. He lay on top of his injured horse, unable to get up lest the animal panic.

"Prince Jobutaten!" yelled Senzar through the loud gusts of sand and wind. "Tiurek!" Senzar buried his head into the belly of his stallion to hide his face from the ravaging storm. There was no choice but to wait out the invasion of the sand as the sky grew black.

Streaks of golden sunbeams shone on the ground and a sudden calm brought light as swiftly as the storm had delivered the dark. Nearly entombed in sand, the charioteer rose out of a mound with concerted effort. In the distance were two scout charioteers from the Estate, charging toward him. The downed stallion flailed his legs and whinnied in pain. A quick examination revealed a broken hind leg. Senzar looked to the sky. "The gods have abandoned me today!" He shouted. There was no trace of the Prince or the Prince's companion, and there was no returning without them. His duty was to search and find them. Worse yet, his gallant stallion must die at his hand. To a military man, this amounted to dishonor.

"Scout the area until you find Prince Jobutaten," Senzar ordered.

His next words were to his companion, his faithful horse. "I have to bid you farewell my friend," he whispered. He removed his head cloth, dampened it with water from his leather pouch and wiped sand from the animal's huge terrified eyes. Weeping, he unsheathed his knife and quickly made a small cut in the large blood vessel at the stallion's neck. The horse snorted softly while life's blood drained from him. When his friend had gone to the gods, Senzar called loudly to Osiris, who governed afterlife, death and rebirth. "Osiris, grant me the

194

privilege to ride my stallion again in the afterlife!" He shouted. Tears filled his eyes as his fists pummeled the sky.

The two scout-chariots' drivers scoured the area for mounds that would conceal a body, when one driver pointed to what looked like a stick protruding from sand. The men rode closer to find that an arm was jutting from the mound. Digging furiously in the grit, they unearthed a young man. His boyish face was encrusted with blood and grime. With a hole in the side of his head the size of a quail egg, he was obviously dead.

They returned to Senzar to hold their lathered steeds hard before him. "Stable Master, we found the Prince nearly covered in sand, and he is no longer living," one rider said in raspy tones.

Anguish in his eyes, Senzar dropped to his knees. "Prince Jobutaten? I am ruined!" he said, sinking to the ground beside his dead horse.

"He arrives!" Becataten heard the calls from her chamber and she adjusted her wig and stood, her heart racing to see her beloved Jobu safely home. She went with her slave to find Lady Nagara in her receiving room sitting on a large bench that had been placed on a platform. Princess Becataten and the Heka Priest stood nearby, anxious to receive the returning prince. Becataten's eyes scoured the

195

room. "Where is Jobu?" she asked as a disheveled and grim Stable Master Senzar entered, dirty and sand covered as if bringing all of Egypt inside with him. He dropped to the floor in a formal prostration. When he rose he said, "My Lady, I deliver tragic news. Prince Jobutaten was thrown from my chariot during a severe sand storm that downed my chariot. He was fatally wounded. We found him nearly buried with his head embedded on a sharp-edged rock."

Lady Nagara's face grew dark as she turned to look at Becataten. Becataten felt all the feeling in her body leave. She collapsed trying to grip Lady Nagara's chair as her slave jumped forward to hold her up. The priest assisted as Becataten sobbed. Becataten fell against the Priest. "No, no. Not Jobu! Not my dear brother! Are you sure he is dead, Stable Master?" Senzar nodded with enflamed eyes and a face full with remorse. The Priest lowered Becataten as she sunk to the floor.

Nothing had ever happened like this at the Estate. If sadness filled Lady Nagara, it was soon replaced by anger. "By the Gods, do not let a Princess of the Royal house linger on the ground!" she shouted.

The Butler, who was listening at the door, rushed into the chamber and helped to lift Becataten to a nearby lounge chair, where the trio worked to revive her senses. Soon Becataten could sit by herself, but she was in shock as devastating sadness consumed her.

Lady Nagara stood on her platform firing accusations at the Stable Master. "You incompetent fool, you were entrusted to return from the Palace, but with *one* passenger, and you failed. You failed so badly a Prince of Pharaoh's is dead. I will demand the removal of your nose and ears."

"We won't be delivering punishments today," Suti's voice said as he crossed the room in a speedy stride. He strode up to Lady Nagara and placed his reassuring hand on her shoulder.

Lady Nagara's jaw dropped. "I thought you were in Thebes."

Suti looked at the Stable Master. "Please take a seat for a moment, I have questions for you." The relieved Stable Master collapsed on a floor pillow. To Lady Nagara, Suti said, "I've returned with news from Hor that we must all be aware of."

Becataten, who was barely able to see or understand the realities happening before her, appeared dazed by the events.

"Butler, remove the Princess to her quarters," Suti said in a hurried voice. He and the slave assisted the fragile Princess out of the room. Becataten could feel herself being lifted and walked out when all went dark again.

Lady Nagara stared at Suti. "This is a most

distressing moment! I can barely take more bad news, Suti. Please tell us what you have to say and be done with it!"

Suti nodded to Lady Nagara before turning to the Priest and said, "It's good to see you again. Heka Priest. I will share the news of course. It seems we have quite a tangle of affairs, don't we, old friend? The death of Becataten's twin is a blow to this house, as it will be to their own."

"It is indeed, Architect Suti," the Priest agreed.

Suti moved to sit on the bench next to Lady Nagara and ordered a chair for the Priest.

He continued, "Before I share my news from Hor, I have many questions, Stable Master Senzar. Have you seen the prince's body and the wound that killed him?"

Senzar was still shaken but he seemed to pull himself together to answer the architect. "Yes, Architect. It is a deep head wound above the ear."

"And how do you believe this head wound happened?" asked Suti.

"My Lord, the Prince was found head-down as though he had stumbled in the sand storm onto a stone, yet I have seen many battle wounds, and I am not convinced falling on a stone would have made such a deep cut." He bowed and asked if he could speak further.

Suti nodded. "Anything else? Was it just the two of you in the chariot?"

198

"Master Suti, the young Prince rode back from the Palace with a companion. He was a royal scribe," Senzar said.

Suti looked meaningfully at the Heka Priest. "Where is the scribe now?" asked Suti.

"He disappeared during the storm, and my men could not find him again during the calm." Senzar looked down. "When I left the scene, he was still missing."

Suti said, "Thank you, Stable Master Senzar, you may leave us." Senzar left the room escorted by house staff.

Suti noted more servants clustered near the doorway, many of whom had been huddled outside the receiving room door mumbling that intrigue was in the wind. "All of you go your own way. Do not linger in doorways and listen in halls where you are not invited!" He clapped his hands and the servants scattered.

With caution, Suti looked about the chamber then motioned Lady Nagara and the Priest to gather close to him. "Hor tells me there is a rumor in the Palace that must be taken seriously."

The Heka Priest interrupted, "Let me assume it involves the Amun Clergy in Memphis, and a plot."

Suti looked surprised. "How did you know, being so distant from the Court?"

The Priest rubbed his nose. "This has gone well beyond a rumor, for Becataten had heard mention

199

of it from her own brother. Let me reveal what I see. Prince Jobutaten was killed, not just because he was aware of this plot but also because he was a Royal Prince. To overthrow a crown, royal children must be eliminated, especially boys. My guess is that this is why Pharaoh's firstborn lies dying in his bed from a vague illness. Becataten's instincts were correct when she said she believed the boy's death would not be a natural one."

"By the Gods, you know about that, too. Everyone knows Pharaoh's first born is gravely ill with a fever. The news is that the royal physicians have done all they can do." Suti blurted.

"What can we possibly do to stop all of this?" Lady Nagara asked.

In hushed tones, Suti leaned in close and whispered, "I would be willing to bet that because the young Prince Jobutaten, who ran with Abu's Court scribes learned of the plot, he was killed."

The Priest shook his head, bent forward and spoke in a solemn tone. "We all know when Pharaoh relocated the capitol from Memphis to Thebes he left behind the God Amun. Once embedded here, he began to embrace the God Aten. Most of us have failed to realize that this has had a ruinous effect on the Amun Clergy in Memphis. They have been brooding about this for many innundations, hoping that Pharaoh would return to God Amun. They have

200

lost income, land holdings, even credibility, and have been reduced to begging in the streets. They must finally be seeking retaliation."

Lady Nagara sat taller and whispered, "Still, I am shocked that a few priests in Memphis think they can plot Pharaoh's overthrow, and now the twins are entwined in this horrible chaos? These are horrible tidings indeed."

Bending forward, Suti said, "Hor has information from Dwarf Beset that someone tried to poison the twins when they were quite young, but their nanny drank the brew instead and nearly died. So, this plot has been in place for a long time. Hor also learned from scribe-gossip that the birth charts of the twins are stellar and show a great alliance with Pharaoh that rivals Abu's power. And we all know how Abu covets power."

"And how he employs it at Court," added Lady Nagara.

The Priest rubbed his head. "When I studied the heavenly stories of the twins, I saw an almost mystical kinship with Pharaoh. Now we know why the Prince and Princess were denied access to Pharaoh and why one was murdered. What I don't understand is why all of this has been brewing so long before it has come to a head."

Suti shook his head. "And I want to stress that we do not have all the facts."

Lady Nagara turned to the Priest, "So Becataten

has the gift of second sight, the twins have a link in their heavenly charts to Pharaoh and that link is stronger than Abu's?"

The priest nodded.

Lady Nagara made fists of her hands and said, "And after all my work with Becataten, it looks more and more distant that the Princess will ever be received by our Pharaoh, now that his son and her brother has been doomed."

Suti and the Heka Priest looked blankly at one another.

Suti continued, "I have more disturbing news. The royal scribe that disappeared in the storm is one who works in the household of Abu. I fear he is the one who murdered Jobutaten."

Lady Nagara pounded her fists on her lap. "By the Gods, who would want to deliver this treacherous and entangled news to Pharaoh?"

Suti replied, "I think you would be the perfect one, my Lady."

Suti and the Heka Priest stared at Lady Nagara. She shifted uncomfortably in her chair, aware the task would be hers.

Chapter 22

♊

Princess Becataten awoke the next morning after a deep sleep that only a poppy potion could have delivered. She had a vague memory of the butler helping her down the liquid as she sat in a stupor and the heaviness of Jobu's death filled her being. Uncomfortable in the clothes she had worn the night before, she sat up. Her slave came toward her carrying honey tea. As emotion took over completely, the horrible thought of Jobu's untimely end flooded her emotions and sent her back to her pillow, where she sobbed until she was out of tears.

Becataten's mood was dark, and her attendants who wanted to offer help were skirting around her. Ready with her chest of cosmetics, the facial artist finally asked in a hushed voice, "Do you wish a bath, Princess?"

Becataten sat still and didn't answer. She didn't know anymore what she wanted. Her head was filled with far too much ominous information that she had learned about herself and Jobu. How could she now go to Pharaoh's bed and be the happy Princess everyone expected her to be? A slave cautiously approached her, took her hand and led her to her drawn bath as though Becataten was a small child.

The tub of hand hewn stone from the quarries at Aswan had been filled with tepid water, and the usual lotus oil laced her bathwater. Vases of long stemmed iris added aroma to the bathing chamber. But no fragrance could smell good today, and no flowers could appear beautiful while Becataten was mourning her dead brother.

Staring blankly into space and trying to think of nothing, she experienced a moment of clarity and soberly asked, "Where is everybody? How long was I asleep?" With no answers from her slave, anger seized her and she brusquely stepped away from her bath. "Bring me the coldest water you can find and bring it fast, and ask for Butler." The slave ran from the room, never having heard the Princess speak in such a demanding tone, and ran for the Butler. The slave continued running to complete her task.

As Butler strode into her room, he calmly addressed her. "May I serve you, Princess?"

"You may. Where is Lady Nagara?"

"She is in her chamber, readying herself for a trip to Thebes."

"Oh is she? Bring me the Nubian who escorts and trains all the slave girls that come from Kush. I am going to go and speak with Lady Nagara, but I want the Slave Trader waiting here when I return."

The Butler of the house bowed and backed out of the room. As he left the room he snapped his fingers at Becataten's slave, who was returning with a bucket of well water. The slave brought the water to Becataten and bowed away, submissively.

Becataten splashed her red swollen face and felt soothed by the coolness of the well water. "Dress me quickly in my finest linen sheath and jewelry," she commanded her slave. She turned to her painter she said, "Paint me a perfect face, and bring my best wig." As Becataten's makeup was being applied, a stolid expression altered her face as she crafted a plan. Her impassiveness lasted throughout the coloring of her face. When kohl was applied to her eyes, they no longer shone a bright and glistening green but dark, like two murky pools.

Lady Nagara hummed as she and an attendant packed her clothing, jewelry and personal items for her trip to the Palace. She had already decided to take the easy way out and not approach Pharaoh first with the news of this plot by the Memphis Clergy. She would tell instead Vizier Huy, but not before she had a lengthy discussion with Hor. She wanted to be sure if Hor knew if the Vizier was involved in the plot. The gods knew that if the Vizier was involved, they were all doomed.

Her chamber door flew open and Becataten stood

squarely in the entrance. Lady Nagara was surprised to see her so well dressed and looking refreshed.

"Where *are* your manners? You seek permission before you enter my chambers!"

An expression of defiance filled Becataten's eyes. "What was discussed after I fainted last night?"

"You need not be included in *all* that happens at the Estate. I am occupied planning a mission that is more important than you can imagine. Now leave me."

Becataten stepped boldly into Lady Nagara's bedchamber. "I will not. My brother is dead and all you can say to me is you are occupied with a mission?"

Lady Nagara softened. "Of course, the entire household is saddened about the prince's death. You must know Suti will do all in his power to see that Prince Jobutaten's funerary arrangements are befitting a Royal," she said.

"I am not here about Jobu's funerary arrangements." Becataten's voice almost broke. "Tell me what was discussed after I fainted, and why are you readying yourself for a trip to Thebes without me?"

Lady Nagara's condescension returned. "As I said when you so rudely entered my chamber, you need not have privy to all that happens here."

Becataten stepped toward Lady Nagara close enough to touch her. "Yes, I think I must. It appears that much of what is happening includes me. Both Jobu's death and my invitation to go to Pharaoh certainly involve me."

Lady Nagara was surprised. "I regret your twin's death, Becataten, but information Suti delivered at the last Ra reveals trouble at Court, and that's all I can tell you. So you see, I have no time for your interruptions," she said, examining a silk shawl in an effort to dismiss the agitated Princess.

"You mean trouble at Court that involves Priests."

Lady Nagara straightened her body and turned toward Becataten. "Where did you hear that?"

"I just know. You may call it my second sight."

"By the Gods, this is getting more involved by the Ra. I suppose you must know, there is a plot to overthrow our Pharaoh by the clergy in Memphis, if you can believe that. I am on a mission to forewarn our Living God."

Becataten took another step forward. "I am going with you."

With a false laugh, Lady Nagara moved back. "You, go with me? Preposterous! But I do note that you have found your tongue. If you like, you can try and carry on some of my myriad Estate duties during my absence."

"I am going with you," Becataten continued,

"Jobu told me many things about this plot," she lied, but she knew she must get to Court. "And Pharaoh wants *me* in his bedchamber and that is where I can summon his sympathy. You can caucus with Hor as though you were accompanying me, learn how big this plot is and no one will suspect what we are doing."

Lady Nagara looked over her pupil, who had fire in her eyes looking beautiful and well bred. "Well, haven't you developed a scheming mind overnight?" she asked in a quiet voice.

"You forget who my teacher is, Lady Nagara."

Lady Nagara stood tall. "I have told you that you are not quite ready for Pharaoh when it comes to pleasuring him. I haven't even told you about the Royal foot!"

The eighteenth dynasty had been plagued by this deformity, and although Lady Nagara hadn't remembered if Pharaoh had inherited it or not, she was trying to hold up her part of the argument.

With a loud and clear voice that turned the heads of all the attendants listening, Becataten responded, "I am going to the Palace with you, Lady Nagara. Remember *I* was royally summoned by Pharaoh's scroll, and I have one other thing to say, so hear me. One of the reasons you have not found time to school me in pleasuring a man is because that man is Pharaoh and a God, but he is also a man you still love. So, I have arranged for the

Nubian who trades in slave girls to school me in pleasuring before Ra leaves, and then I will be ready. It will be a short time with him, I know, but it is all the time I have."

Lady Nagara picked up a copper mirror then soon dropped it, and as it clattered on the floor, Becataten swiftly exited the room. Lady Nagara's servant quickly retrieved it as the Lady looked at the empty doorway, a small amount of pride welling up inside of her at the woman Becataten was quickly becoming.

Chapter 23

♊

Becataten felt stronger, having told Lady Nagara that she must accompany her to the Palace. She hoped that meant it was the right thing to do. The second-sight the Heka Priest said she had now spoke to her and drove her to understand the mystery surrounding her birth. After learning the Nubian slave trader had not yet arrived, she began to prepare for her trip. But first she had to complete a dreaded chore.

Becataten reached for her inkpot, dipped her stylus in the black liquid and paused. Less brave now and shaking, her eyes filled with tears knowing what she had to write. How could Jobu be dead? How could she not have seen him before he died? She turned to write her scroll to Beset.

Beset,

The saddest news of my life – Jobu is dead.

My new friend, the Heka Priest, has been very kind to me during my sorrow. He tells me I have second sight, Beset, and that it had been written in my heavenly chart. The Priest requested that Jobu come to the Estate in great haste because he knew he was in danger. But it was too late, and he never arrived. It is believed he was murdered along the way.

A tangle of horrible events has entered my life Beset, and I will be with you soon to tell all. Lady Nagara has tried to keep me here and go alone to the Palace, but I have forced my way into traveling with her.

I think I am beginning to use the Heka I have been given. I will be with you again in one or two Ras...

May all the Gods Keep You, Taten

Turning to her slave, she directed her to have the missive sent immediately to Beset. As the servant left the room, she started to select the items to be packed in her chests. "I cannot think about clothes and wigs, now. You," Becataten said, pointing to the awaiting makeup artist, "You help my attendants select my finest items. You know how to select a special wardrobe, don't you?" The makeup artist nodded and left the bench next to the cosmetic chest to take charge.

Traveling to the Palace with the honor of being presented to Lord Pharaoh was no longer her singular mission. She also had to learn what Jobu had uncovered. But she had no time to dwell on Jobu. As she walked the room wringing her hands to calm her thoughts, Becataten soon realized she couldn't leave the important packing details completely to others and began to oversee the operation as servants rushed about to help.

"Not that wig. Go and find my newest wig. I think someone has it and is weaving gold beads into the plaits," Becataten said as she motioned to another attendant. "Add these four pieces of linen, and that cloak. Also, get my gold belt and bring all my jewelry." She looked around the room. "Oh, and my sandals, don't forget my beaded ones."

The makeup artist politely suggested that a second chest was needed. "Of course, add a second container if need be."

How things had changed, when she had arrived she carried one small bundle and now she was overseeing the packing of two large chests, maybe three.

"Well, I think that is everything," she said.

The makeup artist shook her head, and pointed to her makeup chest. "Of course, my chest of paints, how could I forget that?" Becataten said.

Becataten began to worry that she was attempting more than she could handle. But she must go for Jobu's sake and discover the secret of their birth charts. As Beset had once said, attempting great things was often frightening.

Later that evening, Becataten followed the Butler

and two attendants holding high-held torches into the black of night. She watched the butler order her chests loaded on a conveyance. Walking back to the Estate she saw the Heka Priest seated alongside the large fishpond. The pond was lined with lighted pots of burning oil. The ripples of reflections danced across the water where he soaked his feet. Next to him, a quartzite statue of Thoth stood, who represented the moon. The priest waved her to his side. "Little Princess, I see you are joining Lady Nagara on her trip to the Palace."

"I am making every effort to go with her. She did not truly sanction that I make the trip with her, and I *was* demanding about going. But she has kept me at the Estate for two seasons and taught me over and over again how to be perfect when I am presented to Pharaoh."

"You are a woman with her own mind now, I see," said the priest in a quiet voice.

"I have grown weary with my tutoring and want this part of my training to be finished. I want another life to begin, especially since I have lost the love of my heart, Jobu. I feel that if I do not force myself to go on this trip with Lady Nagara, my life will not carry on. And I so want to know what Jobu was investigating. What do you think, Priest?" Becataten bit her bottom lip, and caught herself and stopped the behavior she had abandoned with her childhood.

213

The Priest motioned her to sit next to him. "I spoke with Lady Nagara after you and she talked. She has curbed her anger considerably. She wanted to know if I thought this was a favorable time for you to go to Pharaoh, and for her to be the envoy of the news of the plot."

"Oh, please tell me what you think, Priest?"

"I think the God Thoth has placed the moon in a position favoring the journey that you undertake, and you must know that Thoth is a favorite deity of Pharaohs."

Becataten nodded as she stared into the luminous pool, shimmering brightly. *How I wish I would find Jobu at the end of my travels,* she thought.

"When you go, Princess, it must be swift. It is important that you arrive before Pharaoh's son dies, and I say this with great sadness, because it will happen. Sadly, I think Pharaoh's first born will cling to life for some time, but in the end, I believe he will join Osiris in the afterlife. Princess, you and no one else will be received by Pharaoh if he is a grieving father. I am sorry to mention death, Princess, as I know you grieve for your twin."

Becataten stared into his understanding eyes and nodded slowly. Her body began to shake from his words.

The Priest put his arm around her and said, "Lady Nagara will deliver the news to Pharaoh about

214

this wicked scheme conspired by my own clergy in Memphis. She wishes to meet first with Hor, who lives among Court people, and will no doubt have current news about this plot that threatens the Court. If there are no conspirators in the Royal Court perhaps she and Hor can meet with Pharaoh together, and maybe Suti should be there, too. But I cannot stress enough that they must meet quickly. And about the love of your life, Prince Jobutaten, he would be happy that you are taking up his noble effort to unfold the mystery of your heavenly charts. I also stress caution, little Princess. In one or two Ras, I will be following you and Lady Nagara to the Palace."

Becataten sighed and said, "Oh, I will be careful, and it has meant so much to me, Priest, to talk to you and that you have entered my life. I've lived on the Estate too long without my twin or Beset or Maja. I have not had one confidant until you..." Her voice trailed and her eyes welled with tears. The Heka Priest drew her near as she quietly sobbed. Becataten regained her composure. "You must think I am a weak one," she said.

"No, I do not believe that. I believe you are a very strong, young woman. I have come to understand both your rearing and living conditions in the Palace were in no way illustrious. As twins, you even lived through an attempt on your young lives. Although Lady Nagara believes she has mentored you

215

properly, I know it has been a strict life that you have experienced here. You have lost your beloved twin and yet you want to move forward in life."

Becataten dried her eyes and said, "Talking with you has helped me do that. And I have to say, it is Lady Nagara who has made me into enough of a lady to be accepted by Our Lord Pharaoh." Becataten paused at length.

"What is it child?"

"I just have a question about Pharaoh."

"Perhaps I can answer it."

"Do you know what the Royal Foot is?"

A thin smile creased the Heka priest's lips before her spoke. "Yes, Becataten, I do."

Becataten sat attentively.

"Pharaoh and many of his dynasty have been born with a foot shaped like a small box. It has come to be called the Royal Foot. As I understand it, no one ever speaks of it, nor is it to be looked at with curiosity. Does that help, little Princess?"

"Yes, and thank you, Heka Priest. I was worried that it was something serious I should know about and maybe it would have been, before Jobu died. But it isn't important now. What is really important to me now is seeing my nanny and Dwarf Beset when I arrive at the Palace."

"How long has Nanny been with you?"

"She was my mother's slave before me, and they traveled to Egypt together when they were twelve seasons old. My mother was Princess Attah and sent by her King in Mitanni as a gift to our Pharaoh."

"How long has Dwarf Beset been with you?"

"She was a gift from Pharaoh when we lived in the Royal Nursery. I think she was about twelve innundations old when she came to us."

"So your nanny and Beset are about the same age?"

"Yes, I think Beset is Pharaoh's age, too, because they used to play together as children."

"Has Nanny ever talked to you about your mother?"

"No, and I have asked Nanny Maja many times, but she does not want to remember that time. Maybe it was too painful for her. Maybe it is because she and my mother grew up together. I think they were like sisters, even though Maja was her slave."

"So she tells you nothing about your mother and the time they spent in the harem?"

Becataten shook her head.

"Princess, have you ever had any other dreams about your life that have repeated, like the one about Pharaoh's child?"

"No, well, yes, it is just a dream of Jobu and I playing." She choked on her words, and had to pause. "I have dreamed it many times. We laugh and play together by one of the ponds at the palace.

We wrestle, and he gets mad if I win, then his eye wobbles, and we stop and laugh again. One of Jobu's eyes always wobbles when he gets mad or very excited." She added with sadness in her voice, "It used to."

Hearing her comments, the Heka Priest stood, and with hardened eyes said, "I have decided that I must accompany you to the Palace when Ra rises."

Becataten was confused at his sudden seriousness and decision to depart with them instead of coming a few days later as he had said earlier. Why had the Priest changed his mind?

"I must go prepare for the journey, Princess. We will talk more on the way."

The Heka Priest left abruptly, leaving Becataten alone with her thoughts as her servant waited a short distance away with a torch to light their path home.

It was dark but nearing dawn when Becataten entered her chamber. She gasped upon seeing a man. A sinewy ebony figure stood in the low light of the single candle, bowed, and in the deepest voice she had ever heard, said, "You requested me, Princess?"

"If you are the Nubian slave trader, I did." Princess Becataten drew a nervous breath and steadied herself. "I...I need to know how to pleasure

218

a man, a very important man." Becataten tried to sound authoritative. She tried to speak as Lady Nagara might as the servants lit more candles and readied her chambers to receive the visitor.

When the Nubian lowered his head, it was to conceal a smile. Everyone at the Estate had gossiped about her being beckoned to the Living God's bedchamber, so certainly he knew who the important man was.

"I am armed with experience and the blood of Nubian royalty. I offer my empirical services," the Nubian said, standing tall and dignified.

Early dawn's golden rays from the Ras light began to creep in and shine on the statuesque Nubian. His black color also shown with blue, and reminded her of the dark purple grapes from the delta. Becataten had heard that the women he traded had to be beautiful, sensual and accommodating. She was also told they needed to be quick to learn, as many went to the homes of Royals. She felt shy in his presence but made herself look into his dark eyes as he appraised her. She looked around and saw servants lined up, staring in awe at the stranger.

"Leave us!" she commanded, with a voice too high from her nervousness. The servants scampered out of the room.

"May I ask you a question, Princess?" he asked in a silky deep voice as they exited.

How would Lady Nagara respond? Becataten asked herself. She cleared her throat and said, "You may, but I have little time. Ask quickly."

"What made you choose me for this task?"

She raised her chin high. "When I was last at the Palace, I overheard the Viceroy of Kush praising you to another noble. The Viceroy of Kush does not need to praise."

"Viceroy Merymose spoke favorably of me, did he?"

"Yes, he did. Now I am in a hurry. You wouldn't have a scroll about pleasuring, would you? If I could only read about it, it would hurry the matter."

The Trader's face tried to conceal another smile. "The only scrolls that explain this activity, Princess, are ones that are –how should I say, not refined."

"What do you mean?"

"They are records not of words, but pictures of unusual positions that some people like to take when they couple."

"Do you have any of these illustrations?"

"Princess, with respect, I don't believe that these scrolls would benefit us at this time, but let us begin." His wide smile revealed glistening teeth, which seemed to Becataten as white as cow's milk.

She felt a tinge of apprehension that lessened her courage. He would see this as a sign of weakness, she thought, and willed herself to show confidence as Lady Nagara had taught her.

The slave trader placed his hands on his hips as the room brightened in the growing light. "Let me begin by telling you what attributes you have that men find interesting, Princess." He squinted, as though considering an item at a purveyor's stand. "Your green eyes are rare. They are not dull in color, but sparkle like dew drops on lotus leaves. And their shape is like an almond. It gives you the look of a sensuous wild cat, and that is very pleasing to a man's eye."

Becataten was taken aback. "And resembling a wild cat is interesting to a man?"

"Oh, yes, very interesting, and I will tell you how to use those attributes. Men like to stare at beautiful women and drink them in like a fine cool beer on a hot day. Not many women stare at men in the same way, but the women who do are always remembered."

"So I must learn to stare. What else?"

"It is not that easy. This is a lesson, Princess. Now stare at me, into my eyes, and deeply."

Becataten was amazed how difficult it was to hold his gaze, and especially into the eyes of someone so confident. She blushed. It made her feel silly and disappointed that she couldn't do it.

"You see it takes practice."

"Can we come back to that and go on to another lesson?" Becataten needed a challenge she could handle.

"Yes, but remember staring into the eyes of your lover is very important."

"I will make a note of that on my papyrus. Just a moment."

Becataten gathered a small scroll from the nearby writing desk and her stylus to hurriedly scrib the note and then faced the Nubian again.

"The next lesson is for you to remove your clothing, beginning with your sandals and ending with your wig. Be as graceful as you can and when you are finished, stand straight so your lover can admire your body."

Becataten found this easier than staring as she stripped her clothing off slowly and turned for the Nubian's appraisal.

"You are a young beauty, Princess, with some blood from the lands to the east. Am I right?"

"Yes, my mother was a Princess from the land of Mitanni."

"That blood gives you more curves, like my women from Kush, not like the women from Egypt."

Frowning Becataten said, "Do you think men like women with curves?"

"Oh yes, Princess, men like women with curves, just like yours."

"What proof do you have?"

"I know this to be true because I am paid more gold for women with curves."

She liked the way the Nubian worked with her in

an unemotional way. She looked briefly at the renderings on the wall in her chamber of the goddess Hathor. Yes, she thought, this is the place to learn about pleasuring. She said a quick prayer to the goddess asking for her assistance in pleasing Pharaoh.

The Slave Trader removed his zebra skin kilt but left on his shell jewelry and sandals. Becataten did not often see grown naked men, only boys, and looked away. He walked to her cot and sat down, patted his hand on his thigh and said, "Sit next to me. Now touch me, here, touch my member."

Princess Becataten did as she was told. When she stroked his soft member it began to grow, and she flinched, shocked at how fast it grew. Soon it was the size of a giant pestle, she thought. Her eyes bulged and she asked, "Did I do that, or did you do that?"

The Nubian roared with a deep laughter and said, "Have you no brothers?"

"No," Becataten said quietly.

"This is what happens when a beautiful young woman touches a man. It is very exciting and it pleases him. But, Princess, Princess! Do not examine a man's member as though you were inspecting it at auction."

Becataten realized she was staring and blushed, but managed to look into the slave trader's face to hide her embarrassment. "What else pleases a man?"

"Dancing and singing will also arouse your lover."

"I can dance. I can sing."

"You do not have to dance for me, but when you dance for Pharaoh, do it slowly as you remove your clothes. Sing as you touch his member." The Nubian sang, showing her how to do it.

"What else?" Becataten felt she needed to learn as much as she could, and quickly. Her nerves jangled as her thoughts turned to Pharaoh.

"There are places to be touched on a woman that arouse her, and when both the man and the woman are aroused together, the best coupling happens."

"Touch me on those places."

"Princess, I want to leave here with my ears and my nose, so I am going to leave you instead with a feather."

"A feather!"

"Yes, now lie down and I will point where you are to use the feather on yourself, alone in your chamber."

The bowl of his hair held many falcon feathers. Becataten watched him draw one out. He held it above her naked body as she spread out on the cot.

"This will help me to understand my arousal spots?" she asked, unconvinced. Coupling was not what she had imagined if feathers were involved.

The Nubian nodded and gently touched the feather to her breasts. A chill went through her and she was surprised at the reaction deep inside of her. The Nubian then gently pulled the feather from her breasts down further to the Y between her legs. He lingered there, softly moving it about. A surprising, exotic feeling overcame her. She understood now what he meant and a small smile caught her by surprise.

When the Nubian put on his kilt the bulge of his member distracted her. He smiled and patted himself. "Worry not, princess," he said with a smile. "Your beauty and light touch will arouse your lover. Remember the most important lesson: Enjoy yourself."

Becataten put on a shift and placed the feather on her bedside table. The Nubian took his leave. When she was alone, Becataten did exactly as the Nubian instructed, using the feather on her arousal spots. But she was so distracted by the image of how large and quick his member had grown, she wasn't sure if she was executing his instructions properly. Then all of the sudden she became frustrated, got up quickly and walked about in her chamber.

Her mind whirling, she finally allowed herself to think of Jobu. Deep pain washed over her, and she sobbed, feeling very alone. Her tears were bitter but finally brought sleep as the afternoon waned.

Chapter 24

♊

Abu's royal quarters were beginning to cool and darken as streaks of sunlight receded from the apartment's high windows. Butler Farafar shuffled in silence, going from bowl to bowl to light the wicks in animal fat, laced with salt to reduce smoke fumes.

As Abu ate his evening meal, a man sat on the floor before him. He was a foreigner swathed from head to foot in northern dress, the color of sand. Abu had guessed he was from Anatolia, along the eastern shores of the Great Sea. A sharp nose parted the man's bearded face like a greasy knife blade. Sitting cross-legged, the man opened a pouch Abu had thrown at him. As he emptied a generous handful of gold debon into his leathery hand, his fingers showed the calluses of a bowman. Staring at the shiny pieces, he tried to smile but instead produced a sneer.

Abu sat guzzling a pitcher of well-brewed beer while he watched the man. Their eyes met. Tearing apart a joint of meat, Abu placed it in a warm flatbread and bit off a large mouthful. Then mumbling through his food, he said, "You're the assassin the Amun Clergy in Memphis sent me. You have your debon, now go, do your job and eliminate the girl twin." The man rose to stand tall and arrogant before Abu, not fully prostrating himself before leaving. Abu's lip curled as he watched the man depart.

An Amun priest, who had accompanied the assassin to Thebes, emerged from a dark corner whispering. "Good, Abu, you have paid the assassin, and sent him to do his work. As you know, we Amun priests are so poor we could not afford to pay him. And you tell me the boy-twin is dead."

Abu nodded. "I have a senior scribe who made it look like a chariot accident. I have promised to make the scribe Royal Astrologer when I am Pharaoh," said Abu quietly.

"Good, and this assassin will take care of the second twin," said the priest.

Abu nodded with a resentful look. "Yes, but I don't like killing women."

The priest shrugged. "The boy could have become regent, and you never know about a woman. They can become strong and work behind the throne. Look at Queen Tiy."

Abu shifted in his chair then took a large draft of beer. "And Pharaoh's first born, does he yet live?"

"One of our priests who attends him says with the poison he is ingesting each Ra, he will not live

228

through another moon."

Butler Farafar entered to arrange a table, a bench and an abundance of food for the Amun priest, who sat with enthusiasm to dine and further engage Abu in conversation. "You have done well to give the assassin the gold that will end the life of this Princess Becataten, named after the God Aten," the priest said with distaste. "The clergy believes twins close to the throne should be eliminated, especially in Amenhotep III's Court where they are held in such high esteem. And they can sometimes have the magic of Heka."

Abu grunted.

The Priest drank his cup of sma with greed and reached for more. "I am surprised, though, that we have not heard about these twins in Memphis before this, Abu."

Abu explained. "When the twins were born, I produced false uneventful heavenly charts for them, and saw that were never granted a royal audience."

The priest looked perplexed. "But that was thirteen innundations ago, well before we knew Pharaoh would choose God Aten over our true God Amun."

Abu placed his hands in his finger bowl then wiped them with a large square of linen. "I hold a long grudge against my half-brother. Pharaoh and I were good friends as children but soon after his crowning, that all changed."

"What changed?" The priest stopped eating, folded his hands on his round belly and said, "I must hear this story, Abu."

Abu showed annoyance that he had allowed personal facts to slip into his conversation, and answered quickly. "My scribes were in charge of inventorying women for the harem in the early days of building the Palace. Some went into the Palace, while others stayed in a tent waiting for completed quarters."

The priest said, "And let me guess, you coveted one of the women."

Abu nodded.

"Did you couple with her, Abu?"

"Briefly," said Abu. What Abu held silent was that he had asked for Princess Attah in marriage and been refused. Within an inudation the foreign princess died delivering her royal twins. And upon her death, Abu held an unbridled hatred for Pharaoh blaming him for seeding Princess Attah with twins. As a result he had cast the twins into obscurity, never again to mention the name of the mother, Princess Attah.

The Priest smiled. "You have held a grudge for a long time, Abu, and clearly now I see you have no compunction about eliminating these twins."

Abu shrugged his shoulders, and looked away. "I still don't like killing women."

"It is a necessary part of the plan if you want to

230

become Pharaoh," reminded the priest.

Abu nodded again, and with more conviction, said, "I want to become King," but seemed to regret his admission about Princess Attah. Changing the conversation, he added, "But that was a long time ago, and what is far more important now is to minimize the God Aten and resurrect our almighty God Amun," Abu said with conviction that he did not share with the priest.

"You are correct, Abu, and thanks to you, that plan is in force. You should be Pharaoh well before Egypt sees another inundation," said the priest as he held his goblet in tribute to Abu.

Dwarf Beset had retired for the evening when a runner appeared at her door with cryptic scribble on a potshard. She knew what it said, to meet immediately. She knew it was from Dwarf Heby and paid the man who delivered it with a small debon of copper. Trying to tread lightly didn't work, and Maja was awakened. She called out, "Something wrong, Beset?"

"No, I just have to see someone right now."

"It is very late and very dark Beset. Take a torch."

Beset followed her advice and brought a flame to meet Heby at their usual spot. Beset waited for Heby in a garden midway between their apartments.

231

She knew he would come, but he didn't arrive until nearly dawn. And when he did, he was out of breath. "There are no litters to be had at this hour. I had a lot to clean up, I couldn't get away until everyone was asleep and I ran all the way," he panted.

"Take your time, Heby. I know this is important, but sit and rest a moment."

"There is little time, Beset." And then, in hushed tones, he said, "An assassin has been sent to kill your Princess. I heard this conversation as Abu dined with an Amun Priest from Memphis, long after Ra left us. Abu paid the man in gold debon."

Beset sat very still. She seemed to be absorbing and mulling Dwarf Heby's news. "I must leave immediately to warn Taten and of course Architect Suti, but I am not sure if they are at the Estate or in transit," said Beset, talking quickly as her mind raced.

"It makes sense that they are on their way, Beset. I sensed that this hired killer was going to strike when Ra rises. Isn't this the time that the Princess has been summoned to be with Pharaoh?"

Beset panicked. She couldn't have dreamed her beloved Taten would be caught in the middle of this treacherous plot. Abu was a fool, and she didn't have time to tell him that he had fathered the twins. He was clearly blinded by his hate for Pharaoh. But she must protect Taten.

232

"You may be right, Heby. Becataten's last scroll did not speak of her exact arrival time. Either way, I must get word to her conveyance as soon as possible. I wonder what would be the fastest way to warn them."

She and Dwarf Heby sat for a moment in silence. Heby jumped off the bench and said, "I know, we need a Royal who can discharge a speedy chariot to warn them. Royal Architect Hor, Suti's brother, could. Could he not?"

"He could indeed, Heby. His apartment is down the colonnade from the Astrologer. I think it best you talk to him, Beset."

"Heby, you are right. Let's find a litter. You must get back to your household, and I must get to Architect Hor."

Back at the Estate, Suti walked to the lead chariot in the first light of dawn. "Stable Master Senzar, take care of my ladies, and may you have a safe and speedy journey to the Palace with the protection of all the Gods of Egypt."

Senzar bowed deeply. "Thank you, Royal Architect, I will make every effort to do so."

Suti walked to the second chariot bearing the Heka Priest and his scribe. "I received scrolls from Hor, Priest. We have been staying in touch about the plot and Prince Jobutaten's death. They are keeping it a secret for now at the Palace. Few know of this new intrigue."

The Heka Priest indicated concern. "Suti, do you and Hor not fear interception of the messages you send one another?"

"Do not worry about that. Hor and I communicate in a tongue that we developed as children long ago. It has proved very useful of late."

"I should have known you would be cautious. When we were young cubs raising the wrath of the gods, you were always the sensible one."

"Hor says he has arranged for a large apartment where the women are to stay in the Palace. He also mentioned that the Royal Gardener Sennejem is a man who spends time with Abu. Talk with him about the Astrologer's movements. He may be someone we should suspect." Suti added, "Why did you decide to go with my ladies on this Ra, Priest?"

"I wish to confirm something with Lady Nagara about Abu, along the way," said the Priest.

"Be careful, she isn't too fond of Priests, old friend."

A smile and a nod came from the Priest. "I will remain cautious, and I will say goodbye for now."

Suti waved saying, "I will follow when Ra returns."

"Why not travel with us now? I wanted to have a conversation with you too about Abu, Suti."

234

"No, I'll go on alone. I plan to stop and have a long talk with the Royal Gardener," Suti said in a serious tone. "I feel he will have some insight into this intrigue. I will see you after that. Safe travels, my old friend."

Becataten parted the fabric of the opening in the covered chairs, held by slaves she and Lady Nagara shared. She thought the Stable Master standing in his chariot, signaling his caravan forward, looked proud. She noted he was in full military dress, complete with his medals of Golden Flies. She remembered reading that they were awarded to soldiers who showed themselves courageous in combat. They were likened to the tsetse fly that tenaciously swarmed their enemy. It was good to see Senzar vindicated of all accusations, and she was glad he was in charge of their trek to the Palace. Senzar's chariot took the lead, followed by the Heka Priest's chariot and then by the transport she and Lady Nagara shared. On the ground to the rear were armed men who provided additional protection. They were armed with sturdy wooden shields, battleaxes and spears. As the caravan moved forward, jogging bowmen flanked their transport. Becataten felt excited, nervous and covered with the shroud of sadness that she would return home, and Jobu would not be there.

The large and enclosed conveyance she and Lady Nagara shared was fitted with silken pillows and

235

sheer window coverings. Behind them sat a slave fanning them with white plumage studded to a pole. As the guards checked in several times as the caravan rolled out, Becataten's feeling of safety turned to fear.

"We will be fine, Becataten," Lady Nagara said, as she observed her anxiety. The two women sat in silence as their slaves tended to them. The rocking of the vehicle soon put Becataten into a light sleep.

Halfway through the journey, Senzar maneuvered the caravan slightly east, coming to a stop at a small oasis. Laden with palms, the respite offered a nearby basin of water and shade, as well as replacement bearers. Runners soaked their feet in the wet mushy sand, and passengers stretched their legs. Becataten noticed the Heka Priest called Lady Nagara to his side for a walk.

As they strolled around the sandy waterfront, Becataten could sense secrecy in their conversation. Were they concerned about her safety because of Jobu's death, or were they keeping something from her? And why were the horses so unsettled in this calm place? She watched the Stable Master try to soothe his new lead horse, stroking him and speaking to him with gentleness. Then turning away from the animal, the stable master drew his hand to his brow, shading his eyes to scan the vast horizon of Egypt's scorching sands. Becataten looked out over the bright dunes too, recalling a scroll she once read about equines and their keen intuitions. Maybe they had second-sight too. She wanted to get to the Palace where she knew she would be safe, and where she could be in the loving arms of Maja and Beset. It would be comforting to be in her apartment again, even though her beloved Jobu wouldn't be there - would never greet her there again. She hadn't been in a joyful place in a long time, but wondered if she could ever find joy in her old home again. Watching the restless horses, she stood nearer to a close-by guard and waited for the break in their progress to end.

Nearby the Heka Priest and Lady Nagara had stopped in the shade provided by a collection of palm trees. "Your Ladyship, do you remember when Suti, Hor, and Abu were young boys and used to taunt the sentries outside Pharaoh's chamber?"

Lady Nagara nodded, her fingertips brushing sand from her light cape.

The Priest continued, "Do you recall that one of those sentries gave Abu a beating because of his pranks? And Abu became enraged. I know you may not remember. You were younger than the boys."

Lady Nagara raised her head. "I remember that the four of you were always in trouble, and that Abu was even chased out of the harem tent once. My father said your parents often made contributions to

237

Pharaoh's war chest to compensate for the trouble you boys caused."

"True enough, my Lady. My question is, do you recall any unusual facial movements Abu displayed when he was angry?"

"Of course, we children were all afraid of him and called him Jelly Eye. Why do you ask?"

The Priest rubbed his hand back and forth across his mouth, and asked no further questions.

Back on the road to the Palace, Becataten felt the rhythm of the runners transporting her conveyance. She peered out at the Nile and the hard-working farmers building unending irrigation channels to extend the reach of the black floodwaters. She could see the muscles tensing on the legs of the men working the canals. Egyptians had strong backs and were tireless workers. A farmer knew that the farther he could route the thick, black silt into the land, the more crops he would grow. Hapy, the god of inundation and plenty, must love Egypt and Pharaoh immensely, she thought as she watched the workers.

Lady Nagara interrupted her thoughts when she asked, "What did you learn from the slave trader?"

Becataten cleared her throat, startled by her question, and answered, "A few things."

"What, specifically?" asked Lady Nagara. "I'm

curious."

Becataten blushed. "He showed me where my arousal spots are, using a feather, and he let me feel his member so I could see it grow. He also explained how important staring is."

"Well, he was brazen. I should punish him."

"Lady Nagara, please do not think of punishing him, it was what I asked of him, and he was very respectful. He said he could give me no more instruction as he wanted to leave the Estate with his nose and ears."

"Hah, and rightly spoken." Lady Nagara looked closely at Becataten.

Becataten turned away to peer out her window opening. She squinted at the sparkling desert, and on the horizon spied a rider, surging at a fast gallop. He was headed toward their caravan, or was it an illusion? Both mount and horse were sand colored. She turned and said, "Lady Nagara, I think I see a steed racing toward us, or is it a mirage?"

Lady Nagara leaned to look, then grabbed Becataten and pushed her to the floor, following on top of her. She shouted to the fan bearer, "Run for the stable master. Attack!" she cried. "Attack!" Then Becataten heard what sounded like a loud pluck from a lyre string. But it was no pull of an instrument. It was the sound of an unleashed arrow that pierced the back of her cedar chair and was reverberating like the growl of an angry animal. Its

239

mark came within a finger of where she had been seated. The palanquin was dropped hard with a jarring thud, and Lady Nagara and Becataten stayed low.

The voice of the Stable Master strongly called orders. "Stand firm!" She heard the rattling of the chariots as the horses danced in place and coming to flank her litter. Another command brought bowmen into position. "He flees!" someone shouted. Becataten sat up and peered outside cautiously. In the distance she could see the lone rider had turned and was galloping away, whipping his mount into a frenzied retreat.

Lady Nagara held Becataten down. "What is happening, Lady Nagara?" asked Becataten, near tears.

"I'm not sure, but what you saw was no mirage. It was a bowman aiming to take your life! But for the moment, we are both safe. Stay down until we hear otherwise from the command."

Becataten could feel Lady Nagara shaking as she held her close.

Becataten looked up when she heard the Heka Priest's drawing his chariot alongside their conveyance. She saw his great relief when he found them alive.

"My ladies," he said, bowing his head. "All is safe. Senzar has gone after the bowman."

Becataten sat up straighter and watched the

Priest turn his chariot toward the Stable Master, who was racing away to pursue the would-be assassin. Cupping his hands around his mouth, the Priest called, "Return! Get us to the Palace as swiftly as possible."

The order was given for two chariots to flank their conveyance as they sped on to the Palace.

Both women remained crouched on the floor, for the duration to remain safe, their wigs toppled at their sides.

"They have killed Jobu, and now they want me dead too," whispered Becataten from her cramped position.

"Shush, shush, Becataten, we are safe now. We are in the hands of trained men who are Pharaoh's soldiers. Very soon we will be at the Palace." Lady Nagara's own voice shook, her words an obvious attempt to comfort not only Becataten, but herself as well. From the floor of their litter, Becataten never saw the Palace materialize like a fine mirage in the distance.

241

Chapter 25

♊

Princess Becataten and Lady Nagara's litter bearers were fatigued but still running at their fastest speed toward the Palace. Once at the gates, Lady Nagara dared to look up and see Hor anxiously waiting in a chair with a small retinue of armed guards to greet their caravan. Hor's expression froze when he saw the speed with which the vehicle approached, its curtains flying.

Becataten heard the Priest shout at his charioteer to drive toward Hor. The Priest nearly fell off his chariot as his driver abruptly drew his horse to a halt. The men spoke frantically to one another. She heard Hor loudly call, "Are the ladies well?"

Breathing heavily, the Priest nodded.

Hor rushed a covered palanquin to move alongside Becataten's vehicle. "Dwarf Beset alerted me of this, and I had just dispensed a runner to meet and warn you. But we were obviously too late. Are you unharmed?" he said.

Becataten was on her knees, not yet able to get to her chair.

"Yes, Hor, we are unharmed," Lady Nagara said

as she got to her chair, "And what did Dwarf Beset know that we did not?" she snarled.

Becataten shook with fear still, but she knew it was rage that consumed Lady Nagara.

Exhausted and dripping with sweat, the Heka Priest chariot joined Hor's. "This is horrifying! But thanks to all the Gods, you ladies are well," he said.

Becataten took Hor's firm hand as he escorted her, and then Lady Nagara, to the waiting transport. As they hurriedly rearranged their wigs, Becataten knew how disheveled they looked and how frightened they must have appeared when she saw people staring at them. She felt Lady Nagara cling to her as they changed vehicles. She saw Hor's face change to a look of horror, when he saw the arrow that struck Becataten's chair. He stood tall and turned to his aides. "Get us inside the Palace walls now! This caravan has been attacked! Lead the ladies' litter to their apartment, and arrange for extra sentry guards when they arrive!"

Once safely within the Palace walls, Lady Nagara looked stone-faced as their litter grew closer to their apartments.

Once at the apartment Hor had arranged, Lady Nagara called loudly to an attendant, "Bolt that door. You are to let no one in unless you speak with me."

Becataten eyed a muscular slave. "You must guard the door!" The slave bowed deeply and took up his post, his back to the secured door, arms folded. Lady Nagara nodded in approval.

Exhausted with legs shaking, Becataten called to a nearby servant to draw them a bath. Hor had arranged for many vases of flowers, bowls of exotic fruits and braziers burning the finest of incense for their arrival. They went unnoticed and untouched by the servants that scurried to ready the apartment for the worn travelers.

The overseer of royal apartments had secured the quarters for the Princess and the Lady, housing them near Hor on the long colonnade, per his request.

"How far is Pharaoh's house from here, Lady Nagara?" asked Becataten.

"Too far," answered Lady Nagara. "We are not as safe as we could be if we were closer."

Security measures had not been taken into consideration when their location was assigned, but now it was a priority. They would need protection, as they would have to cross grand gardens to arrive at Pharaoh's House of Rejoicing for Becataten's audience.

Lady Nagara's fear abated some when the two women were seated together in their bath. Becataten dismissed their attendants when, with a quiet resolve, Lady Nagara looked directly into Becataten's eyes and said, "We are to be very careful about talking near the ears of our attendants. We are to take no food for fear of being poisoned, and we must protect ourselves in every way. I solved our dining by sending a message to Queen Tiy, requesting the favor of taking our meals from her chef, Bakenamun. I have also ordered a tasting slave. We will dine that way, and that way only. Do you understand?"

Wide eyed, Becataten nodded.

"As you know, Queen Tiy and I grew up together, and I believe her to be my friend. We can trust no one until we learn who the enemy may be within the Palace. As to our safety, I have done what I can, but we are in the hands of Hor, and I will feel much better when Suti arrives. I will feel far more secure under their dual protection."

Becataten added, "And the protection of the Heka Priest, Lady Nagara."

"Yes, and the Heka Priest. The trouble is we have all grown older and know not who to turn to for protection among the younger and more able in the Palace."

"Your Ladyship, are we going to be murdered?"

"Do not worry yourself about this matter..."

"Your Ladyship, please do not treat me like a child. I am nearly three inundations older now, and have come into my womanhood. I have been invited to Pharaoh's chamber by royal decree. I have already lost my beloved twin. Do not keep things from me that concern me directly."

245

It was time that Becataten explained her feelings. She was not just someone to groom any longer. She was a woman trying to become involved in her future. For too long she held no control over her life, and someone had just tried to take it away before she lived it. She wanted to know why and who was doing this.

Lady Nagara's face twisted into a displeasing shape.

Becataten continued. "The only time you have ever listened to me was when I was rude to you and insisted on making this journey to the Palace. I respect you and appreciate all you have done for me, but I deserve to know about this treachery that surrounds us, or rather, me."

Lady Nagara expelled a long breath. "You are quite right. You are no longer a child. I will tell you what I know."

Becataten sat up in her bath water.

"I know you talk to the Heka priest, Becataten, and his insight into this treachery is probably the most accurate. Not only is he a Heka priest, but he has also cast your true charts." She reached for a ceramic bowl, tilted her head back and poured water over her shaved head, and dirt from the road dripped down her breasts into the bath water. "But let's begin at the beginning, as I know it. You have undoubtedly heard of Pharaoh's father before him, the great King Thutmose IV?"

246

Becataten nodded, and cupped water in her hands to spill over her face. *Why am I getting a history lesson at this time? And why do I feel so much has been kept from me? I need Dwarf Beset, but I must listen to what Lady Nagara is saying. Does Lady Nagara know who this person is that wants me dead, too? Has she been keeping it from me?*

Lady Nagara continued. "Let me try and explain. It was Pharaoh's father who first began to favor the God Aten. He influenced our Pharaoh to do the same, so now God Aten takes precedence over all the Gods in Thebes. And Pharaoh continues that decree as sure as we sit in this bath together. As the God Aten has come more into favor, the Amun Clergy in Memphis have lost their worshippers their offerings and status, while the new priests of Aten are flourishing. When Pharaoh moved his capitol from the delta here and built his Palace of the Dazzling Aten, the Amun Clergy grew angrier than anyone knew, until their ire escalated into a plot to overthrow our Pharaoh."

Becataten nodded and began to think like a scholar. "I have read scrolls about this, but I had to read them in secret."

Lady Nagara nodded. "Yes, my dear, I sometimes forget about your great appetite for reading."

"The rest I know from the Heka Priest, Lady Nagara. Jobu and I have charts that show great and favorable influences in the life of Pharaoh, and so we must be involved in this plot in a helpful way."

I say we, and yet Jobu is gone, Becataten thought as great sadness replaced her fear.

"Then you know of this treason as well as I, my dear. However, what we don't understand is who is driving this plan and if people close to Pharaoh are involved? I think if I were a man, I would ask, where does the militia stand in this matter?"

Becataten relaxed down into the water of the bath, trying to push Jobu from her mind. "There is something I would like to ask you. What did you and the Heka Priest talk about at the oasis?"

Lady Nagara frowned. "Why?"

"Just tell me," asked Becataten.

"Let me think, we spoke about Suti, he and Abu growing up and raising the anger of the Gods with their pranks."

"What else?" asked Becataten.

"We talked about how Abu was the worst of them, how he even snuck into the harem once and took a beating from one of the guards for doing so."

"What else?"

"Well, I think that's it, my dear."

"No, there was something else that shocked the priest," said Becataten.

Lady Nagara looked off into space. "I reminded the priest that when Abu took his beating, or grew angry, his eye wobbled and we called him Jelly Eye."

248

Becataten froze, the shock of the words permeating her body. "Oh no! No, no!"

"What is it, my dear?" Lady Nagara, now clean, sat up taller in the large tub.

Becataten stood up. "I must leave this bath and see Maja and Beset!"

She climbed out of the tub and scurried for a linen wrap. Lady Nagara was right behind her.

"Stop, you may not leave this apartment, Becataten, it is unsafe! Why is it so important you see Maja, now?"

When Becataten heard Lady Nagara reveal the discussion about Abu's wobbly eye, she was more determined than ever to talk to Nanny Maja about the origins of her birth. Becataten rushed to open her dusty trunks as Lady Nagara argued that she was not to leave. She told the room guard to inform the others that the women were not being attacked but having an argument.

"I must go!" Becataten insisted, yelling, her voice on the verge of hysteria as if all the anguish she hadn't yet unleashed was coming out in this instant. "There is much you do not understand yet, but I need more answers."

"I am telling you, what you propose is quite unsafe!"

Their voices rose to a high pitch when they were distracted by an abrupt knock.

Becataten investigated. "Who is there?" she

249

asked, still clutching the wet long linen wrap from the bath. A royal envoy, from Pharaoh himself, had arrived with a beautifully scripted and illuminated scroll, formally inviting her to his apartment.

Becataten sat on a lounge, leaning into the light provided by tall candles. She unrolled the papyrus and scanned the document. It formally greeted the Princess and her Ladyship, requesting their pleasure when the next Ra left Egypt. This meant there was no time for her to take a chair to her distant apartment and meet with Nanny Maja. Time now must be spent on but one thing, the preparation of her visit to Pharaoh. The argument was mute.

Becataten handed the scroll to Lady Nagara and said, "I suppose I can do nothing more but prepare to meet with Pharaoh. You have been included in the invitation, as you can see," Becataten said with resignation.

Lady Nagara sighed. "Yes, to show proper Court etiquette. He will convey to me his good wishes and respect, then I will be dismissed. You will stay, and I pray to the Gods that you are ready."

"So I go to Pharaoh to reveal the attempt on my life, to discuss the Court plot, as well as to couple with him," Becataten said.

Lady Nagara shook her head. "It is a task I would not have set for you, my child," she said with sympathy in her eyes Becataten had not before seen.

"At least in Pharaoh's chamber I can assume I will be safe," Becataten said. Then she quickly returned to the present. "I still must find time to meet with Maja and Dwarf Beset! I need to ask Nanny Maja what my mother's last words were. I know she has kept something from me about that time. And Beset, Beset knows all."

"That may be true, but that time will not come. Ra will be leaving us soon and we must ready you for your audience with Pharaoh. It will take at least another Ra to prepare you. Now let us return to your bath."

"Return to my bath! No. I am leaving." Becataten walked to her nearest trunk, now opened, and rummaged through her clothes. She found the simplest shift, reached for a shawl, and covering her head and shoulders, rushed to the entrance. "Open this door, I wish to leave!" she told the large sentry.

"Do not allow the Princess exit," Lady Nagara insisted, pointing to the sentry on guard.

"I am a Princess, she is but a Lady. I demand you open this door, now!" said Princess Becataten.

Lady Nagara pulled on her wrist. "You may be a Princess, but you are acting like a child. Stop and think. We do not know who wants you dead, Becataten, and leaving may be a sure way of finding that out."

Becataten twisted her arm free. "And it is my life,

251

my own risk I take. My brother is dead. I need to get more answers before I speak with Pharaoh on the next Ra. I must go!"

The sentry manning the entry waited as the two women argued. She marched up to the sentry, and stood her full height. "As Princess, I demand you let me free!" she said. Shrugging, he opened the door for Princess Becataten upon her second demand. She rushed out and hurried to put distance between her and Lady Nagara.

Once in the long colonnade, it wasn't clear which way to turn. She saw what a distant walk it was across a vast garden to the halls of the Palace. And she needed to walk much further to the opposite end of the compound to her own apartment. With an unpainted face, no wig and being commonly dressed, transports didn't stop for her. She hurried toward what she thought the right direction when a man approached her from a large garden plot. It was dark, and although torches were being lit, the lighted ones hadn't reached her. "Hello, little one, can I help? You look frightened."

"No, I must hurry to the west gate," Becataten said as she experienced a bad feeling about the man.

"The west gate, that is a long way," said the stranger, stepping into her path. He was wearing a soiled kilt, the wig of a worker and had bad teeth.

"Please, let me pass. I must go," she said.

"Not so fast," he said, as he backed her against a column. He ran his hand down the side of her body, then under her shift. "You smell fresh, an attendant to a lady would be my guess," he said, as his other calloused hand rubbed hard against her breasts.

The wanton man was mauling her, and she knew she didn't have the strength to fend him off. Maybe she could outwit him. "What kind of work do you do?" she asked.

He smirked, "What do you care," he said as he began lifting his kilt. She could see his member harden just like the slave traders had. His dirty hands revealed he must have worked in the rich black soil.

"Are you a garden worker?" Becataten asked.

"And what if I am?" he said.

"You should know that my lady is with the Royal Gardener Sennejem, now, in that apartment over there. I was sent for a lotus blossom for their lovemaking. I was to be quick," she lied.

The garden worker's member grew limp at her words and he stepped back, then disappeared into the dark. Becataten's enthusiasm to find her old apartment wilted, and she returned to the Palace apartment feeling fortunate she got away, yet full with anxiety about being so close to Maja and Beset and being unable to reach them. Did they know about Jobu yet? How would they ever know where she was in the vast Palace?

When Becataten re-entered the apartment, she and Lady Nagara spoke little. Becataten allowed one of the attendants, schooled in massage, to rub her with scented oils. Soon after, she requested an inkpot and stylus wrote quickly to Dwarf Beset to give her the news of where she was staying. Looking at her attendant through hot tears, she said, "This is to be sent to Dwarf Beset immediately!"

Going into her bedchamber, she lay on a lounge, covered her eyes with her arm and said, in a soft voice, "It is a strange time, one of sadness mingled with joy, as I prepare to meet with Pharaoh." *I don't think I can tell Lady Nagara that I believe the Royal Astrologer is my true father.*

As a runner showed up to deliver the scroll to Dwarf Beset, Lady Nagara, now perfectly adorned, oiled, painted, and wearing her wig, sat next to the plain Becataten, taking her hands. "I heard your words, Becataten, and it *is* both a sad and beautiful time. I know everyone around you has expected much from your visit with Pharaoh, especially me. I have looked upon this event selfishly. But I want you to know I have come to love you, my dear, and whatever happens, that affection will remain true." Her words brought Becataten to tears. "Now, I have one last thing to tell you that I don't believe the slave trader would have revealed." She cleared her throat, pulled her stool close and continued, "It is simply this, my dear. When you and Pharaoh finish

254

with touching and all the tenderness that Pharaoh will bestow upon you, his royal member will grow very large, much like the slave trader told you – although you must not expect Pharaoh's member to grow quite as large - and when this happens he will thrust it inside of you. You know that. Correct?"

Becataten nodded.

"When that happens, a woman feels a quick stinging sensation, and even a few drops of blood are shed. This is a joyous time, a time when Pharaoh knows you have never been with another. I understand in other countries men don't want a woman after her first coupling, and deem her spoiled. In Egypt, that is not so."

Wide eyed, Becataten replied, "I have never read about that."

"No, I doubt that you have. Not everything is written in a scroll, Becataten. I wanted you to know about this for two reasons. This has happened to every woman since the beginning of Egypt, and you are not to be frightened because of the event. Do you understand?"

Becataten nodded again.

"Pharaoh is a god, but also a man, Becataten. The god in him worships and keeps close all of Egypt's female goddesses. The man in him adores his female companions and reveres them. Because of this, the time you spend with him will be a loving experience."

255

"You describe this time with Pharaoh very differently than the slave trader did."

"There are two points of view about lovemaking Becataten, one from a woman's point of view and one from a man's. These two points of view are what make us an alluring mystery to one another."

Becataten looked into her eyes and said, "And, you know all about this because you spent time with Pharaoh in his bed chamber a long time ago, did you not?"

"Yes, Becataten, I did."

A faraway look consumed Lady Nagara. She placed Becataten's hands onto her bosom. "And now, because I was with Pharaoh once, I am able to offer you to him, as you are my grandest prize."

Beset quickly paid the runner a few pieces of copper debon and with anxiety unrolled the scroll and began to read. She whispered to herself, "She knows who her true father is, and someone is trying to kill her now! First Jobu, and now Taten! How did that happen?"

Maja padded in after a night stroll with Sennejem, as Beset sat with the scroll in her lap, anxiety covering her face. "Beset, is something wrong?"

"I am unsure," said Beset, "But there is something to this that I fear may be more terrible

256

news, although little can be worse than losing our dear Jobu. It is a scroll from our beloved Taten."

Maja hurried beside Beset and sat down. "Oh I miss her so! What does she say?"

"She says she is here! Now! In the Palace, but she must prepare for her coupling with Pharaoh and that she cannot come to us right now."

"Here!" Maja asked, hopping up and down.

She says she hopes the last scroll she sent did not distress us too much and that she would come to talk to us in person about Jobu, and to try not to be too sad."

Both women lowered their eyes, tears flowing as they thought of their beloved Jobu.

"She also then says something very strange, that she is in danger, and that she knows about her father and Jobu's father, and she must find a way to get away to visit us and tell us in person, for scrolls are not safe. Do you think she knows who her real father is?" Beset wiped her tears as she sat staring at the scroll. "This concerns me greatly, we should see what we can learn on our own," Beset said as she stood up and rolled the long scroll back up, fear creeping into her mind.

Chapter 26

♊

A nervous Princess Becataten and a composed Lady Nagara stood at the portal to Pharaoh's royal apartment waiting to be received. A pair of towering Nubian sentries flanked the doors wearing kilts of panther skins and armed with spears. The women had arrived in the nearing darkness as Pharaoh's scroll requested. Rank demanded that Lady Nagara stand behind Princess Becataten. They waited for only a short interval when the doors flew open, and swiftly out walked Abu. It was difficult to know whose face expressed the most surprise.

Becataten had never before seen Abu, but when their eyes connected, she felt a cold chill run down her spine. She turned to see Lady Nagara's heated face. Becataten shook her head. She had to get the sight of Abu removed from her mind as she felt regret at not having asked Maja her questions about her parentage. *How could this man possibly be our father?* she wondered as the man ducked upon seeing her, wrath in his eyes, one wobbling, just like in her dreams.

Abu pounded his heels into the sand, taking long

and determined steps to his royal apartment. An attendant outside Pharaoh's chamber had fallen asleep but was awakened by Abu's exit and rose to catch up. The small man had difficulty keeping up with the long strides of the royal astrologer. Well behind Abu, the bearer hefted high the heavy linen canopy, trying to catch up and shade Abu from the waning sun at the same time. Not lessening his pace, Abu turned and growled through his teeth, "Return to your post, you incompetent."

When their master stormed into the apartment, Dwarf Heby and Butler Farafar stepped aside. Overtaken by his temper, Abu leaned on a table, breathing heavily and muttered to himself. "Why didn't the Anatolian dog, with the supposed strike of a snake, do his job? Now the clergy will make me find another means." He rose in a wrath, and with the sweep of his hand cleared the table surface of candles and scrolls. Grunting and snorting, he stomped nearby storage pots into shards. He tore open the lid of his bed chest, flinging its contents into the air, then held it over his head and threw it to the floor where it crashed into a broken mass. He stood panting like one of Pharaoh's sighthounds on a lion hunt, his fists held tight to his sides so hard they had grown white. His left eye wobbled uncontrollably.

The staff of his household ran crying from his apartment save for his old eunuch butler, who, after a time of silence, entered Abu's space. He hobbled into the main room to clear the floor of debris and place unbroken items back in order.

"After you have cleaned this room, send me a runner. I wish to inform a guest he is to join me at my late meal." Abu said with calmness.

Dwarf Heby rushed out the door to find Beset.

While waiting to be announced, Becataten stood very straight to ensure the pleats of her shift would remain unwrinkled. The fine linen had just been removed from a board with long V shaped grooves, where it had dried in the sun to create knife-edged crimps. She was shaken from seeing Abu but knew she must swiftly recover, lest her time with Pharaoh be tainted.

The sentries allowed them entrance, and as she walked through the entry she passed a highly polished copper mirror. In it she saw a reflection of a beautiful woman who wore a shining wig, not too large, decorated with scores of refined plaits and adorned with a tasteful number of gold and turquoise beads. Becataten was taken aback with the beauty of her image. Her confidence bolstered.

Lady Nagara had insisted she wear minimal jewelry, especially not a necklace, as Pharaoh would remedy a bare neck with a gift. Becataten could also see that Lady Nagara had instructed the facial painter well. And most important, no special perfumes, as she had been told more than once that Pharaoh preferred his own scent to prevail. Together they stood waiting to be announced. Lady Nagara took Becataten's hand and squeezed it to divert her attention from admiring her image. Then the announcement came, and Pharaoh sauntered toward them, with a face that grew lively when he saw Becataten.

Both women bowed appropriately then rose to greet Pharaoh. A gold collar, replete with rows of beads made from turquoise, carnelian, and lapis lazuli surrounded his neck. Large polished emeralds studded his gold cuffs. A long tunic of a foreign weave with a decorative fringe fell upon his hammered-gold sandals. The kilt tied just below his belly, in the latest fashion, copied by his male court. His brown body glistened and kohl elaborately outlined his eyes. He was heavily perfumed with morenga oil, laced with frankincense.

Standing erect before them with his majestic nemes covering his head. A striped head cloth, topped with the sacred cobra, defined him as the true Pharaoh.

He penetrated Becataten's eyes with a long, deep gaze.

Here comes the staring, just like the slave trader said. I must not weaken and look away. He is gazing on me like a cat fixed on its prey, but his smile is

261

kind, Becataten thought. She held her gaze to his.

Still she shook as the Living God took her hands. *I am meeting the God of all the lands of Egypt. I can little believe this.*

"What a beautiful young Princess you are, Becataten. The goddess Hathor has favored you greatly," Pharaoh said in a gentle voice.

Becataten felt her knees weaken. "Thank you, my Lord."

Pharaoh turned to Lady Nagara and greeted her warmly, then led her to his sitting area. Becataten turned to observe Pharaoh's magnificent chamber, laden with objects that beguiled the eye. Standing on a panther skin, she noted that much of the wooden furniture was covered in hammered gold. Elaborate foreign tapestries adorned the walls, and observing the designs, she thought they must have come from the traders who crossed the Great Sea.

She saw Lady Nagara giggle and act like a child in Pharaoh's presence. Becataten felt a brief sadness for her. *I have never seen Lady Nagara react like this toward any man. She must still be in love with Pharaoh.*

Looking away to give them privacy, Becataten was overwhelmed by a grand map of Egypt covering an entire wall. It depicted Pharaoh's many vassal states and was painted in bright colors. Gems, embedded into the thick brick walls, identified certain cities and states. She was so engrossed by it that she failed to see, or hear, Lady Nagara's departure. A warm hand clamped her shoulder causing her to jump. Lady Nagara gone, they were alone.

"Is the map of Egypt more interesting than your Pharaoh, Princess Becataten?"

"Oh no, of course not, My Living Lord."

"Architect Suti tells me you are a learned young woman; you surely have seen maps of Egypt before."

Becataten relaxed a bit and answered honestly. "I think it is the sheer scale of the map that overwhelms me, the vassal states and the grandeur that is Egypt."

"Spoken like one of my scholars."

I am talking like an academic, which Lady Nagara and the Slave Trader both advised against!

She tried another phrase. "But the beauty of your presence and surroundings truly makes the map pale by comparison, My Lord."

"Spoken like a governor. Would you like to try for the voice of a bureaucrat?" He smiled again.

He was teasing her, and she noticed how handsome he was with his gleaming chest and golden adornments. Becataten felt her insides clench, then before she could stop herself, words poured out.

"I am overwhelmed to be here with you and in your private quarters. I am thrilled to have been invited by you to view parts of Egypt that I have never seen. It is humbling to know that I am to be your companion for a time." Becataten's eyes misted with emotion.

"Come here, child. I believe you are about to cry."

"I am tearing a little only because I am so happy, and so relieved."

Pharaoh pulled Becataten close to him. She could smell not only his perfume, something else, his maleness. She knew now why Lady Nagara had told her not to wear perfumes or ungencies. He liked his essences to overpower, and they did. He wiped her tears with his thumbs and held her at arm's length. "We can't have kohl running down your beautiful plump checks. A face painter has taken the time to do your emerald eyes justice. But tell me, Becataten, why do you speak more like a scholar than a young princess?"

Becataten hesitated. *Lady Nagara wouldn't like where this conversation is headed! But she had told me to do as Pharaoh asked.*

She took a deep breath. "My scholarly life began when Suti taught me about architectural drawings, which he knew held great interest for me." Pharaoh seemed interested, so she continued. "Suti mentored me and took me to his Estate where Lady Nagara tutored me in dress, music, song and deportment. I loved the Estate because I got to see how Pharaoh's land is channeled after inundation, to see farming

264

take place and the great herds of cattle tended."

"And Lady Nagara let you go into the fields and see this?" Pharaoh asked.

"I did, for a little while."

"Why did this interest you so?"

"I think to see seasons come and go with the great Nile inundating and bringing Egypt the gift of black water, to watch farmers plant, to see crops come to life, ending in the great harvest is a beautiful cycle. It must require you and all the Gods to work in magnificent concert for this to happen."

"How many inundations have you lived Princess?"

"Thirteen, almost fourteen."

"You are a very deep-thinking Princess for such a young one. Come to me, Becataten."

He held her to him for several breaths, his body warm against hers. Then he stepped away from her and said, "I want my jewelers to see your eyes, so they will polish my emeralds accordingly to match them."

She was beginning to feel comfortable with him when his butler appeared and offered her date wine. Pharaoh took a cup of his sma and motioned for the removal of his nemes. With his head bare, his eyes were penetrating, especially since he smiled more with them than he did his lips.

In a distant corner Becataten heard the soft notes of a lyre. Pharaoh clapped his hands and two beautiful women entered his chamber and quietly danced to the music, now joined by a flute. The rustle from the dancers' garments and jewelry was soothing. More wine was served, and Becataten thought the only thing left to do was sing and begin to fondle his member. As the dancers were dismissed, she hoped she could sing after drinking two cups of wine. She set her drink aside and wavered just slightly. "Pharaoh would you like me to sing, you a song, then fondle your member?" she asked.

"Who told you to say that?" Pharaoh asked, his smile showing amusement.

"Ah... a man."

Pharaoh's amusement quickly left.

"What man?"

Becataten was stunned for a moment. *What to say? What to say? Dwarf Beset says never tell everything.* "Oh... a man that comes once a year to the Suti Estate."

"What does this man do at the Suti Estate, princess?"

"Oh... He rests his caravan there for a time before moving on to Thebes."

"What does his caravan contain?"

She held her lips tight. *What to say, what to say.* "Slaves."

"What kind of slaves?"

"Women slaves."

"And what is this man called, Becataten?"

"I don't know his proper name."

Pharaoh tried to conceal his smile. "Would this man be called a slave trader?"

Becataten nodded and spoke softly, "Yes."

"What possessed you to talk to a slave trader, Becataten?"

Trapped, she now had to speak genuinely, as promised. She straightened, looked him in the eye with a contrite expression. "Lady Nagara helped me so much to make my time with you perfect, but she would never really tell me how to couple with you, or entice you, or exactly what to do when we coupled, and there was no scroll that I could find no..."

Pharaoh interrupted. "So you took it upon yourself to engage the slave trader for answers?"

Becataten nodded her head ever so slightly.

Pharaoh slapped his leg and roared with laughter. He paused, looked at her again, then roared a second time.

"You have entertained me already more than my musicians and dancers, Princess. I find you to be quite amusing." He clutched her wrist and pulled her toward him. "Come to me, Becataten. Show me what you have learned."

Chapter 27

♊

Suti's chariot was swift to arrive at the location where Sennejem's crews were in the long process of planting an elaborate garden. He waved demandingly for Sennejem to join him. The Royal Gardener took quick steps toward Suti.

"Where can we talk?" Suti sharply asked.

"Please follow me," answered a concerned Sennejem, bowing with respect.

They entered a small, makeshift palm shack and sat on discarded building stones, facing each other. "I am going to be frank with you, Gardener, I believe you are associating with a man who is plotting against Egypt." Suti said in a condescending tone.

With a shocked look, Sennejem's jaw dropped, not knowing how to respond.

Suti continued, "It is known that you visit the Royal Astrologer often, and it is believed that he is driving a plan to overtake Egypt's throne."

"That cannot be true... I mean I am not a traitor, and yes, I see the Royal Astrologer from time to time, but it is just when he calls me for an occasional dinner," Sennejem said, finding his tongue.

"You are a foreigner, are you not?"

"Yes. I am originally from Mitanni, like many people in Egypt. The Royal Astrologer was my mentor. What is it that makes you believe that he is a traitor?"

With a look of judgment, Suti chose to ignore the question. "And what favors did you give the Royal Astrologer for your position?"

"I gave none."

"I know you dine regularly with Abu, and you have spent much time with Prince Jobutaten and Nanny Maja. What knowledge are you trying to gain from them?"

Sennejem looked confused. "I dine occasionally with the Royal Astrologer, and what does spending time with Jobu, I mean Prince Jobutaten, or his Nanny Maja have to do with anything?"

"It has to do with the fact that the Prince Jobutaten is dead, and you were one of the last people to be with him."

Sennejem's eyes lowered in response to this news. "I had heard unconfirmed rumor it was so and hoped it was not true. I just saw Jobu a few Ras ago." Sennejem's large black eyes grew with disbelief. "It is unclear to me what happened to him. How did he die?"

"He died under very mysterious circumstance, and we suspect a royal scribe." Suti said.

269

Interrupted by an envoy that poked his head into the shack, the two looked up. "I arrive with a message for you, Royal Gardener."

"Yes, what is it?" Sennejem asked, showing annoyance at the interruption.

"The Royal Astrologer Abu requests you join him at dinner as Ra leaves," said the envoy.

Suti stood, with a sneer on his face and an order for Sennejem to accompany him in his chariot to Hor's apartment. Suti drove the chariot hard and rough, making Sennejem hold hard to the rails as they raced for the Palace.

Once on foot and within the Palace walls, Suti waved down a double-chair litter and told the runner to advance with speed to Hor's apartment. As they were stepping on to their conveyance, Suti saw Dwarf Beset's sad face as she flagged them down.

"Follow me," she said. They stepped off the litter, and followed her to a secluded corner.

Suti looked concerned and spoke first. "Greetings, Dwarf Beset, I was sorry to hear the tragic news about your Prince."

Beset's face swelled with sorrow. "Yes, the Princess sent me a scroll right after the tragedy. And I thought life could never be so cruel." With her small hands, she wiped away tears. "But more shocking news awaits, Suti. Someone has tried to murder Princess Becataten as well on her way to the

Palace! Thank the gods the plan failed. The assassin has fled."

Suti and Sennejem stood immoveable. Suti looked about and whispered, "Do you know anything else, Beset?"

"A friend of mine who is an attendant in Abu's household told me that he overheard a Priest, an Amun Priest talking to Abu. The Amun Priest wanted gold to pay an assassin to take the life of Princess Becataten, just a few Ras ago."

Covering his mouth with his hands, Sennejem faltered.

Suti's shoulders fell. "This must have happened on the way to the Palace from my Estate?" he asked in a panic. "And my Lady, is she well?"

"Yes, and they are both well guarded in an apartment on the colonnade near Hor, taking no visitors," Beset said.

Before Suti and Sennejem returned to their chair, Sennejem leaned down to put his arm around Beset in a comforting way. "I, too, am so saddened about the loss of Jobu, Beset." He climbed in after patting her shoulder. Suti glared at him.

Walking slowly back to their conveyance, Beset whispered, "Suti, you seem upset with the Royal Gardener."

"That is an understatement, Dwarf Beset."

"I wouldn't suspect him of any wrong doing, Suti. I have looked into his life, and he has

271

perpetrated no harm."

Suti looked at her unconvincingly, but said nothing. He stepped back on to the conveyance and ordered the bearers to rush them to Hor's apartment.

After traversing the short distance, they arrived and Hor's butler bowed to Architect Suti and Sennejem, announcing them as they pushed past him into the apartment. The apartment appeared spare and unwelcoming, even with Hor's collection of art and fossils. The smell was dusty, like an unused room. In the impending darkness, Hor's butler lit the wicks of several bowls of oil and a few floor candles then discreetly exited.

Both Hor and the Heka priest stared at Suti and Sennejem in their disheveled and soiled dress.

Suti went to the flagon of wine, downed a cup and collapsed his plump body on a lounge, comfortable in his brother's apartment. The four men's eyes exchanged suspicious glances while Sennejem stood in the middle of the room, nervously.

Hor addressed Suti, "You've heard the shocking news of the attempt on Princess Becataten's life?"

Suti nodded, and poured more wine. "Heka Priest, meet Royal Gardener Sennejem, a great friend of Abu."

The men acknowledged one another, nodding

272

but without speaking.

The four men were silent until Suti sat up and spoke in an angry tone. "I am here to tell you that Sennejem was mentored by Abu, who secured his position as Royal Gardener. For years he has been friendly with the twin's nanny, and always had information about Prince Jobutaten and Princess Becataten. I believe he regularly passed information to Abu about the twins."

Sennejem interrupted, "Royal Architect, that is untrue."

"Then you were naïve and stupid to remain friends with Abu. You have known and been close with this family since the poisoning of their nanny!" Suti fired back.

"That is true, and I even discussed that poisoning with Abu those many seasons ago. I asked him if he knew of any scribes with the knowledge of poison, as the drink was delivered by a scribe."

"And I suppose you learned nothing."

"I remember that I succeeded in angering the astrologer with my questions."

Suti stood, shaking, and poured himself more wine. He turned to Hor and the Heka Priest and said, "They even took the blue lotus drug together and went into states of dreams and fantasies. At least Sennejem thinks Abu took it. Am I not correct, Sennejem?"

Sennejem bowed and spoke solemnly. "It is true we sometimes ate and drank together, and yes, we used the blue lotus on occasion to go into soaring states. We usually spoke in our shared, native tongue. Abu was instrumental in getting me the position of Royal Gardener, so of course I thought he was my friend, not someone he was using. Please, brothers, believe me when I say I would *never* bring harm to the household of the Prince and Princess or their attendants."

In disgust Suti said, "Sit down, Sennejem. Have some wine and convince us."

Sennejem refused and instead stood at attention while sweat ran down his back from under his dusty wig. With pleading eyes, his eyes shifted from Hor to Suti and then to the Heka Priest.

Hor looked hard into Sennejem's face and spoke with great volume. "So are we to believe you had no hint that information was being extracted from you during these dinners?"

"Yes, Architect Hor, that is true. I swear by all the gods, I did not know or mean to give any information about the twins to the Royal Astrologer. Over the years he may have asked me questions about them, but very general ones, about how the twins were faring."

"Did you ever hear Abu mention a clerical plot emanating from Memphis?"

"No, Architect Hor, I did not."

274

Now Hor's voice was booming off the clay walls. "Then you believed a man as powerful as Abu, one who has the king's ear, liked and embraced you as his friend."

"Yes, I think I did, because of our shared tongue, Architect."

Suti stood and began to pace in anger and impatience. "Has anyone learned who else may be a part of this plot at the Palace? And has Pharaoh been approached about these rebellious acts?"

With composure, Hor turned to Suti and in low tones bent to his ear. "I have tried to speak with Vizier Huy. He requests I place in writing what I wish to discuss with Pharaoh before he will grant me an audience. He is the same bureaucrat he has always been, protecting Pharaoh from any business he does not know about first." Suti nodded as Hor angrily added aloud, "Chancellor Ptathmose, who may have gotten us an audience, is in Kush."

Meekly Sennejem said, "May I interrupt, brothers? I remember one evening Abu had wax dolls on his table and quickly covered them when I entered his apartment. They were the kind you use in magic and pierce with wood splinters. Also he had a visitor once who wore eastern robes, a man who appeared most unsavory."

Suti, still angered, shook his head incredulously. "Ah, you finally remember more about your visits with Abu? I've always said a stupid man is the most dangerous."

The Priest perked up and reached for his amulet depicting the magical Heka snake. "So, Abu thinks he can perform magic with wax figures to destroy lives. I for one believe Sennejem when he says he is not in collusion with Abu," the priest said looking at the twins. "I would like us to reveal to Sennejem all we know. He may be able to add some hidden facts."

Suti and Hor looked at one another. Hor nodded to the Heka Priest, but Suti's face showed doubt.

"Sennejem, you know that Pharaoh's first born lies dying with an illness healers cannot cure," said the Heka priest.

"Yes, I had heard the Prince was seriously ill," said Sennejem.

"We in this chamber believe that Abu's magic is an attempt to make that happen. And we suspect someone is administering poison to the young Prince as well."

Sennejem finally sat down on a bench. "Architect Suti, you mentioned earlier that you suspect a Royal scribe was involved in Jobu's death."

The three men looked at Sennejem.

"I think I know the Scribe. It would be Tiurek. He once told me that Abu promised him the title of Court Astrologer if his loyalty remained absolute.'

Suti stood. "This has gone far enough. I am going to Lady Nagara. I told her that when she and Princess Becataten reached Pharaoh that she should deliver the news of Prince Jobutaten's death. That also put her in the position of explaining the assassin's attempt on Princess Becataten's life. Where is her apartment, Hor?"

"Taten, pardon me, the Princess Becataten is here in this part of the Palace, this close to Abu?" Sennejem asked.

"Yes," Hor hissed through his teeth. "You ass of a donkey, you're finally beginning to grasp the gravity of this plot that you have abetted?"

The Heka Priest interrupted. "Do not worry about the Princess, she is protected by Goddess Hathor, and my spells. No harm will come to her. She has the Heka herself."

"Humph, you priests are always so sure of your predictions," said Hor. "Why don't you tell Suti what you learned about the bloodlines of the Princess. That is no prediction!"

"It seems a certain princess Attah of Mitanni and Abu became brief lovers in the harem tent, as women's quarters were completed within the Palace. This was in the early days when Pharaoh was still young and could not always procreate. That woman bore twins and died in childbirth. Her only slave became Nanny Maja to those twins. The trait of the wobbling eye was recieved by Jobutaten, and of course we have all seen Abu's eye go askew, especially when he's angered. Abu is the twins' father."

277

Suti looked as though he was struck in the stomach with a stick after the Heka priest spoke.

Sennejem covered his mouth. "It is true. One of Abu's eyes quivers when he grows angry."

Suti stammered, "Does the Princess know of her parentage?"

Hor replied dryly, "We know little, as Lady Nagara and the Princess just arrived. Her ladyship demonstrated wisdom by sequestering herself and the Princess in the apartment I arranged for them. As a result we have not communicated with them. For all we know they may have already seen Pharaoh."

Suti rushed to the door, "All the more reason I should speak with Lady Nagara."

Chapter 28

♊

Princess Becataten felt comfortable with Pharaoh and was pleased the matter of the slave trader was out of the way. She was especially relieved he did not judge her wrongly for engaging him, but instead found the event quite amusing. She decided she had much to learn about men.

Another group of musicians entered Pharaoh's chamber and played more lively music. As she and Pharaoh nibbled on sweets and indulged in more drink, they talked and laughed into the night. Now he was sitting on his lounge and patting a pillow next to him, beckoning her to come and sit. *This is what the slave trader did. It must be the coupling time.* She walked to his side and sat next to him, the wine steeling away her anxiety.

"Remove your shift, Princess. Let me see your bare beauty. We have spent enough time on your mind."

She did as Pharaoh asked.

"You have not painted your breasts with henna designs."

"Does that displease you, Pharaoh?"

"No, I think I like you in your natural state."

She experienced the feelings of arousal when he fondled her nipples with his thumbs, and thought that this was a little like the feelings she had gotten from the feather on her arousal spot. She wished she'd experimented more so she would know what to expect.

Pharaoh's butler approached and indicated that he would take her wig. She lifted it off her head and handed it to him. With his eyes averted, and handling her wig with care, he vanished behind the sheer linen curtains.

Nearby, on a small table, Pharaoh reached for a pot of lotus oil and handed it to her. "Rub this around your nostrils. It enhances the desire to make love, Becataten."

She did as he asked.

"Now, rub some on my member."

And when she did, it grew like the slave traders, although not as large. She watched in amazement.

"Now rest on my lap, one leg on each side of me. Look into my eyes and slowly sit on my member."

He adjusted her hips, as she did what he asked. There was a catch in her breath and a sharp sting. As he pushed himself into her further, tears splashed from her eyes onto his chest.

"It is over, Becataten. You will not feel pain again. Do you know what just happened?"

Her chin quivered as she nodded with wide eyes,

"I think so." *If this if coupling, I don't know if I will like it,* she thought, but she struggled to keep her demeanor neutral.

Pharaoh gently lifted her off his lap and placed her onto the lounge.

An older woman appeared with a copper bowl and a damp cloth to help Becataten refresh herself, then left as quickly as she had appeared.

A large Nubian man quietly entered and sat on the lounge. Pharaoh said, "Now, Becataten you will feel no pain, just delight."

After the Nubian gently settled Becataten back on the lounge, Pharaoh spoke. "Part your legs, Princess, and my Nubian will caress your arousal spot."

She knew she must have looked frightened because Pharaoh took his hand in hers and said, "Look at me, Becataten, and fear not." The Nubian, who firmly held her legs apart, began to make her writhe. The massaging of her pad of beauty, as Egyptians called it, titillated her. She stared at Pharaoh in disbelief from such wonderful pleasure as her pelvis rose once, twice, and then it was over. And then Becataten noted that the Nubian vanished, just like the butler. She took a breath, feeling sated and happy.

"Now we will have pleasure together," Pharaoh said.

Becataten stared into Pharaoh's eyes. *There's*

281

more?

Pharaoh clapped softly. A faint drum beat in the background while Pharaoh moved on top of her. He entered her easily this time with his member and began moving rhythmically to the drumbeat as it grew louder. She picked up his rhythm and together they were moving each other as a masterful rider gallops on an elegant horse.

A new sensation came alive within her, a deeper one, and it was thunderous. She was thrusting forth with bolts of energy she never knew she had, while Pharaoh was exploding inside her.

Now she knew what everyone had been talking about.

Chapter 29

♊

Beset stood with a small torch in one hand, leaning on her cane with the other, and staring into a pond of lotus lilies that had closed with the absence of light. Bearing Jobu's death diminished her. But conspiracy involving her twins was not over, and she would find the strength to rally - the vigilance she needed to know all. She had just scripted a scroll to Becataten and had it rolled up in her fist, ready to send to her sequestered apartments.

My Sweet Taten:

I will explain what I believe you may already know. I have also learned that when your mother entered Egypt, she had an affair of the heart with the Royal Astrologer Abu. He even asked Pharaoh's permission to wed her but was refused by a young, and then arrogant, King. It would appear Abu has been trying to punish Pharaoh ever since, and as a result, leads the plot to overthrow the crown. I know this is all a great shock, but Nanny Maja tells me they cared a great deal for one another, and I believe Abu has never reasoned that you and Jobu are his children. Tell Pharaoh about the plot, but you may want to omit that Abu is your true father. It is my guess that Pharaoh already may know this, and it matters not, as today he is a fair and just ruler. And remember Abu is Pharaoh's half-brother. You will know when the time comes whether to reveal this information or not. Destroy this scroll, my Sweet Taten...

From the dark came her name. Beset looked up with a wan smile. "Greetings Architect. I would have expected you to be with Lady Nagara. But why have you traveled from one end of the Palace to another?"

In an angry tone he said, "I just pounded on the door of my Lady's apartment and was told that she and the Princess are with Pharaoh."

Suti silently took the torch from her. "Shall we walk and talk about all of this conspiracy and madness?"

After several steps, Beset stopped. "Why didn't someone come to me about all of this intrigue a long time ago? I knew the scribe that Jobu ran with was a bad one. And yes, I know all the tragic news about my sweet boy, and how he died. Becataten and I managed to scribble scrolls to each other as often as possible." She rubbed away tears with the back of her stubby hands. "I should have told you, or someone, who could have protected Jobu from that Scribe Tiurek."

Suti's words grew kind as her rubbed her back.

"Don't fault yourself, Beset."

Beset went on in an exasperated voice while Suti patiently listened. "That scribe used my boy. Not until Jobu's death did I surmise that he endured his company sexually, but to learn of his and Taten's true birth stories! If I could have just seen earlier what was happening. I learned too late that Tiurek was a tough and angry child." Beset clutched the scroll, one eye looking for a Palace runner to take it to Becataten. "You know Abu bought him on the slave block," she continued. "Probably because he was from the same area in Babylon. I heard that he ran away from Abu's household more than once until Abu finally enrolled him in scribe school. There, they beat his back until he understood he had to learn reading and writing, and stop street fighting. But, of course, he was still mean inside."

Beset wiped a tear. "There were clues, of course, ones I did not pay close attention to. I should have listened when Maja told me that Jobu sadly gave up a sweet relationship with a girl in our apartment building to run with Tiurek. Maja had asked me at that time if men had to give up women to become scribes. But I didn't take a proper hint from Maja's observation. I should have."

Beset began breathing heavily from exertion. They seated themselves on a secluded bench. Once in private, Beset cried openly while Suti held her small hand.

285

"I can hardly believe that we have experienced a murder of a Royal child! Are we to expect another attempt on Princess Becataten's life?" he sighed.

Dwarf Beset collected herself, and said, "No, I don't believe so Suti."

Softly Suti asked, "Do you know of the parentage of Princess Becataten?"

"Of course I do," blurted Beset. "Don't you know by now we dwarves know everything?"

They removed their sandals and sank their feet in the pond water. Beset put her small hands on her thighs and rubbed them. "Becataten will most likely be on the Royal barge sailing the Mother Nile south to Kush when Ra next shows himself," she whispered.

"But that is very distant," exclaimed Suti.

Beset waved her small arm and said, "With Pharaoh's strong rowers, they will be back at the Palace in a few returns of Ra. It is probably the safest place for her to be right now. And Pharaoh will not be away too long while his firstborn lies gravely ill. I believe he thinks his son will recover, but I have my doubts."

Suti nodded. "My friend, the Heka Priest also believes that Pharaoh's heir will not survive."

They sat silent for a time until Suti spoke. "I worry so about Becataten's welfare, and now the possibility that Pharaoh may learn of her parentage. I am concerned about her safety, Beset, even at

Court! We still do not know who else may be involved in this plot or if they can be counted among Pharaoh's advisors."

Beset calmed some. "The Princess has grown to be a strong woman, Architect," she said, as she patted his hand. "I do not wish to offend you, but most young women living under the tutelage of your Lady Nagara for two seasons would be devoured as a water bird gulps a marsh fish. But Becataten has survived to be strong and resilient. Perhaps there is something to be said about having inherited the shrewd strengths of Abu."

"How long have you known that Abu is the twins' true father?"

Beset took a deep breath. "I plied Nanny Maja with sma and learned the truth one evening, many moons ago."

"You are clever, Dwarf Beset. May the gods love and care for you always. You bring clarity to this confounding situation."

"Is there anything anyone can do to stop this?" Beset asked.

Suti shook his head. "Hor and I have been unable to pierce Pharaoh's bureaucracy, let alone speak with him, and there is also the possibility that the Vizier and the Chancellor may be involved in this plot. But what really concerns me is that we have no real facts to present to Pharaoh of Abu's involvement in the murder of Prince Jobutaten, the overthrow of the Crown or even the attempt on Princess Becataten's life. And I am not sure I want to be the messenger of the fact that Abu is the twins' father. I do not yet know if my Lady had an opportunity to speak with Pharaoh as I instructed her."

Beset sat mute for a while. "My feeling is that the Vizier and the Chancellor are not involved in this overthrow." She lifted the scroll in the air to show Suti. "I am sending this to my Princess now."

Suti sat rigid and serious, then turned to her. "Do you have a plan?"

"Of course," Beset said. "And Becataten is going to be the messenger of my plan."

Several Ras later, Becataten and Pharaoh slid across the water. On a platform strewn with silken pillows, Princess Becataten lounged next to Pharaoh on his royal barge, their hands intertwined. A fan bearer pumped a pole of ostrich feathers over their heads as rowers moved the royal barge gently back to Thebes. Pharaoh had dozed off, while Becataten closed her eyes.

But crowding her mind were the words she was to deliver to Pharaoh that had come to her on the scroll Beset had sent to her. *Why was this so difficult? Am I afraid that Pharaoh will learn that his half-brother slipped into his harem and fathered me? Oh I have to stop thinking, and just tell him.*

288

She opened her eyes, realizing how new it was to fully comprehend the recent status imposed upon her, both as a Royal Princess and as companion to the Lord of the Land. She knew and felt like a different person, one of prominence, confident of her womanhood and of her sexuality.

She sat up and watched the Nile banks slip past. It was amazing how full her life had become. She had traveled with Pharaoh to the great desert plain, accompanied by hundreds of chariots where lions abound, and where she couldn't turn away as he led the grand hunt, killing thirty-two lions. She watched Pharaoh's soldier's rush out to the mortally wounded beasts and slice off their tails for their Lord, the Royal symbol of kingship. He would use them to swipe flies in the bush, to dangle from his kilts and adorn his robes. The lion and Pharaoh were as intertwined in sprit as was the falcon. Images of the hunt and the fascinating structures she had seen in her brief travels filled her memory. Pharaoh opened his eyes and turned to Becataten, "You look so serious, Princess."

She took a relaxing breath. "Oh, I was just thinking of our tour of the Karnak Temple. I was stunned by the immensity of the sacred complex, and the grand improvements you made to the walled center of worship. They were all magnificent, Pharaoh. The sanctuary must be the size of a large town."

Pharaoh rested his arms behind his head and said, "Larger."

Becataten went on. "Egypt's Pharaohs have been adding onto Karnak for over a thousand innundations, haven't they?"

Pharaoh nodded.

"When we raced the long causeway to the Tenth Pylon that you had Suti and Hor build, I almost couldn't believe my eyes. And next to those huge columns is your statue, brightly colored and bejeweled. Is it the largest statue in Egypt?"

Pharaoh affirmed that to be true also.

Becataten knew she could go on and on about the Karnak Temple, describing the poles sheathed in gold that reached to the sky with highflying flags. She could describe the enormous and artfully carved wooden doors that allowed them entrance. She could mention, which she didn't think was fair, that the people of Egypt could never gain entry to Karnak, but had to worship from outside the temple walls to its gods within.

And she could also speak about the bark built for a cult god to float the Nile on festival days, made of cedar wood that had been dragged from the mountains near the eastern coast of the Great Sea. And that Pharaoh had had it lined with pure silver worked with gold.

But languishing in all these thoughts that interested her had to stop. She must tell Pharaoh what she knew about the threat he faced before they arrived in Thebes.

Pharaoh had dozed off again. This time when he awoke, Becataten was ready.

"Still you are awake, your mind always full of the wonders of Egypt," he teased.

"Yes, I was thinking about the places you have shown me, but especially Kush, and how it is governed in the same administrative style as Egypt. You have given Viceroy Merymose extraordinary powers. There must be much trust between you," Becataten.

"You are correct, I do trust the Viceroy. The Viceroy and I quelled a rebellion in Upper Nubia together. I returned triumphant with thirty thousand Nubian slaves. I secured Egypt's mines of gold, galena, and malachite," he said, sitting up with interest. Becataten knew Pharaoh enjoyed her for her mind as much as her body.

Becataten's mind went to a scroll she had once read, "And on your *stale,*" she said, "It is carved that you came down upon the enemy with the 'wind stroke of a falcon.' That is why you have Nubian slaves etched into the soles of your golden sandals."

"True," he said smiling.

Becataten grinned, "And I think you like exotic imports like pygmies, ivory, ebony, and panther skins, too." Becataten realized she was having trouble saying the words that wanted to come out.

"Why did you ask about Viceroy, Becataten?" Pharaoh said, changing the subject.

"He seems to be an able overseer and statesman, too."

"What do you see in him that you think makes him an able statesman, my little scholar?"

"He was firm but civil to his men, and I noticed that he likes to delegate responsibility to those who learn quickly, somewhat like you administer your Court."

"You notice a great deal, Princess. Where does all this wisdom come from? Surely Lady Nagara and Architect Suti were not the only contributors of your thoughts."

"I think my royal bloodlines have some bearing on my thinking." She swallowed hard, reminded now of her true bloodlines. "And Lady Nagara did teach me, in a stern way, what not to be. Suti, I think, schooled me in what to be. And I must add Dwarf Beset to my life's learning, because she taught caution."

"Ah yes, caution. Reflect before you act. Tell me what reflections you have about my Court?"

"My Lord, I could not presume to comment on your Royal Court."

"It is my command that you do."

I need help from Dwarf Beset now. Her mind raced with what she wanted to tell Pharaoh. *This is probably the moment to begin the telling.*

292

"I see our great lord as a benevolent god who is fair with his administrators..."

"You are using the voice of a governor, Becataten. We talked about this once before, remember?" He smiled, tapping his his finger against her nose.

Becataten lowered her head and when she lifted it, she gazed at Pharaoh, her face intense.

Pharaoh frowned. "Becataten, your green eyes are so hard they seem they may shatter. What is wrong?"

"Will you please ask your attendants to leave us?" she asked softly.

Pharaoh swept his hand to his consorts, and they left his side, except his mute fan bearer. He motioned her close. "Speak. I give you pardon before I hear your words, if they displease me."

"I do not fear displeasing you, Pharaoh. I fear you may not believe me. I am about to tell you of a web of events, interwoven as deeply as you are with all the gods of Egypt. First, I must start with the story of my twin, Prince Jobutaten, who is now dead."

"I am aware of his tragic accident and have not mentioned it so sadness would not enter our time together."

"I beg you, Lord, let me describe the entire web."

He sat back, motioning for Becataten to continue.

293

Becataten met his stare and summoned the courage that Beset said she would find to deliver her grave news. Her voice grew stronger. She was thankful they were on board the royal barge. It was a private place. But the Nile currents were steadily moving them toward Thebes, and she had to hurry now with the telling.

When Pharaoh saw how distraught she was, he took both of her hands in his to lean close.

Becataten began. "Many inundations ago my Nanny Maja was poisoned. Dwarf Beset learned that the poison was intended for both Jobutaten and me."

"You are sure of this, Princess?"

Becataten nodded.

"As my brother grew to be a young man, he became friends with young, royal scribes who told him that two sets of heavenly charts had been cast at our births, one ordinary set, and our true, illustrious set that was hidden. The quest Jobutaten was on was for the truth about our charts and that ended in his murder."

Pharaoh's eyes narrowed. "Continue."

"An attempt was made on my life when traveling here to the Palace by a bowman. His arrow struck the back of my chair."

Pharaoh straightened in his chair. "My little Princess, this you should have told me. I will..."

"There is more, Pharaoh. It is believed that there

is a plot to take your kingship by the Amun Clergy." And the saddest news she held back – that she was born with second sight, and saw that his son would not live, nor could she include that Abu was her father.

Becataten thought it was a sad story to tell on such a beautiful day on Pharaoh's royal barge. She sighed and lowered her head, signaling the end of her tale.

Pharaoh's jaw was set firmly as he sat stony-eyed for a few moments. "Captain," Pharaoh commanded. "The fastest drum beat!"

The skipper turned and immediately implemented the order. The rowers pumped hard to the quickened beat as the Ka-em-Matt moved swiftly toward Thebes.

"I want the strongest runner from my Royal Guards," Pharaoh called then motioned for his document scribe. "I am dictating two missives, scribe fast." Pharaoh said, with the eyes of a shrewd schemer.

As all this commotion was taking place, Becataten unobtrusively lowered Beset's small and tightly rolled scroll, down and into the Mother Nile, to be swallowed by her forever.

Chapter 30

♊

Becataten observed another facet of Pharaoh just before the royal barge docked. He briskly told her that she would be sent to Hor's quarters once they moored, to wait there while a new suite would be secured, one closer to his apartments. When she asked if Lady Nagara, Dwarf Beset *and* her nanny could join her, his answer was a curt "yes". He added that in their new location, no one was to leave the suite. Palace guards would flank the entry, and their food was to come only by way of Royal attendants. Those were his last words to her as he turned to swiftly disembark.

When Pharaoh stepped off his Royal barge and onto the stone quay, his waiting administrators greeted him with expressions of concern. Because Pharaoh's vessel arrived in haste, his waitingadvisors knew that there could be cause for alarm. The Egyptian people crowded around his entourage and threw flowers for The Living God to tread upon. Pharaoh acknowledged his subjects quickly, but moved on.

296

Vizier Huy stepped forward. "You arrived with great speed, Pharaoh. Is all well?"

Pharaoh stepped onto his golden chariot and with a braod smile said, "I requested the captain to allow my rowers to show me how swiftly they could move the Ka-em-Matt. Do you not think that they did a splendid job?" But a skeptical expression darkened the Vizier's face at Pharaoh's contrived smile.

Once in the Palace, Pharaoh rushed to the bedside of his first born, a son not quite into his manhood. He knelt and touched the boy's hand, finding it cold and clammy. He spoke to him but received no response. With gentle hands Pharaoh adjusted his side lock as nearby healers intoned curative chants. Pharaoh remained near the bedside of the dying heir apparent, and wept.

The following night Pharaoh requested common street attire from his Butler in a gruff voice. As it grew dark, he exchanged royal dress for that of a flamboyant merchant. His butler showed nervousness and confusion as he struggled to hold a large silver mirror before his master. A cynical smile crossed Pharaoh's face when he tied the cords of a rough linen cape that covered his bare chest and hide kilt. Securing a dagger in a garish red sash, his image was that of a rogue. His reed sandals squeaked with each step he took as he slipped behind a hanging tapestry. Using an almost forgotten secret passage, Pharaoh disappeared down a long dark chamber. Through many turns, brushing cobwebs aside, he finally arrived outside the Palace walls. Waiting in the dark with a donkey was a tall Nubian guard. He too was garbed in unrefined dress and with concealed weapons on his person. The black man made eye contact with Pharaoh, offering a slight nod, then shadowed his king into the streets.

Pharaoh quickly traveled on the small animal to the barracks of his army, where he approached the shelter of the Lieutenant-Commander of Charity. This was his father-in-law, Queen Tiy's father. He had been a loyal appointee, and an adroit trainer of men, especially during peacetime when armies would grew lax.

The Nubian, upon the order of his Pharaoh, surreptitiously entered the commander's tent and handed him a ring. Clearly, it was Pharaoh's jewel. That the Lord of the Land was nearby was unthinkable. Next, Pharaoh entered the tent and the shocked leader of Pharaoh's Royal army dropped to one knee lowering his head. "My Lord," he said.

Pharaoh stood in a wide stance, fingering the dagger at his waist. He scanned his surroundings and in a rough tone, said, "Rise."

Tonight there was no familiarity between the two

men as there often was at Court. The Commander spoke. "Yes, my Lord Pharaoh, how may I serve you?"

"You are in charge of my Theban Army, and I consider you loyal, but I ask, is my Memphis Army as loyal? Think before you answer me, Commander." Pharaoh had little contact with the Memphis Army as it was five hundred miles north, and had been left behind when Pharaoh moved the capitol to Thebes.

"Yes, I believe your northern army is loyal, but I will summon the Memphis Head of Charity to my side immediately to add surety," answered the Commander with concern.

"And is my Admiral of the Royal Fleet here in Thebes loyal?"

"Yes, My Lord," the Commander said with conviction.

"Is anyone under your command engaged with the Royal Astrologer in any way?" Pharaoh said.

The commander paused at this unusual question before answering. "One of my generals in the field recently informed me that the Royal Astrologer sends his scribes to cast heavenly charts with no charge for the soldiers. Should I have them tortured to learn more?"

Pharaoh's eyes narrowed and grew dark. "Yes, and come to me in two Ras with any knowledge you have gained," he said in a guttural voice. He then

299

turned and exited as swiftly as he entered.

Pharaoh's Butler stood worriedly awaiting his lord's return. When Pharaoh slipped back into his chamber, the old manservant's anxiety was replaced with relief. Pharaoh's face was hard-set as he ripped the merchant attire from his body. "Bring me a sleep potion, and wake me with the return of Ra," he barked.

The Butler brewed his master a tonic of herbs with a modicum of the poppy for a proper rest, but not so much as to cause drowsiness when Pharaoh awoke. After draining his cup, Pharaoh lay down on his royal bed while three slave women sang him a lullaby.

The following Ra seemed to quickly overtake the fleeting night, and after an elaborate bath, Pharaoh emerged in a fine and cheerful demeanor. His mood always dictated the atmosphere around him, and today it evoked a cordial mood. Pharaoh had been dressed extravagantly this day in a long kilt made of a purple woven cloth, edged with a gold rope and an attached lion's tail. His large jeweled collar was strung with rows of turquoise, carnelian and gold beads. He strode to his gilded chair gleaming from Ra,s rays and the lather of his favorite morenga oil, laced with frankincense.

The assembly was gathered in a smaller chamber

with only his close friends and Court officials. Pharaoh had Abu summoned, who as usual was in a waiting chamber, and he responded immediately. Briskly walking to Pharaoh's chair, Abu paused and bowed.

Abu stood while Pharaoh smiled broadly, displaying unusual friendliness. It was common knowledge that he had just had a long romp with the young and beautiful harem twin, Princess Becataten. One old, androgynous advisor leaned into another and whispered, "Rather disgusting, don't you think, that it takes a woman to lead a man to such cheer."

Abu appeared short on sleep, as communiques from Memphis had kept him working well past Ra's leave. The last scroll read that the Amun Priests had placed the Memphis Royal Army at his command. It also revealed that Abu was to take the crown after the heir apparent's demise and during Pharaoh's long mourning period thereafter.

"Abu, come and take some sma with me. I want to talk of a date for a grand Court celebration, a time only you can forecast." Pharaoh gathered up his kilt then rose from his informal throne.

Abu straightened, "Of course, My Lord, I will plan a date immediately."

With a wide smile Pharaoh stepped toward Abu. "I am sure you will. How long have you been planning dates for me, Abu, deciphering messages, casting heavenly charts?"

Abu shuffled his feet a bit. "It has been since My Lord came to the throne, when your father died, may all the gods bless him."

"Ah yes, that is when my Palace was not yet complete, and my harem women had to endure a tent. Do you remember that time, Abu?"

"I do, My Lord," Abu replied, with a placid face.

"And how old are you now, Abu?"

"I have lived through thirty and six inundations, my Lord."

Pharaoh looked at his gold cuffs, studded with lapis lazuli, and adjusted them. Into Abu's face he spoke in a louder than usual tone. "So you were born out of my father's harem, were you not?"

"Yes, My Lord."

Disdain covered Abu's face when this matter was broached. Some of Pharaoh's Court women whispered and giggled to one another when the subject was mentioned, and a surprised Vizier raised an eyebrow. Reminding one of harem parentage, especially at Court, was rude.

"So you must carry the bloodlines of my father." Pharaoh added, "It is good to know that he lives on in his offspring, even though your mother was not an Egyptian."

The Vizier's expression grew more suspicious as Pharaoh continued. Abu acknowledged Pharaoh's comment with an uncomfortable bow. Mentioning that his mother was not an Egyptian cut deep into the expression on Abu's face, a brutal reminder that he was not a full Royal.

Pharaoh adjusted the lion-tail sash below his belly, and circled Abu, his silver sandals rasping on the limestone floor. Pharaoh smiled at Abu, baring his teeth, unlike when he smiled at a woman. "My father, Thutmose IV, was a great and formidable warrior. Do you not agree, Abu?"

The Astrologer nodded and bowed again in agreement. As Pharaoh circled him he made an effort to walk tall, expanding his chest and sucking in his beginning paunch. He was the shorter of the two men yet, Abu was less fit and sported a rotund middle.

"My father was a shrewd King," Pharaoh continued. "During his reign, he crushed a rebellion in Kush, much as I did. He also took foreign princesses into his harem. This mix of bloodlines with our Royal dynasty quelled wars. But he was best served by his shrewdness when he staved off several Court intrigues. Do you know all this history, Abu?"

Pharaoh did not usually stand and face his subjects. Today he came close and spoke to Abu head on. Abu's nostrils flared at the strong smell of Pharaoh's body oil.

"Yes, My Lord," Abu said, trying to avoid Pharaoh's eyes.

303

Pharaoh continued, "I would measure you inherited some of that cunning. Is that not true, Abu?"

"You honor me, My Lord."

Pharaoh's eyes danced as Abu's discomfort grew. The mood of the guests had changed from pleasant to strained, and those gathered became quiet and still.

Pharaoh crossed his bronze arms and flexed them against his gold armlets.

"Tell me, Abu, what would you do today if you were Pharaoh, and found an intrigue within your Royal Court?"

"Pharaoh, I am no Lord of the Land. I have no answer to that question."

In a loud voice, Pharaoh said, "Imagine it, Abu."

All eyes were on Abu for a response, "I... I would call for all my advisors and generals, speak to them and try to judge from where the plot was emanating."

"And tell me, Abu, how would you determine who was lying and who was telling the truth?"

"I... I would torture those I suspected, My Lord."

"Well done, Abu. Now return with the dates for my grand Court celebration."

Abu bowed then marched out of Pharaoh's chamber with sweat running down his body and perspiration spotting his upper lip, his dignity seriously diminished.

Chapter 31

♊

Although Pharaoh had grown to be a fair and generous king, when threatened by an enemy, he would first wound his opponent, then pursue him for sport as though he was on a lion hunt. Pharaoh had called Abu shrewd, after their father Thutmose IV, and if there was a time to employ that characteristic it was now, because Abu had just become the hunted.

After his critical meeting with Pharaoh, Abu swiftly crossed the Courtyard, pounding the sand toward his dwelling. He stormed into his apartment, roaring for Scribe Tiurek, who came running. Abu raced through his words. "We are going to sail to Memphis now. My plans have accelerated. But first I want to take a late traveler with us, and it is you who will arrange that she be on my barge. We will sail in the last of Ra's light."

The scribe stood at attention, and with a smile lowered his head in servitude.

Nearly out of breath, Abu continued, "I will dictate a scroll, which you will take to the royal apartment of Princess Becataten, accompanied by two Nubians in royal-guard dress. All you have to do is deliver the document, and leave the Nubians I send with you to handle the rest. Remember how I had you once copy the words of Pharaoh to mimic his style?"

Scribe Tiurek nodded.

"Good. Now in that form, but with more familiarity, I want you to say the following: You will address the Princess Becataten requesting that she meet with Pharaoh well before Ra leaves Egypt. Explain that he will have Royal Nubian guards waiting outside her door as her personal escort and that it is urgent she come to him immediately. Present the script for my review, but scribe quickly."

The scribe rushed toward the library chamber. Abu turned to sit at his table and in haste wrote a brief scroll to his Nubian foreman, head of his slave trade operation. His order was to launch the barge loaded with as much human cargo as it would hold for the slave markets in Memphis. One last task was to eliminate two of his scribes who knew too much of his private business.

Abu turned and was startled to see a man who sat in a dark corner on the floor.

"Oh, you have arrived. Come," Abu said in a surprised voice. The short and squat man stood and moved into the light with a modicum of arrogance. He walked with a limp and, though small in stature, he was powerfully built. His teeth had been filed down to sharp points, and resembled Abu's baboon. The diminutive man emerged from the shadows bowing with limited respect, and said, "I have thought about your offer, Royal Astrologer, and as you ordered me, I will bring you the hearts of the two scribes you wish killed. I will weigh them and expect the same weight in gold debon as my payment."

Abu appraised the lowborn. "What do I call you?"
"Call me Pygmy."
"Are you from the land of Punt?" Abu asked.
"My mother was."
"You are a rare oddity." Abu's eyes drifted from Pygmy's face to his torso and on to his loins with a lewd pause. Then, returning to business, he said, "I have thought twice about these hearts. How will I know they are from my scribes?"
Pygmy narrowed his eyes. "Tell me how you could identify these scribes and I will bring you that body part."
Abu thought a moment. "Recently, these two had their hands painted with henna designs. Bring me their hands."
"One or two hands each?"
"Since you are charging me by weight, send me one hand from each scribe."
Pigmy's upper lip curled as he paused to meet Abu's vulgar gaze. "You will have their hands late

tonight. Am I to deliver them to your barge?"

"You are, and we will be ready to sail as Ra leaves." Abu added, "Would you like to join us?"

Abu enjoyed bargaining, but it was clear the pygmy did not. Soon Abu was being looked at as a deceiver, one not to do business with.

Abu was interrupted by Tiurek to review the scroll with the message to activate his slave trading craft and crew. After approving the missive, he turned to Pygmy. "Well, will you be joining us?"

Ignoring the invitation, Pygmy said, "My brother owns a small boat, and he will sail me to your barge."

"I also want to know how you will dispose of these bodies so no trace of them remains," Abu asked.

"That is simple, Astrologer. I will leave them where Pharaoh hunts lions. But first, I request a small amount of debon."

Lying, Abu told Pygmy that his well-guarded treasure was on board, and he would be paid there.

Pygmy offered a slight nod before exiting Abu's apartment where a short man stood waiting in the shadows. "Did you get the gold?" his brother asked.

"No," replied Pygmy.

The second man stared at the closed door. "I do not like the feeling of this transaction."

"Royal Astrologer has much gold. We will get it later. Come." The pygmies hurried off to carry out their duties.

Relocated in an apartment closer to Pharaoh's quarters, Becataten, Lady Nagara, Dwarf Beset and Nanny Maja were made secure. However, there was no enclosed wall garden, and their quarters were sequestered from foot traffic. The only people allowed in were food bearers from the Royal Kitchen. They could not leave their confine, and the absence of an outdoor area left the atmosphere in the apartment cramped and warmer than usual. Outside their doors were two royal sentries in tiger skin kilts, armed with spears.

Lady Nagara fidgeted in a small chair and said, "Becataten, why are you dressing and having your face painted so early? We cannot leave the apartment."

"I just want to be ready when Pharaoh summons me. He likes me to come in haste to his chamber. We may go sailing or walk in his gardens," replied Becataten in a childlike voice.

"My dear, the plot within the Palace threatens Pharaoh's very crown. You must understand the weight of this conspiracy. Pharaoh has to learn who may be conspiring with Abu. Everyone around him is a suspect now: his advisors, his military, even his nobles could prove to be untrustworthy."

"I know, but still he may summon me. Beset, don't you think he would want me during this

309

time?" she said, restless and pouting.

"Princess, Our Great Lord has much on his mind as Lady Nagara explained, and don't forget that his son lies critically ill. This is probably not the time he would wish to invite you to his chamber," Beset said.

Lady Nagara nodded in agreement.

Maja had a frightened look on her face and although she didn't understand everything that was happening, her empathy for Becataten showed. "Taten, come and sit and I will get one of the attendants to paint your breasts with henna designs," she said.

Becataten was sulking like a spoiled child now. "No! I don't want my breast painted with henna. Pharaoh likes them as they are. He told me so. I'm his Princess now. We are no longer at the Suti Estate, Lady Nagara," she added defiantly.

The chamber was stifling with heat, Becataten's makeup was running, and when her whining words came forth, Lady Nagara and Dwarf Beset's faces both showed that they were looking at a lovesick child.

Later in the day, the sentries were having a loud discussion outside the doors of Becataten's apartment. Lady Nagara stood with concern, her ear to the door.

"Who is it?" Becataten anxiously called. "Is it

word from Pharaoh for me?"

Lady Nagara motioned for silence. "Be still, Becataten. I am trying to hear what is being said."

Beset hopped off her cot and scurried toward the door to listen at her height.

Lady Nagara whispered to Beset, "I think it is an envoy from Pharaoh with a scroll, but I'm not sure."

Becataten stood with stiff arms at her sides, her hands forming fists. "This is ridiculous. Just open the doors. If it is an envoy, he has a scroll for me, and I am being summoned."

Lady Nagara turned toward Becataten and said with authority, "We are not to open the doors from our side. Only the sentries are to open them."

Becataten stomped her foot and said, "But why is it taking so long?"

Beset spoke softly. "I think they are arguing about the authenticity of the envoy or the scroll, Taten."

"Just let me see the scroll, I will tell them if it is from Pharaoh or not," Becataten said impatiently.

She walked quickly to the entrance, knocked hard on one of the heavy cedar doors and called, "This is Princess Becataten, and if there is a scroll for me, pass it to me, and I will decide if it is from Pharaoh, or not!"

A time of quiet ensued, then one door opened with just enough room for the scroll tube to be passed through.

311

Becataten grabbed the jeweled cylinder, quickly opened the canister and unrolled the papyrus as her gold cuffs shook on her wrists. She scanned the scroll and said, "You see, he has summoned me, and where it is written that I am to join him in his chambers, red ink has been used."

Lady Nagara stood behind her, scanning the scroll as well. "Becataten, this could be a forgery. Abu is a man who has written many scrolls on Pharaoh's behalf."

"But look," added Becataten, "here is Pharaoh's personal seal."

"That too could be obtained by someone as clever as Abu," said Lady Nagara.

Becataten raised her chin and said, "Well, I do not think it is false, and I am going to see Pharaoh now!" She knew Pharaoh would want her at his side and was frustrated by these meddling women.

Lady Nagara and Beset pleaded with her not to go as she turned to Maja. "Hold the mirror for me Maja, and dab that bit of running kohl from my eyes." Maja did as she was told. Becataten adjusted her wig, admiring her reflection in the polished copper oval, then turned and briskly walked to the entrance. She banged on the door, it opened, and she was free. The Nubian envoys were quick to escort her, a little too quickly, she thought, to a secluded garden area and then into a heavily curtained chair. Was she going to meet Pharaoh in a place other than his chamber? That was not what the scroll said.

Once in the chair, she felt a dagger at her throat. A Nubian demanded silence. He reached for something out of his carrying pouch and gagged her with it. She trembled with fright when the wad of linen, treated with a poultice of the poppy, was forced into her mouth. She could smell and taste it. *I am trapped! And this man is tying me to my chair. I hear directions but can't quite make them out. I'm going to die just like Jobu. How could Pharaoh not know of this?*

She was frightened and shook uncontrollably until the drug took its course. The jogging of the litter lulled her thoughts as the drug blurred her senses. In her clouding mind she could hear Beset saying, *stay calm*. Soon her eyelids fluttered and she felt death coming. *Is this death or is it the potion?* Vaguely she heard more instructions being called to the chair bearers, something about a quay, then nothing more.

Chapter 32

♊

The large litter that Abu ordered had arrived at his apartment. With a chair at the center, and eight robust runners, it abruptly stopped and hit the ground for boarding. Abu stepped from his domicile, snapped his fingers ordering his household attendants to quickly load his treasure chest, and a basket of food. He rushed to the conveyance, with Butler Farafar and Huni following. Abu quickly settled himself, ordered Farafar and Huni to sit, and shooed Dwarf Heby away. "Run at full speed," he commanded the bearers, directing them to a certain quayside. Sitting in the wicker seat, his expression was determined. His head jutted forward as he gripped the arms of the chair. Butler Farafar tugged on Huni's tether as the baboon tried to climb onto Abu.

A confused household staff was left behind. Displaced Heby roamed around, wringing his hands as he paced the floors. Then he stopped and rushed out the door.

Abu's litter moved swiftly to their location, and a

rare smile crossed Abu's face when his giant slave-trading raft, crowded with human cargo, came into view. A captain and several pole-men stood waiting to cast off.

The huge barge was made of bound papyrus reeds that were lashed together resembling logs. The tree-sized logs were attached to one another with thick leather straps to create a platform. The lashings and dried stalks swelled, and with ease the hefty foundation floated the large craft.

Looking around in the muted light and seeing no one of consequence, Abu breathed a heavy sigh as he stroked his treasure chest beneath him on the litter. He ordered it taken on board.

Rolling his heavy body off the litter, Abu walked toward the raft as river currents, tamed from their rapids in Kush, rippled across the Nile. Two Nubian traders came forward and whipped at the crowded humanity to forge a path for Abu. He followed his chest to his chair located at midship. Here, human cargo surrounded him as the last light of day was robbed by the night. Not only was he running from Pharaoh's wrath, but he was also transporting runaway Nubians he had long ago promised freedom. They appeared edgy and frightened. He planned to use many of them as attendants in his new life in Memphis, knowing that he could buy their loyalty and offer them a measure of freedom.

The liveliness of the boat was limited to restless

traders surveying their bound slaves for market. Huni, Abu's baboon, squealed and bared his teeth at the strangers. Abu sat on his chair and took a wet linen cloth from his butler to wipe Huni's face and hands. After feeding him a bunch of grapes, he handed him off to his butler. Attendants drew curtains around Abu's chair.

But no order was given for the barge to move. The night grew still as the gentle tide of the river pushed the raft against the quay, an agitating reminder that they were still docked. The captain was told they would cast off directly after a specific package was delivered, and not until then. Abu asked if a pygmy had arrived. The captain said he had not.

With an impatient scowl, Abu turned to glare out his curtained window where he saw in the low rising moon a rider come into view and halt his horse at the river's edge. An expression of eagerness lit Abu's face. With ease, the man lifted a goatskin roll from the front of his saddle to his shoulder. Next he urged his mount into the water to swim toward the barge. The unwilling animal reluctantly entered the Nile. Once the two were close to the barge, several Nubians dove off the raft to retrieve the horseman's load. Skillfully, the roll of animal skin was handed off to several Nubians who were treading water. Together, they deftly held the well-bound bundle above their heads then paddled in unison toward

316

the barge. The rider turned his mount and the horse willingly swam for the Nile's shore. The rolled cargo, hauled on the shoulders of a muscular Nubian, was carried to Abu's curtained platform and placed at his feet.

He shouted to the captain, "Sail, now!"

Heby panicked when he realized there was no time to reach Beset and tell her what Abu was about to do. He rushed to the closest apartment he could think of and knocked hard on the door.

The Royal Gardener opened his door with surprise. "What is it, Dwarf Heby? You seem greatly disturbed," a weary Sennejem said.

"Please Royal Gardener, help. I heard Abu giving orders to abduct Becataten, and sail to Memphis tonight on his barge. He is even killing off his scribes, and..."

"Slow down, Heby, this sounds serious. Are you sure of your facts?"

"Yes, I am. I beg that you get news about this to Dwarf Beset as fast as possible. My small legs cannot get me there in time." That awakened Sennejem's senses, and, setting his jaw, he grabbed his wig and flew out the door.

Sennejem hurriedly thanked Dwarf Heby as he ran to the nearest litter, commanding the runner to carry him to the Chancellor's office. Once there, the Royal Gardener pushed through the guards, yelling for them to let him in and pounded on the door. "Chancellor, let me in, it is a life and death matter I must speak to you."

The sentries and office scribes stood in shock at the raucous display of a man who had always been polite and courteous. "Royal Gardener, we cannot grant you entry. The Chancellor has just returned from a long trip and has retired," explained an official as concerned guards stood at the ready due to Sennejem's furor.

"Not until I speak with him," insisted the Gardener.

Sennejem's quick appraisal of the facts urged the Chancellor from his bed.

Awakened to a loud conversation between Chancellor Ptahmose and his Butler, Pharaoh sat up in bed.

"Enter, Chancellor Ptahmose," said Pharaoh, sensing more than a common disagreement between his Butler and his Chancellor.

The Chancellor approached and bowed, deeper than usual. "I have grave news... the Royal Astrologer plots against the throne, and has apparently abducted the Princess Becataten. It is believed that they are on a slave-trading barge moving toward Memphis where Abu is in command and well-guarded."

Pharaoh sat up rigid, as his cat Lady Mui flew

318

from his bed. "Where did you learn this?"

"The Royal Gardener revealed to me that Abu leads a plot to overthrow the crown, and I investigated further to learn that the Princess is absent from her apartment."

As the Butler hastened to light some nearby candles, the glow that lit Pharaoh's face revealed a mask of rage. Naked proof now exposed Abu. Slowly Pharaoh turned to the Chancellor and spoke in a low growl. "Then you have questioned Abu's household attendants?"

"We have, My Lord."

"And the guards posted at the Princess' doors?"

The chancellor nervously answered. "Yes, My Lord. They said Nubians posing as Royal Guards escorted the Princess to a chair. A false scroll invited her to your chambers, but she was taken elsewhere."

"Kill the posted guards."

"Yes, My Lord."

"Has Abu relatives or loved ones that you know of in Thebes?"

"None, My Lord."

"How many people does the barge carry?"

"It is crowded, we estimate one hundred."

"Where are they getting their food?"

"They have a brassier on the after deck and plan to buy the catch from boats of local fisherman."

Pharaoh stood, quickly slipped into the robe his

Butler held and began to pace. "Assemble a few modest fishing boats. In each boat, I want one seasoned fisherman and two of my finest royal sailors, disguised as fishermen."

"Yes, My Lord, we have Royal Naval boats standing by." The Chancellor exhibited adroit answers to every question, keeping pace with his King.

Pharaoh turned to the Chancellor erupting with rage. "I don't want royal ships anywhere in sight. Instruct my sailors to board the barge, I repeat, from fishing boats, and when most passengers are asleep, take Abu prisoner! The men who capture Abu will have enough gold debon to spend until they die."

Pharaoh stopped pacing. "The Princess is to be returned unharmed, if it is not too late." More rapidly he added, "Instruct Viceroy Merymose to have my Nubian sailors fall back. And advise my Royal Navy, who are ahead of the barge, to move further away. I want Abu to think he has been successful and outwitting the mastery of his Pharaoh."

"My Lord, does the Viceroy and the Royal Navy know of this?"

"Yes," Pharaoh said, with cunning, "They each received missives from me when I was sailing on the Ka-em-Matt, and first learned of this plot."

Pharaoh looked at his Chancellor with a

venomous glare, and through clenched teeth hissed, "See that Abu is taken alive."

The Chancellor nodded, bowed and swiftly backed from Pharaoh's chamber. He prepared scrolls immediately and exactly to Pharaoh's specifications, wondering how his King knew of this conspiracy.

Chapter 33

♊

With shaking hands, Abu unleashed the goatskin roll placed at his sandaled feet. He cut the twine that bound the roll, and out tumbled a petite woman in fine linen, golden cuffs, anklets and earrings. Sleepily she looked back at him, her wig at her feet. His mouth dropped open, his head jerking back as though he was looking at a spirit. His face took on dumbness. "You are Princess Becataten?" he asked wide-eyed.

Bound and gagged, Becataten struggled to sit up as she reeled from being drugged. Still feeling the effects from the poppy, she looked at Abu with confusion. Struggling against the bindings at her hands and trying to spit out her gag, she was helpless. She now remembered being abducted at dagger point by the Nubian. With some composure, and as much fortitude as she could muster, she tried to mask her fear and shock. *I guess he isn't going to kill me. He had his chance.* But when Abu pulled a dagger from his sash, she decided she was wrong and held her breath.

Abu moved toward her and cut her restraints. He nicked her wrist, and in doing so immediately yelled, "An attendant!" A man in a loincloth appeared. "Bring me a cloth to tend this cut," Abu said, looking regretful for having drawn her blood. With more care he freed her hands. She pulled the gag from her mouth, and rubbing her bloody wrist, glared at him. He seemed confounded when he stared into her eyes, even weakened by her beauty. He looked uncertain upon seeing her, and Becataten felt uncomfortable at the way he stared, as if he recognized her. Returnng to the present, Abu adjusting himself in his chair and loudly cleared his throat. With a forced demeanor he sneered, "So I have Pharaoh's prize, or at least his current one."

Becataten couldn't find words, and she was beginning to shake.

"Are you mute, whore?" he asked.

The rude comment caused her to find her tongue, "I am neither mute nor a whore, Royal Astrologer," Becataten said, stretching her back as an attendant bandaged her cut wrist.

Sitting back against cushions of leopard hide and collecting himself, Abu gave her his full appraisal. She sat opposite him, cross-legged, at his feet. They evaluated one another, each not revealing their emotions. She tried to view him as her father but could not, even though it pained her to see a strong resemblance of Jobu in him.

323

He spoke with regained sureness, "You are a beauty in face and body, Princess." Continuing with less conviction he added, "You will bring me much gold debon on the slave platform."

Becataten was trying to gain strength to speak when Abu clapped his hands for an attendant. His baboon stuck his head between the curtains. "No, Huni, not you," he snapped, as his butler yanked the animal away. Abu turned to Becataten and said, "If you are quiet you may stay on my platform. If not you sleep on deck with the slaves."

As the influence of the poppy began to wear away, she found her tongue and asked, "Why have you brought me on board this craft, and where are we going?"

Abu adjusted his seat to sit taller. "You are my bargaining power, Harem Princess. Pharaoh will think twice about halting my sail to Memphis with your life in my hands."

She shook her head to gain clarity. "Why are you taking me to Memphis?" Becataten asked.

"No more questions."

She wanted to keep him talking and calculated he might listen to her if she began a dialogue. "You know that I am not Pharaoh's daughter."

Abu sneered at her and with a mock laugh said, "Are you saying I abducted the wrong Princess?"

"No, I am saying I am *not* Pharaoh's daughter."

Abu snickered. "You do not appear to be stupid,

Princess Becataten, so why do you speak with a double tongue?"

"It is true I am a harem child, as were you."

This comment made Abu stiffen. Becataten saw anger in his eyes. *Be calm,* she thought, *as Beset always advised.* She took a deep breath. "My mother was a Mitanni Princess that Pharaoh took to his bed chamber but once. Her name was Princess Attah."

Abu crossed his arms and narrowed his eyes.

"In childbirth, my mother told my Nanny Maja never to speak of the lover she took in the harem tent. She asked Maja to raise us as Pharaoh's twins and never reveal our true father."

Abu remained still, his breathing shallow and his jaw slackened. Without expression, in measured tones, he spoke in a voice lacking his earlier authority. "If this is a story of fantasy to persuade me to release you, it is a very poor one. And what do you know of a harem tent, so many inundations ago? I am the one who knows of that tent. It was my staff who inventoried the women in that place."

"Then you know that my mother's last words were true, and that her lover is the father of her children." Becataten said, with anger in her eyes.

"But you admit that this Princess Attah went to Pharaoh's bed," countered Abu.

"My Nanny said that my mother told her that Pharaoh was but a boy. That he could not yet properly couple with his harem women, even though he invited them to his chamber. And she also said her lover asked for my mother in marriage, but Pharaoh said his women were scarce and no one was allowed to leave the harem."

Speaking almost inaudibly, Abu's voice trailed off. "*Not one woman was allowed...*" He sat back in his chair, reassessing Becataten with slit eyes. His chest heaved for air, and with his exhale, he seemed to grow smaller.

Becataten had hit a cord and knew it, and some of her fear waned. She searched Abu's face and thought he must now see that he fathered her and Jobu.

Abu's reply was cautious. "Let us say this fantasy you construed is true. Then who is your true father?"

Becataten began to say things she wished she never had to say, but her words soon flowed with the same currency as the Nile.

"My father is the man who ordered my Nanny Maja poisoned. He is the man who arranged that my loving twin, and his own son, Prince Jobutaten, killed. He is the man who ordered my death, using an assassin whose arrow barely missed me. I can only ask the gods if he knew that he had tried to kill his children."

Abu turned to look away from her. His face had turned mottled and grey in the low flame light.

Collecting himself, he struggled to return to a hardened demeanor. "You tell a good mystical tale, Princess. Too bad you cannot prove it." Abu's upper lip filled with sweat.

She saw his left eye wobble, and pain welled up inside her as Jobu came to her mind. For a moment she wanted to lash out at Abu. Instead sadness consumed her.

A commotion arose on the afterdeck, and Abu turned willingly toward it. He picked up a short whip, cut from the tail of a zebra, and walked through the reek of humanity across the crowded deck, sharply hitting anyone in his way with it. Male slaves were in loincloths, their upper arms behind them, bound with straps just above the elbows. Women were not secured as they were to be sold in pristine condition. Abu walked nearer the commotion. His baboon followed close behind, stretching his tether, making it difficult for Abu's aged butler to keep Huni in tow. On deck, a woman was crying hysterically about wanting to go home to her tribe in Kush. She prostrated herself when Abu approached, grabbing at his ankles and pleading with him to return her. He glared at her then whipped at her backside. The bound men groaned and struggled against their bindings. Huni screeched and danced on his leash, further terrorizing the captives. Then Abu turned and whipped his baboon into silence, and when he thought the animal might turn on him, he ordered fruit thrown to him by the frightened-looking butler.

As soon as Abu left her, Becataten clutched herself to find some comfort. In Abu's absence a familiar slave trader's head poked into the curtained platform where Becataten was sitting on the floor. "Princess, Princess, remember me?" he whispered.

It was the trader at the Suti Estate that she had asked to inform her about intimacy. Her eyes brightened, "I remember you well," she answered weakly.

"You, Princess, are in trouble. I will help. I will swim to the Palace shore to tell Pharaoh that you are a captive of this cruel hippopotamus."

"No. Pharaoh knows by now. Of that I am sure. But please don't leave my side. You are my only friend."

He entered the curtained chamber and crouched beside her and said, "There is talk that Abu is going to sell you like a common slave when we get to Memphis."

"I don't think that is his plan anymore." Becataten prayed he would not get rid of her in such a savage manner.

The Slave Trader pulled his dagger from its scabbard and handed it to her. "Take this for your protection, Princess, and do not trust him. He is a forked tongue."

Becataten slid the dagger under her as the trader slipped away, but he remained close outside the curtain and whispered what was happening on deck to her until Abu came back. When Abu returned to his platform lathered with sweat, she thought he looked older and not as in charge as before.

He plopped into his chair where he sat dripping. "Did you hear that, Princess? Abu means to have discipline on this barge, discipline among his slaves and in life."

She was horrified by the sounds of a poor sobbing woman she knew he had beaten. His butler arrived with a fresh kilt to replace the soiled one, and with no regard for her presence, he changed before her. Then she saw it, the birthmark on his left buttock just like her own.

Abu saw horror and disgust in Becataten's face. "I don't think you want to try and claim me as your long-lost father any longer, do you Princess?" he said wiping sweat from his body. "Or are you still making up magical stories about me?" he said, breathing hard, his power renewed.

Princess Becataten felt she had nothing to lose now. She stood, turned her back to him and lifted her shift to show the replica of his birthmark on her. "You are my father!"

He produced a false laugh, still out of breath. "Well, you are so interested in making me your father, Becataten, you have given me an idea. I will not sell you. What I will do is proclaim you my Royal Daughter and Queen when I am Pharaoh. You will not go to the slave market. You are going to serve a larger purpose than I had originally planned, Princess Becataten of the harem. Together we will return from Memphis, back to Thebes, with an army. I will rightfully take the crown from my half-brother Amenhotep III, and reestablish God Amun supreme. History and the Memphis clergy will praise us both." Pausing to take a breath he added with a strong voice, "And it was the Amun clergy who ordered Prince Jobutaten's death and yours, not me!"

Abu then instructed his butler to bring him pickled meats, cheese and flatbread. He looked exhausted, and with a tight throat she realized she could no long engage him in conversation. Ignoring Becataten, he gorged himself on food and beer. Sated and drowsy, Abu drifted into sleep as the pole men moved the barge toward Memphis on the black, silent Nile.

Becataten knew Abu's loud snoring signaled her chance to use the slave trader's knife. She reached for the dagger, feeling her courage diminishing, but stood to bury the knife in Abu. With a shaking movement, she took long steps toward him and struck her toes hard on his metal treasure chest. She winced at the pain and that woke Abu. He

330

looked up, at first confused, then his eyes grew large, and he reached for her wrist and squeezed. He held it so hard she dropped the knife. But large black hands clamped Abu's arms, forcing them behind him. It was a Royal Nubian sailor who motioned for Becataten to leave the platform with escorts. Given the order, Pharaoh's soldiers moved to swarm the raft. The Royal Navy escorted Abu from his slave barge with bound arms. Huni jumped and screeched while the weary butler tried to restrain him.

Chapter 34

♊

A poised Pharaoh stood at the Nile's edge in his golden chariot that glistened under a half moon. Behind him was a force of Royal Infantry standing as densely as papyrus stalks. Torches lit the king's entourage.

As Abu was presented before Pharaoh, Becataten saw a great vengeance in the King's face as he looked down on his half-brother, and she felt a great vindictiveness coming. When her eyes met Pharaohs, she read no message in them. She could see him for the Ruling God he truly was.

A heavily veiled chair awaited Becataten. She had hoped Pharaoh would have stepped off his chariot to meet her. But he did not. Before she could lament further, her chair bearers were off at a fast jog to return her to the Palace. Still shaking, she curled up into the position of an unborn as her transport traveled a rough road to safety. Her thoughts drifted. Did Pharaoh now know Abu was her father? Certainly he would plan an even more torturous fate for him, if he did. When she began to count the people who knew of her real parentage, she realized how many there were. Jobu, Nanny Maja, Dwarf Beset, Architects Suti and Hor, maybe even the Royal Gardener, and of course, the Heka Priest. Would any of them tell Pharaoh? Her thoughts slowed and her shaking eased as sleep began to overtake her.

When she awoke, the three women in her life were at her side. Nanny Maja was holding her hand. Dwarf Beset lay at her feet as she had when Taten was a child. Lady Nagara sat erect on a bench next to her bed. Becataten smiled when she saw them.

Beset squealed, "The gods, bless the gods you are back safe and with us. We will celebrate with beer and food. What do you want to eat, Taten?"

Becataten smiled at Beset, who forever wanted to consume food to celebrate happy occasions or as a comfort against sad times. Maja stood and kissed her forehead, her smile saying all the words she could not. How old Maja's face had become. Her bent posture and sagging eyelid seemed more prevalent than ever from the poisoning long ago.

Lady Nagara looked exactly the same. "Are you well, Becataten? Did that vile beast harm you?"

Becataten sat up. "Let me hold you all. I thought I would never see you again. It means so much to be with you. How long have I slept?" A vague memory of being led in from the chair and put to bed by attendants and her doting family came back to her.

333

"A long time, and I hope you are rested," said Lady Nagara. "Pharaoh has called for your presence as soon as you feel well enough. You must bathe, dress and be taken to Court."

"Do you know why he wants me at Court?"

"Yes," Lady Nagara frowned. "Pharaoh has tortured Abu, and before he dies, he wants him to prostrate before you and beg your forgiveness."

Becataten felt miserable and distraught. "But I do not want that."

"It is Pharaoh's request, Becataten. As a Crown Princess, you must assume this responsibility. You are to receive the Royal Astrologer as he begs for your pardon. And you are not to forgive him."

Becataten's face twisted. "But it is all such a pretense."

Poised on her bench, Lady Nagara's posture leaned forward with emphasis. "Pretense or not, you are expected to play the role of a Princess, Pharaoh's Royal Princess! Did it occur to you that it is an honor to be called to Court for the condemned to beg your forgiveness?"

"It is just so, so brutal."

"Becataten, you are sounding like the unpolished child Suti delivered me seasons ago."

Beset sat up on her knees at the end of Becataten's cot. "May I speak, Lady Nagara?"

Lady Nagara nodded.

"Taten, you and Abu are both Royals, and that

is why you have been chosen." She locked eyes with Becataten as if to say, *stop talking about this in Lady Nagara's presence or it will be revealed that Abu is your father.* "He and Pharaoh have the same father, Thutmose IV. That means Pharaoh and Abu are half-brothers. And perhaps that is why Abu wanted the crown so much." She threw Becataten another knowing look.

Lady Nagara nodded. "Well said, Beset. Now, does that help you to better understand your Royal status, Becataten?"

"But honor or not, I don't want to see him tortured."

Impatient, Lady Nagara's indignance began to show. "Becataten, he tried to overthrow the Crown! He was rightly punished. Pharaoh, Abu, Suti and Hor all grew up together. Abu was jealous of them all because he was the only one who didn't have an Egyptian mother. My mother was an Egyptian, and I could have become Queen if chosen. But it wasn't to be. Instead I became Lady Nagara. Yet I didn't try and overthrow the Crown because I wasn't chosen."

"That is probably why Pharaoh didn't come to me when I was rescued, because I do not have an Egyptian mother, and he never really saw me as his Queen," Becataten said.

Lady Nagara looked taken aback. "My dear, few women are ever considered by Pharaoh to become his Queen, especially when he has such a strong first wife like Queen Tiy."

"But she has given him but one child."

"She has given the Pharaoh two sons, sadly one lies gravely ill clinging to life. The other we know little of."

"And didn't you say that her parents were of a noble class, not Royals."

"Well, yes that is true, but of course, she had an Egyptian mother," Lady Nagara said.

Becataten fidgeted in her bed. "I have read all about the Royalty lineages in the library, and I still don't understand the rules."

"What you don't understand, Becataten, is that Pharaoh makes the rules and amends them as he chooses. Now ready yourself."

Becataten sighed and shakily stood as attendants jumped forward to create the stunning beauty that Pharaoh was expecting.

After a brief wait at the doors of Pharaoh's receiving chamber, Becataten was announced. She walked in with dignity in a pristine linen dress wearing a necklace of polished emeralds that Pharaoh had given her. Following her, in order of status, walked Lady Nagara, then Dwarf Beset. Nanny Maja had asked to be excused, not realizing she hadn't been invited at all.

Entering Pharaoh's formal receiving chamber,

Becataten wondered as she passed a brazier with a forger stoking his fire, and on such a hot day. They were escorted to stand to the right of Pharaoh. Becataten felt some comfort when she saw Suti and Hor along with the Heka Priest standing there too. Also in attendance were Pharaoh's Vizier and Chancellor. *Why is Viceroy Merymose here?* Sennejem also stood among the group. She would just have to see what came next. It was hard not to expect the worst. The air in the chamber grew rigid with protocol.

Pharaoh, seated on his golden throne, wore his most formal crown. His crook and flail he held across his chest. The crook reminded his subjects that he was a benevolent ruler and shepherd of his people, while his flail spoke of thrashing grain or the disobedient. Today it was clear that his flail would speak. He, his Chancellor, and Vizier had never looked so serious.

When everyone was settled, a Royal Nubian Guard banged a staff on the stone floor, and the chamber doors opened. Two Nubian guards aided Abu into the room, his feet dragging, his head downcast, marred with dark and dried blood from torture. Becataten felt him to be a heartbreaking sight. Her stance faltered at the sight of his mutilated body. The Heka Priest moved to her side and Beset squeezed her hand. Lady Nagara stood erect as a column.

337

Pharaoh bellowed in a voice she had never heard him use. "You are here for one reason, Abu. Do you understand that reason?" Abu's head bobbed slightly. "We are waiting," Pharaoh called.

With a face rutted with pain, Abu raised his head to Pharaoh's voice and spoke inaudibly.

"Speak louder," called Pharaoh showing impatience, "And address your statement to Princess Becataten!"

In a raw whisper, Abu said, "I beg your forgiveness for abducting you, Princess Becataten."

Becataten clutched at her heart, feeling Abu's pain. She had never seen someone in such agony, and she wanted to run from the horror of it.

Lady Nagara turned to look directly into Becataten's eyes. She shook her head ever so slightly, careful not to rattle her wig beads, making it clear that Becataten's forgiveness was not to be offered.

Becataten looked hard at this almost unrecognizable man in a loincloth, sullied with blood and filth. She guessed they had castrated him and could see they done something to his fingers and toes, as they were raw and bloodied too. Her eyes welled with tears. Pharaoh could have just ended his life, not tortured him with such cruelty. The sight was too much for her to bear.

Why has death always danced about me? My mother died at my birth. My loving twin was

338

murdered before he became a man. And my true father awaits Pharaoh's edict to slay him. This killing all seems endless.

Her eyes darted about the audience for help, but she knew there was none. Her checks ran with tears. She decided she would say what was in her heart and deliver it like the Princess Beset convinced her she was.

Addressing Abu she said, "I forgive you, Royal Astrologer."

Abu strained to raise his head and catch her gaze. She thought she saw gratitude in his pained stare. Then he fell unconscious.

Pharaoh, without moving his head, said, "Are you sure you wish to forgive the traitorous and evil acts this man has perpetrated on you and Your King? In a matter such as this, forgiveness is reserved only for a relative."

Lady Nagara's eyes grew wide as she glared long and hard at Becataten. Nodding affirmatively, Becataten's checks streamed with kohl. Then she realized that shaking her head would not do, and she had to say the words again.

Pharaoh straightened on his throne. "Becataten has offered her forgiveness. I have not. Put out his eyes and imprison him until I deem his fate."

The man standing at the brazier came forward with two pokers, both glowing red. He deftly seared one eye, then the other, out of Abu's head.

Becataten threw herself into the arms of the Heka Priest to hide from the horror. She covered her ears to stop Abu's piteous howls as they bellowed through the Palace colonnades. A profound silence followed Abu's collapse. What lingered were wisps of smoke that bore the stench of burnt human flesh. Everyone in the chamber averted their eyes from the gore and covered their nose from the odor, except Pharaoh.

To the relief of all, Abu was hauled away amid his own screams of agony and the dismissal of Pharaoh's audience followed, save for Becataten and the Viceroy. A motion from Pharaoh brought his butler who stepped forward and took from him his formal regalia.

Then as if nothing horrific had just taken place, Pharaoh turned to the Viceroy and smiled. "I gift you, Merymose, my most able Viceroy and overseer of Kush, Princess Becataten as your wife."

Becataten fainted.

Chapter 35

♊

Becataten's apartment was buzzing with packing and planning for her new life with Viceroy Merymose in Kush. Lady Nagara had ordered her a sumptuous new wardrobe and offered incessant advice about her role and responsibilities as the wife of Pharaoh's most important overseer. And, for the first time, Becataten felt that Lady Nagara cared for her well beyond the role of a mentor. Yet Becataten remained apathetic about her new life, lounging away her days in a melancholy mood.

Beset sat at the foot of Bataten's cot. "Becataten you must eat something. You are shrinking. Look how lose your armlets and bracelets are! If you won't take food, drink some of Pharaoh's sma. There are so many good years to choose from! Or take beer, from Pharaoh's kitchen. It is much better than what we used to drink."

Becataten smiled as sweet Beset was again offering comfort through food, and as usual, she was trying to be kind. Sma, Becataten thought, is what she longed to be drinking right now, but with

341

Pharaoh. She wanted to see him, feel him next to her and talk to him.

When Lady Nagara overheard their conversation, she walked to Becataten's side. "Dwarf Beset is right. You are withering away. Food is what you need. And, Becataten, you must become interested in this new position Pharaoh bestowed upon you. It is the beginning of a grand new life and carries much prestige. What is the matter with you? You have been moping about for days. Is it that you don't like the Viceroy?"

"No, he is very polite and treats me well. I just..." her voice trailed off.

Lady Nagara said, "You just, what?"

Becataten sat on her cot, staring into her jewelry chest, fondling all the gold items Pharaoh had given her: golden armlet, bracelets, necklaces and rings.

Becataten whined her words, "It is just that I never got to speak with Pharaoh about my, my abduction - no farewell, not even an audience."

She couldn't reveal that she had fallen in love with Pharaoh just as Lady Nagara had years earlier. Never mind that he had a Royal Queen and was planning on marrying another. *Oh if he would only find a special place for me where I could always be in his life.* She didn't need to be the Viceroy's Lady. She would be satisfied just being a concubine of Pharaoh's.

Lady Nagara looked at her with a critical eye and

spoke sharply. "Becataten, listen to me. You had your days with Pharaoh, and they are over. He has passed you on to the Viceroy, and given you a position of great status. You remember I once told you not to become too interested in running an estate, as that would never be your lot in life. I was wrong. You will be mistress of the largest estate in the land, and the richest. Pharaoh and the Viceroy are very similar in disposition, and the Viceroy is a good man. Not to mention, the Gods have placed all of Egypt's gold in Kush in his command."

With the look of a spoiled child, Becataten shrugged her shoulders.

Lady Nagara pulled a stool up to her cot and said, "Becataten, look at me."

Becataten raised her teary eyes.

Speaking softly, she said, "You have been through so much: the loss of your twin, an attack on your life, an abduction and that horrific brutality in Pharaoh's chamber, then abruptly given to another in marriage. I know you feel the loss of Pharaoh. You came to love Pharaoh, and that is your past, Becataten, not your future. Forget that time and be proud and grateful of the position he has bestowed upon you."

Becataten began to sob.

With empathy Lady Nagara said, "My dear, you will never share his bed again. I know it is a shock, and I know he let you go without ceremony, but that is his way." She handed her a linen cloth, and Becataten blew her nose so loudly the servants looked up from their packing detail.

"I hope you will not duplicate that nose-honking when you are married to the Viceroy. You sound like a goose under the knife."

The young girl in Becataten began to giggle. Lady Nagara joined her and the two women had a good laugh, then hugged one another. It was the first time the two had embraced.

A firm knock at the door interrupted them. They were told the Viceroy had come to call.

The scramble to touch up Becataten's facial paint and choose a presentable shift with the proper jewelry and wig was quickly attended. When Becataten graciously greeted the Viceroy it was with a dignity she knew would make Lady Nagara proud.

As the Viceroy stood at the portal of their apartment, she calmly walked toward him with a demure smile. He offered her one red rose, and a tear rolled down Lady Nagara's cheek.

They left the apartment, hands entwined, to stroll through a large walled garden. The Viceroy asked her if all her needs were met for their trip to Kush. She assured him they were and thanked him for his many gifts of flowers, incense and scrolls of poetry. He led her to a stone bench near a small lotus pool. Pomegranate trees shaded the area where they sat. The Viceroy reached up and picked a piece of fruit as a soft breeze moved through the foliage.

He looked straight ahead and said, "Becataten, I know you must think Pharaoh's decision for you to be my wife, unexpected. He did not take into consideration your recent abduction and the torture you had just witnessed. He is not always a tactful man when making business decisions."

Becataten looked down at her golden sandals and felt like weeping. Softly she said, "So you see our marriage as a business decision, My Lord."

"Yes, I do, Becataten. But speaking for myself, I plan to make it much more than that if you will let me. And, please do not call me Lord."

She looked up into his face and saw honest eyes that affirmed his words. "Why do you think Pharaoh made a business decision by offering me to you as your wife?"

The Viceroy took a deep breath and spoke with care. Slowly he began, "I believe he thinks that you would govern with me as a proper Royal. Pharaoh sees you as I do: a bright and regal woman who could share in many of my responsibilities, and understand my status, much as Lady Nagara does as wife to Architect Suti."

Silence passed between them as she took in his words.

"I have a grown child who is being educated in Thebes. You may have seen us at Court. He is from

345

an Egyptian wife who died in childbirth."

Becataten nodded respectfully. But she couldn't help adding, "I have heard that you have Nubian wives."

He turned and looked into her eyes and said, "I do, but I will have no need of them if you and I..." his voice trailed off.

What did he mean, that this was a trial period - or - that I could become his only love interest? "I think I would like to know more about your Nubian wives."

He looked uneasy. "There isn't much to know – just that a man grows lonely in a place far away from his own kind."

"What do you mean by that?

"Becataten," he said with eyes straight ahead while tossing the pomegranate from one hand to the other. "From the time you came to Kush with Pharaoh, and the few times I encountered you at Court, I found you beautiful and fascinating."

"Why did you not speak to me about this before, Viceroy?"

"One does not speak to Pharaoh's women about such things, Becataten"

Becataten turned to him and said, "But I did not know I fascinated you."

"You must understand I had to wait until you and Pharaoh no longer..." his words trailed. "And then when Pharaoh presented you to me, I was overjoyed."

She reached for his hand, gathering strength from his heartfelt words and said, "I promise to be a proper Princess and loyal wife to the Viceroy of Kush." Then she gave him an alluring look and added, "And I look forward to replacing your Nubian wives."

He tossed the fruit aside, stood and reached for her, bringing her into his arms. "You will not regret being my wife, Becataten," he whispered into her ear.

She felt the tensions and formalities of their relationship beginning to dissolve and his warm strength envelope her with his arms.

Walking back to her apartment with him, she noted that he did resemble Pharaoh as Lady Nagara had said, but he was slightly taller. His eyes were not a cool blue like Pharaoh's but a rich brown - the color of carnelian stones. Behind his serious demeanor, she had detected warmth that he had previously kept hidden. His speech was low and soft. She observed that with that voice, his orders were acted upon quickly.

As they arrived at the portal to her apartment, he took her hands in his. "Princess, are you sure there is nothing I can do for you before we sail?"

"There is one thing."

"Anything," he replied.

Becataten made a softly spoken appeal to the Viceroy. It was a bold request and she knew it. She saw a disturbing look cross his face, but he agreed.

"I must leave you now, Princess. My crew awaits my final instructions. As you know, we sail when Ra returns."

"Oh, one last request, Viceroy?"

He frowned with a puzzled look.

"Visit me in my apartment after Ra leaves us, and we will celebrate the beginning of our new lives together."

The Viceroy's face brightened. He moved closer to her and said, "I have a better idea. I will send for you when Ra leaves, and we will celebrate in privacy on my barge."

Becataten blushed and smiled her assent, and was surprised to find that she was looking forward to it.

Controlling her excitement, Lady Nagara dressed Becataten in a seductive gown for her evening meeting with the Viceroy. She motioned to Maja for a long piece of fine linen which she wrapped Becataten in, tightening it at her waist with a hammered gold belt. It fell to Becataten's ankles and had a slit to her hip. Two narrow straps of woven gold were attached to the skirt. Lady Nagara placed them over her shoulders, just covering the nipples of her breasts. Becataten was surprised how sensual Lady Nagara had made her look and how much she enjoyed fussing over her. After the painter applied

348

her facial paint, Lady Nagara asked that no gold dust be used, but to apply extra green malachite to accentuate the color of her eyes, and not to line them too heavy with kohl. Also, she suggested she go to the Viceroy without shoes, for on board a ship that was appropriate. Becataten's wig glistened bobbing with gold and turquoise beads. Jewelry was reserved for her ankles and upper arms. As the Viceroy had handed Becataten a single rose earlier, Lady Nagara guessed it was his favorite scent and choose it for Becataten's body oil. She reached for the finest cloak she owned, one Suti had brought to her years earlier, and draped it on Becataten. The luminous wrap woven of gold and silver threads engulfed Becataten and gave a regal look.

Dwarf Beset and Nanny Maja watched as Becataten's tantalizing new look came into form. Becataten saw them smiling and whispering.

"She dresses her like a doll," Maja whispered.

"She dresses her like she would like to be dressed," Beset whispered back.

Becataten smiled, her heart filling with love for them both.

Standing back to take a last look, Lady Nagara said, "The viceroy will make love to you tonight like you have never been loved before."

Becataten looked at Lady Nagara, and almost spoke the words. *How does she know that?*

It was an ordinary palanquin that came to

transport her to the Viceroy's boat, but manned by his private crew and spread with thousands of rose pedals. Lady Nagara nodded her approval. Four Nubian crewmembers carried the conveyance down colonnades, through a large garden and beyond to a stone quay. She arrived at the Viceroy's ship as Ra was descending. There stood the Viceroy patiently waiting for her like a sentry, at the bottom of the boarding plank to his vessel.

Pharaoh never appeared to be waiting for me when I arrived in his chamber. The litter stopped and she began to step off when the Viceroy, quick to arrive at her side, swept her up into his arms like a kitten. He carried her down the plank onto his vessel where a square compartment had been created using yards of red silk. Two crewmen parted the sheer fabric walls and the Viceroy carried her inside. He stood holding her, her arms around his neck. Smiling, they looked into one another's eyes for a few moments before he put her down. Without speaking, he untied her cape, set it aside then stepped back to enjoy her body and dress. "You are beautiful, Becataten, more so tonight than I have ever seen you." He moved toward her and adjusted the straps of her shift observing how the scant straps were barely wide enough to cover the nipples of her breasts. "Wear this gown often. I like it."

Becataten nodded. They stood close and quiet.

There is no music, and there are no other women

dancing or servants tending us, but I think I like it this way - he and I alone.

He reached for a pitcher and poured her a glass of pomegranate wine and himself a dry red sma. He toasted softly, "To our first night together." She nodded and they sipped their wine.

Becataten did not know why, but she felt no need to speak. *I used to chatter so with Pharaoh.*

He then set their wine glasses on a small brass table and stepped back to look at her with sensual eyes. She felt mesmerized by his gaze.

This is not staring like the slave trader taught me. The Viceroy's staring gives me a warm and deeper feeling.

He reached for her to stand close. Then he moved the straps from her shoulders, bent and kissed each breast. He unlatched her gold belt and let her skirt fall at her feet, then removed her wig. His face gleamed with his appeal for her as he studied her bareness. Raising his arms, his broad smile said, undress me. *I never was asked to undress Pharaoh.* Becataten untied the sash of his kilt and let it fall. He didn't have the round belly that Pharaoh had but was hard and smooth. She struggled to remove his golden collar. Standing on tiptoes to remove his wig brought a smile to his face.

They lay down together on the billowy pillows that covered the floor. He began to caress all parts of her. It was almost an examination, but made her feel so lustful that she just lay back to enjoy his touch until she could no longer be passive. She reached for him, squeezing him tightly, wanting him more than she had ever desired Pharaoh.

He took her hand and placed it on his member. *By the Gods, it was made of stone, not like Pharaoh's, and larger too, but not as large as the slave trader's.* She was pleased.

No drums beat, no music played, no special oils used and no incense burned, but the night went on and on to offer sensual coupling, unabashed lovemaking and tenderness that she would never forget.

It was just as Lady Nagara had predicted.

The Characters of Harem Twins

Egypt: 1380 to 1400 B.C., Middle Kingdom

Ⅱ

Pharaoh Amenhotep III
Amenhotep reigned during this prosperous time and was a lover of beauty, women, architecture and art
(Living person during this period)

Queen Tiy
Pharaoh's first wife who was allowed much freedom
(Living person during this period)

Princess Attah
Mitanni war reparation for Pharaoh's harem and mother of twins Becataten and Jobutaten

Princess Becataten/Prince Jobutaten
(Taten and Jobu) Twins born on an auspicious date related to their destiny with Pharaoh

Dwarf Beset
Female dwarf and greatly revered by Pharaoh's court, as dwarves in Egyptian culture are associated with male God Dwarf Bes

Nanny Maja
Slave to Princess Attah and Nanny to the twins

Royal Astrologer Abu
Brilliant and ambitious court translator and half brother to Pharaoh who created charts for all royal dates

Huni
Castrated baboon with incisor teeth removed who lives as a pet with Abu

Royal Gardener Sennejem
Friend to Nanny Maja as they share the language of her hometown
(Living person during this period)

Royal Architects Suti and Hor
Royal twin architects to Pharaoh
(Living persons during this period)

Lady Nagara
Wife of Architect Suti

Royal Nurse Heqarneheh
Eunuch in charge of the royal nursery
(Living person during this period)

Dwarf Heby
Worker in Abu's household and friend of Dwarf Beset

354

Vizier Amenhotep Huy
Chief advisor to Pharaoh
(Living person diring this period)

Chancellor Ptathmose
Chief advisor to Pharaoh
(Living person during this period)

Heka Priest
Royal priest knowledgeable in magic and astrology

Viceroy Merymose
Administrator of Pharaoh's vassal state of Kush where Egypt's gold is mined, second in power to Pharaoh
(Living person during this period)

Glossary
Egypt: 1380 to 1400 B.C., Middle Kingdom

♊

Ipet Harem

Sma Blended wine from preferred vintages

Irep Wine

Nome Provence

Ka Spirit or soul

Debon Various-sized pieces of gold, silver or copper for trade, prior to coinage

Nemes Royal headscarf adorned with the royal cobra

Kush Probably modern-day Sudan

Stela Flat stone with carved information

Punt Probably modern-day Somalia

The Great Sea Mediterranean Sea

Heka Magic

Discussion Questions

1. How authentic is the culture and era of this book?

2. There are many details of Egyptian life, society, dress, culture, social system, government, food......which ones did you find most interesting?

3. What was your reaction to the way the newborns were handled in the nursery?

4. The age of childbirth started as young as 12 years-old. Egyptians usually lived thirty to forty years, some longer. In this story, did you feel the characters matured rapidly. If so, how and why?

5. How did the imagery in this book help the story and/or add to your enjoyment or idea of Egypt in 1400 B.C.?

6. Discuss the relationship between Princess Becataten and Lady Nagara.

7. What type of relationship did Dwarf Beset have with Nanny Maja? Which character did you prefer and why?

8. Compare the treatment of women in this book to the treatment of women today.

9. Describe Pharaoh Amenhotep III and his development from a young Pharaoh to his adulthood. What did you like about him? What did you not like about him?

10. Lady Nagara was "grooming" Princess Becatatan for the Royal Court to be presented to Pharaoh Amenhotep. Do you think she did this effectively?

11. Discuss how the past shaped the lives of Princess Becataten, Prince Jobutaten and Royal Astrologer Abu.

12. Why do you think the author had Prince Jobutaten killed? Would you have preferred him to be saved?

13. Advice from Nagara to Princess Becataten "There are two points of view about lovemaking Becataten, one from a women's point of view and one from a man's. These two points of view are what make us an alluring mystery to one another." Discuss this quote.

14. "When you are a Royal you are blessed with the blood of the Living God, you are like Jobu and Taten. But when you are Noble in class, you are rich and serve the Royal class." Discuss which you would rather be, a Noble or of the Royal class.

15. Can you relate to these characters? Do they seem real?

16. How did Princess Becataten change or evolve from the time she left home until the end of the novel?

17. Do you think if Princess Becatatan had not left that Prince Jobutaten would have lived?

18. What moral or ethical choices did Pharaoh make that made you like or dislike him? Did you see him as a "good" Pharaoh or a "bad" Pharaoh?

19. Describe the dynamics in the marriage of Lady Nagara and Royal Architect Suti.

20. Were you surprised by the complications, twists and turns of the plot?

21. Did you enjoy the imagery throughout the book?

22. Select one description of a meal and read it out loud? What is the group's reaction? (pg 62,63,106,175)

23, Select one description of the clothing of the time and read it out loud? What is the group's reaction?
(pg 80,111,144,172,260,261)

24. What did you enjoy about the book the most?

25. Who was your favorite character and why?

27. Did this story awaken an interest in Egypt and its culture and history?

To My Readers: A Request!

♊

Dear Readers,

Thank you for taking the time to read *Harem Twins*! I have written two more books in the series, and they will be published soon.

Every book's success depends on you, the reader, and the reviews you pass on. Authors are thrilled by every sentiment shared on their novels and any comment from you would mean the world.

To find the next installments in the series for purchase, and to leave a review on Amazon, google "Dolores Davis Harem Twins."
Thank you.
~Dolores Maria Davis

doloresmariadavis.wordpress.com

Dolores Maria Davis is the author of *Gourmet the Simple Way* published by World Nouveau/Mischievous Muse Press, available on Amazon. She wrote the *Harem Twins* series about a boy and girl twin living in ancient Egypt where secrets, intrigue and danger abound in Pharaoh's halls. She also wrote the soon-to-be-published *Black Angel* series about the rise of a young female lawyer working for the Mob in 1970s Los Angeles and Las Vegas. When not writing or cooking, Dolores enjoys studying about ancient lands and traveling. Find out more about Dolores online at:

doloresmariadavis.wordpress.com